Praise for Jenn Bennett and *Summoning the Night*

"Bennett quickly establishes that her terrific debut was no fluke, delivering another riveting tale featuring gutsy renegade magician Cady Bell. Bennett does a stellar job blending character development with plenty of supernatural mystery and peril. A series for your keeper shelf!" —*RT Book Reviews* (Top Pick!)

"Another fantastic novel. . . . I can't find enough superlatives for the enjoyment each of Bennett's books has brought. She has won a lifetime fan in me."
—*Fresh Fiction*

"Cady, Lon, and Jupe are my new favorite crime-fighting, magic-wielding Earthbound family unit. More, please." —*Reading the Paranormal*

"Jenn Bennett has created another amazing novel filled with strong characters, magical surprises, and quirky humor." —*Tynga's Reviews*

"Hands down, Jenn Bennett writes some of the best characters: They're relatable, approachable, and gosh darn it, near perfection." —*Heroes and Heartbreakers*

"The minute I cracked it open and started reading, I was reminded why I loved this world so much the first go around. . . . If you haven't picked up this series yet, you need to smack yourself and start it right now."
—*Wicked Little Pixie*

"Tremendous phenomenal fantastic! . . . Jenn Bennett proved that she can write with *Kindling the Moon,* and with *Summoning the Night,* she proved that she has staying power." —*Yummy Men & Kick Ass Chicks*

"Well written and full of unforgettable characters. While I appreciate the cliffhanger at the end, I have to lament it with equal fervor. I (not-so) patiently await the next installment of this series." —*Dark Faerie Tales*

Kindling the Moon

"The talent pool for the urban fantasy genre just expanded with Bennett's arrival. This is an impressive debut, which opens the door for a series that promises to be exceedingly entertaining. . . . Plenty of emotional punch, not to mention some kick-butt action. . . . Bennett appears to have a bright future ahead!" —*RT Book Reviews*

"Without a doubt the most impressive urban fantasy debut I've read this year. . . . The writing is excellent, the characters are charming, and the romance is truly believable. . . . Flawlessly original!" —*Romancing the Darkside*

"For the love of things that go bump in the night, this book was FABULOUS! It was the perfect blend of action, intrigue, tension, and the supernatural." —*Reading the Paranormal*

"I was hooked from the first page. . . . The story was fun and original. . . . The twists and turns came at every intersection. . . . I can't think of one thing I didn't like about the book. I didn't want to put it down." —*Urban Fantasy Investigations*

"I was smitten with this book right from the beginning. . . . A fantastic debut to a new series I am very excited over, and a must-read for all lovers of urban fantasy." —*Wicked Little Pixie*

"Jenn Bennett has written a great off-beat debut novel with a likeable heroine and a fun, original storyline. . . . I thoroughly enjoyed it!"

—Karen Chance, *New York Times* bestselling author of *Hunt the Moon*

"*Kindling the Moon* rocks like AC/DC on Saturday night. This book has it all: great writing, action, romance, a strong heroine, a unique hero, and the best teenager ever. I can't wait for the next one."

—Ann Aguirre, *USA Today* bestselling author of *Devil's Punch*

"*Kindling the Moon* engaged me from page one. I loved it! I immediately adored the heroine, Arcadia Bell. This book is packed from cover to cover with unpredictable twists, heart-pounding action, and heated sexual tension. . . . Jenn Bennett has definitely made my 'To Buy' list."

—Anya Bast, *New York Times* bestselling author of *Midnight Enchantment*

"Jenn Bennett takes the familiar ideas of magic, demons, and mythology, and she gives us something sexy, fun, and genuinely unique. Arcadia Bell is a sassy, whip-smart addition to the growing pantheon of urban fantasy heroines, and Bennett an author to watch!"

—Kelly Meding, author of *Changeling*

"Fantastic magic, non-stop action, and hot romance make *Kindling the Moon* a not-to-be-missed debut. Arcadia Bell is a tenacious and savvy heroine who had me hooked from the start."

—Linda Robertson, author of *Wicked Circle*

"Delicious characters, fun twists, and fiendish risks. . . . This smart, stylish debut really delivers. Loved, loved, loved it!"

—Carolyn Crane, author of *Head Rush*

Don't miss the rest of the Arcadia Bell series . . .

Kindling the Moon
Summoning the Night
"Leashing the Tempest"

JENN BENNETT

BINDING THE
SHADOWS

POCKET BOOKS
New York London Toronto Sydney New Delhi

Pocket Books
A Division of Simon & Schuster, Inc.
1230 Avenue of the Americas
New York, NY 10020

This book is a work of fiction. Any references to historical events, real people, or real places are used fictitiously. Other names, characters, places, and events are products of the author's imagination, and any resemblance to actual events or places or persons, living or dead, is entirely coincidental.

First Pocket Books paperback edition June 2013

POCKET and colophon are registered trademarks of Simon & Schuster, Inc.

For information about special discounts for bulk purchases, please contact Simon & Schuster Special Sales at 1-866-506-1949 or business@simonandschuster.com.

The Simon & Schuster Speakers Bureau can bring authors to your live event. For more information or to book an event contact the Simon & Schuster Speakers Bureau at 1-866-248-3049 or visit our website at www.simonspeakers.com.

Manufactured in the United States of America

10 9 8 7 6 5 4 3 2 1

ISBN 978-1-4516-9508-3
ISBN 978-1-4516-9511-3 (ebook)

*To the real-life Kar Yee in Hong Kong,
the epitome of kindness and grace. I miss you.*

BINDING THE SHADOWS

1

I scrambled through the second-story window and balanced on a square section of slanted roofing above a portico on the first floor. Lon followed, biting out obscenities. I'd never seen him move so fast. Fire is a good motivator.

We hugged the outer wall of the house, flanking both sides of the open window. A sharp night wind whipped my hair around my face and shoulders as I butted my shoulder against the siding.

Where is Merrimoth now? I thought.

"Left the room to search for the gun," Lon said in a low voice.

I quickly surveyed our surroundings. A small balcony lay to our left, a couple of rooms away. I risked a glance below and got queasy watching the tide crash and foam around an outcropping of jagged rocks.

Merrimoth's contemporary house was built on stilts over a lonely expanse of Pacific coast. The shoreline that stretched in front of us was studded with crags and driftwood and sea otters, and maybe the occasional wet-suited surfer seeking a thrill. I was neither sea otter nor surfer, and I figured I had a one percent chance of surviving a dive into the threatening waters below.

Long strands of golden brown hair fluttered around the back of Lon's neck as he leaned against the house and listened. Light from the still-burning fire radiated from the open window, creating dancing shadows that deepened the long hollows of his cheeks.

Like Merrimoth, Lon Butler is an Earthbound: demons on the inside, humans on the outside—with the small exception of a wispy halo of light that floats around their heads, marking them as "other." When Lon was transmutated, his demonic halo morphed from the usual nebulous gold-speckled green cloud to an eruption of flames that licked around his head and shoulders. He also sprouted a pair of spiraling ram-like horns, which were currently making a disconcerting knocking sound when he leaned his head against the house.

"He thinks he's spotted where the gun landed," he whispered.

Lon's damned Lupara. He'd only managed one shot before Merrimoth took possession of the gun a couple of minutes ago. I'd shocked Merrimoth with charged Heka—natural magical energy kindled with electricity—causing the gun to fly out of his hand,

and he retaliated by inexplicably creating a wall of fire across the room. Which is why we were now standing outside the window above a rocky shoreline when we should be sitting down to dinner.

Ambrose Dare, the very rich and very powerful head of the Hellfire Club, sent me here to put a metaphysical leash around Merrimoth's neck after hearing reports that his Number Two Earthbound had gone mad. Not usually my business or concern, but Dare was busy at some holiday fundraiser, and I was getting paid to care.

"We can't stand here forever," Lon said in a low voice.

No, we damn well couldn't. I longingly glanced at the nearby balcony. It was several feet away and connected to our roof by a slim ledge of cedar.

"Would it hold us?" Lon asked.

I tested it, easing the toe of my shoe on the ledge. Seemed strong enough, though it was awfully narrow. "I don't know . . ."

"Try to bind him again."

"You think I'm not?" I whispered hotly.

My inherited moon power was stronger than it'd ever been, now that I was using it regularly, but that didn't mean I understood the mechanics behind it. All I knew was that it damn sure didn't work in the daytime and—like the cable in Lon's house up on the cliffs—went on the fritz during storms.

Lon exhaled in frustration. Clever eyes studied

mine as his index finger and thumb moved in unison to smooth the thin pirate mustache that trailed around his mouth and matching triangle in the center of his chin.

"Bind Merrimoth," he finally said, "and I'll do that thing you like later."

"It's not like my power reacts to the reward system," I said, then added, "What thing?"

The corner of his mouth quirked. "On the chair."

"You mean that thing *you* like?"

"We *both* like," he corrected. "Win-win."

I snorted a soft laugh. "I don't think you understand the concept of bargaining."

He held up a hand to quiet me, then whispered after a few moments. "The gun fell behind his piano. He can see it from the landing."

"Perfect. When he heads back downstairs—"

"Cady—"

"—we'll just go back inside and—"

"Ahhh!"

Lon lurched away from the side of the house and nearly toppled off the narrow roof. I felt it a second later: fire on my back, spreading across the wood siding. I yelped in pain, then ducked into a crouch as a sudden *boom!* rattled the house. Flames burst from the open window, a column of orange fire like dragon's breath. It spewed over our heads, just missing one of Lon's horns, then retreated. Mostly. Flames continued to cavort around the window and surrounding wall.

The scent of burning hair wafted. I furiously patted my bleached white Bride of Frankenstein streak, which hung over my shoulders and stood out against my otherwise dark hair. "How is he doing that?" I hissed.

"Hell if I know. Even transmutated, there's no way he should be able to do this."

But Merrimoth *wasn't* transmutated, which made even less sense. Many Earthbounds have a demonic ability, what they call a knack. Lon's an empath. He can read your emotions. Transmuted, like he was at that moment, he can also read your thoughts. Merrimoth possessed a knack I once would've classified as harmless: temperature control. Last time I saw him, he could warm my hand with a touch. But creating giant blasts of fire? This was new.

"Ha!" Merrimoth's joyful voice called out from inside the house. "I am God—no, the Devil himself. I've never felt so alive!"

And I'd never felt so angry. Come to think of it, I'd felt nothing but hate for David Merrimoth since I met him at the Hellfire caves several months back. Not only because the elderly Earthbound tried to feed Lon to a caged Æthyric demon in a fighting ring, but also because he wanted to herd me into an Incubus orgy.

"Stay right there, won't you?" Merrimoth hollered from inside the house. His batshit-crazy laugh was lost in the crackle of flames that licked around the window frame.

Lon pulled me to my feet and craned to see inside the window. "He's going downstairs."

Heat from Merrimoth's fire caused sweat to trickle down my back. We weren't circus lions. No way was I jumping through the ring of a window on fire, but I wasn't going to stand there and wait for Merrimoth to come back and shoot us. I gazed at the balcony and resigned myself to a tightrope act. "I'll go first. Wait until I've crossed."

"Like hell. I'm not going to stand here and watch you fall. We both go."

Fine. If our combined weight destroyed the ledge, maybe I'd get to give him an I-told-you-so on the other side. I flattened my back against the house and gingerly sidled onto the cedar ledge. My heart drummed inside my chest as salty ocean air filled my lungs. I stretched out an arm and guided myself forward with an open palm on the siding for balance. One step . . . two steps. . . . The ledge creaked.

"Slow, Cady," Lon's voice said somewhere behind me.

I was inching forward one foot at a time—how much slower could I go?

Something fell on my face. A sharp pinpoint of cold. Then another. *Plop*.

"Shit." So much for clear skies. A handful of plops, then the heavens just opened up without warning and dumped a torrent of winter rain.

"Keep going," Lon said.

Christmas was next week, for the love of Pete. I should be wrapping presents right now and preparing myself to meet Lon's extended family—not running from fire and tightroping across the side of some nut-job's house in a storm.

At least the anger was motivating. Three more steps and we were halfway there. Or were we? It was hard to tell—I couldn't turn my neck to look back or I'd lose my balance. Blustering wind thrashed my hair and fanned a hard sheet of rain across my face. Vertigo turned my knees to jelly.

"Ignore it!" Lon barked at my side.

He was right. Too late to turn back now. I had to press forward. Had to make it. All I needed to do was slide one foot, fingers reaching, slide second foot, and repeat. But during the next step, I felt the house rumble against my back.

"What was that?" I whispered.

Something behind us, on the safe little island of roofing we'd left. I'd fall if I glanced back. Lon must've detected something with his knack because his hand suddenly gripped my shoulder. All my muscles went rigid as a breath stuck in my throat.

A gun's report cracked the night air.

My back stiffened. Fingernails gouged the rain-slick siding, scrabbling for purchase. Lon swore indecipherably.

"You couldn't hit a buffalo with this old thing," Merrimoth's voice shouted into the storm.

"Keep going," Lon said to me. "The Lupara's out of shells now."

I drew harsh breaths through my nostrils and

took an indecisive step. Then another. Lon was saying something behind me again, but I blocked him out. Three steps to the balcony. I extended my arm. I could do this. Two steps. Almost there. My fingertips reached for the wooden railing—

Glass doors swung open.

A green halo swam in front of my eyes as Merrimoth burst onto the balcony. The gray-haired Earthbound was in his early seventies. He wore perfectly ironed gray slacks and a white shirt that gaped open three too many buttons to expose a plush thicket of curly gray chest hair.

"How stupid do you think I am?" he said breathlessly as rain soaked through his shirt. No horns, no fiery halo. He definitely wasn't transmutated, so how could his knack be potent enough to create fire?

"Merrimoth!" Lon shouted. "Let us inside. We'll discuss this like adults."

"There's nothing to discuss, m'boy. Dare wants to sic his hounds on me? And not even worthy hounds—Jonathan Butler's privileged ragamuffin son and his witchy Sheba, barely old enough to tie her own shoes, much less bind me properly. Don't think I've forgotten that little stunt you pulled in the Hellfire caves. Dare blamed me for the vermillion binding circle you broke. He flayed me for it."

The crazy Earthbound held out an upturned palm. My rain-bleary vision took several seconds to register that his hand was striped with pink scars.

"Dare said I couldn't touch you or I was out of

the Hellfire Club. But I don't need them anymore, not with power like this!" The beginning of a laugh was choked in his throat as his gaze narrowed and landed on Lon. "Get out of my brain, Butler. I feel you poking around. You want to know how I started those fires? I'm not telling. But remember that my knack always went both ways—hot and cold. Would you like a demonstration?"

"Merrimoth—"

"Look at you, little birds perched on my house. The footing on that ledge looks awfully dicey. Would be even more precarious if the temperature dropped a few degrees . . ."

The rain surged and swirled as the Earthbound flicked his wrist. A volley of cold, sharp raindrops flew against my body and pinged off the house, sounding like a thousand marbles had been scattered into the wind. Hail. He'd frozen the rain around us.

Ice quickly formed on both the ledge below and the wooden siding at our backs. My fingers slipped. Merrimoth swooped his arm in a downward arc and a long strip of ice solidified at our feet. It shot out into the night air like the enormous, curling tongue of a mythological Nordic Frost Giant.

Lon's leg banged against mine, then his foot gave way. I turned just in time to see him career down the icy slide. He launched into the air, rocketing into the night sky as if he'd been released from a slingshot. I watched in horror as his body hung for a split second, then dropped, heading straight for the rocky coastline below.

I didn't have time to make a plan. No option existed but stopping Lon's fall. And after all the trouble I'd been having summoning up my moon power to bind Merrimoth, in that single moment—the second Lon dropped—the erratic magick immediately submitted to my will and lashed out like lightning. I had no particular spell in mind, not even a sigil. Only one thought ballooned inside my head and crackled through my synapses: *No*.

Magick whooshed out of me with my breath. I blinked, drowsy and momentarily disoriented. I knew I'd done something big, but it took me a moment to realize exactly *what*.

Time had slowed.

I glanced around in shock. A peculiar silver light swathed my vision. Raindrops hung suspended in the air—illuminated by light from the house's windows, they looked like clusters of misshapen glass beads. And on the balcony, Merrimoth's body stood stock-still, his mouth open, hand poised in the middle of some unrealized gesture like a wax figure. As if I'd pushed a pause button. I peered over the arch of ice at my feet, dreading what I might find.

Lon!

He was suspended in the air a floor below me, caught in my magick, falling facedown, his halo and long hair streaming behind.

I'd never, *never* done anything this big—never even imagined I could. But the amount of energy it took to power it was already draining me.

Screwing up my courage, I chanced a couple of small, cautious steps on the slick ledge until my hand wrapped around the railing. I took a deep breath and awkwardly pitched myself sideways, scrambled onto the balcony, and skidded, almost crashing into Merrimoth. Silver fog swirled around his legs. Creepy as hell. Even creepier when I realized he wasn't completely still. His arm was rising in slow motion, a hair at a time. His angry gaze struggled to shift in my direction.

A wave of dizziness unsteadied me. My Heka reserves were draining and I was running out of time. I shuffled around Merrimoth, spotted Lon's vintage gun in his hand, and pried it out of his fingers. Then I scurried through the balcony doors into the house.

I found myself inside a cavernous bedroom, decorated with restraint and neutral colors, like the rest of Merrimoth's home. Automated ceiling sprinklers doused everything with circular sprays of water. I stumbled across polished wood flooring, frantically looking for a way out, and found more than I wanted: three cameras on tripods, a bed outfitted with black rubber sheets, an object that I initially thought was a curly dildo (and upon closer inspection, was, I thought, a butt plug with one end shaped like a pig's tail), and a gleaming, shiver-inducing metal speculum. I scurried around a black leather swing hanging from an exposed beam and darted into the hallway.

Silver fog eddied around my feet as I galloped down the main stairwell and rushed through the living room. The layout was disorienting. Lon and I had only been in this room a few moments before Merrimoth went apeshit earlier and chased us upstairs. I finally spotted a pair of glass doors. My fingers shook as they flipped a dead bolt and flung the doors open.

A small set of stairs led to the beach. Trudging over wet sand, I slipped the bulky Lupara inside my jacket and scoured the shoreline. Lon's golden halo hummed in the darkness. He was still hanging in the sky over the foaming water, though he'd descended a bit. If he dropped a few more feet, I could reach him . . . if he weren't suspended a few yards out over the ocean.

Minutes ago, the crashing tide would've pounded me to a pulp against the rocks here, but now the water was eerily still, silver fog clinging to the quiet surface. I plodded into the winter-chilled water. My steps left dark holes in the foamy surf. Utterly surreal. I marveled at the way the splashes around my watery footprints hung in midair, how they deepened as I waded knee-deep. Farther away, somewhere beyond Merrimoth's house, I could hear the surf pounding: my moon magick apparently had limits.

Lon was above me now, his black peacoat

billowing at his sides like the wings of a fallen angel. I focused on climbing the rocks to reach him, a task more difficult than I initially thought. They were slimy with seaweed, rough with broken mussel shells, and it didn't help that shivers racked my body. When I got to a point where I could stand without falling, I stretched and nabbed Lon's ankle, then tugged. He moved a few inches. Holy Whore—it was like pulling a box of bricks out of the sky. I tugged harder and, with a series of groans, dragged him through the air, retracing my steps to shore.

My lungs felt close to bursting and I was seriously dizzy from the amount of Heka I was using. But I knew that once I let go of the moon magick, Merrimoth would inflict some sort of insane Narnian winter across the beach. Maybe even turn us into frozen statues. Or set us on fire. I shoved Lon closer to the ground, leaning across his back, then finally sitting on him when that didn't work.

Screw David Merrimoth and screw Dare for calling me up in the middle of the night to bind him. As I considered whether I had the strength to wrangle Lon up the driveway and into the car so we could just get out of there, a figure materialized in the shadows beneath the stilted house.

It was a woman, possibly fifty years old, long and lean. She was wearing odd clothing—a toga-like gray dress. Silver fog clung to her bare ankles. Her dark hair was pinned up and dusted with gray at the crown. She had intelligent eyes, cheekbones that could cut diamond, and a full, sensual mouth. French, through and through. She crossed her elegant arms with an air of superiority and smiled at me like she'd just won the lottery.

When I realized who she was, I screamed bloody murder.

2

Complete shock severed my connection to the moon magick, and the woman disappeared in a flash. Newly reanimated, Lon faceplanted into the sand just as the ocean roared back to life, echoing Merrimoth's angry shouting somewhere above us.

My heart raced around my chest like a fox outrunning a hunter. A terrible feeling of hopelessness took root.

Enola Duval. Never in a million years did I think I'd see her again. Gifted student of the occult and author of multiple books on magick. Infamous former member of the highly esteemed Ekklesia Eleusia esoteric society, or E∴E∴, as it's known in occult circles. One of the Black Lodge Slayers. Number 37 in a set of American Serial Killer trading cards. On the FBI's Most Wanted list.

Mom.

My mother had been gone for months, claimed by a primordial albino demon named Nivella the

White and taken into the Æthyr with my father as payment for crimes they committed. Nasty crimes. Unpardonable crimes. Long before her stint as a serial killer, my mother conceived me during an arcane ceremony that invoked something big and secret and unknowable from the Æthyr inside my cells—all so that she and my father could steal its essence through good, old-fashioned ritual sacrifice.

Mom was evil. She was crazy. And she could *not* be alive—Nivella wanted my parents dead, and had every reason to kill them as soon as they crossed into the Æthyr.

What I saw just now was only . . . a hallucination, or something. Whatever it was, it couldn't be my mother. Period.

Lon's muffled swearing wrenched me away from my panicked thoughts. As he pushed himself to his feet, I bent to help him and brushed sand from his jacket.

"You did that?" he rasped. "Stopped my fall?"

"I'm as surprised as you are."

His eyes quickly narrowed in concern. "What—"

"Don't read my thoughts right now, okay? Later."

He nodded, and with his typical economical way of compartmentalizing emotional situations, promptly tabled his curiosity and focused his attention toward the underside of the house, listening for Merrimoth. "Can you bind him from here?"

"Is he coming? Can you read him? Where is he?"

As if in answer, the sound of the crashing waves suddenly stopped. The nearby surf was white. Not foamy white—snowy white. Not my magick this time. Lon and I cautiously glanced around the stilts.

Merrimoth had created a sludgy, half-frozen iceberg on the ocean's surface. If he had been aiming for us and just missed, I didn't want to risk him trying again and succeeding.

Time to get this over with.

I zeroed in on his voice and called up the moon power again. How could I have had so much trouble reaching it earlier? It came so naturally now. Power hummed inside me, ready to be wielded, as I warily scanned my surroundings for my mother. Not there. Good. Whatever had caused her image to appear earlier, it must've been a product of my mind—some sort of witchy glitch. At least that's what I told myself.

The blue dot of light that marked my starting point appeared in my line of vision. I expanded it, molding the light into a standard binding triangle with all the proper seals and symbols. Then I shut my eyes, concentrated, and projected it upward through the house, searching for Merrimoth.

I lassoed him, but something felt wrong. He should be trapped, unable to do anything but pace and moan inside my binding, but he was moving. Lon shouted something incoherent. My eyes snapped open. I saw the blue light of my binding nose-diving through the night sky, spinning in circles around Merrimoth. I tried to yank the binding toward me like a leash. Tried to will him to stop—to slow time again. It was too late.

Two terrible realizations twined inside my head. Merrimoth had already jumped from the balcony when my binding trapped him—he'd constructed the snowy iceberg as a landing pad to soften his fall. Whatever he'd done to amp up his knack's once meager power, he now believed himself to be infallible. Godlike.

And by yanking on my binding—even though I'd been trying to save him—I'd pulled him off course. His grotesque scream was abruptly aborted when a sickening *crack!* pierced the air.

Like an afterthought, the iceberg melted all at once into the sea and the renewed surf pounded against Merrimoth's torso, impaled on a jagged point of rock.

I'd just killed someone. Again.

Shock silenced us for several heartbeats as we stood in the rain. Lon finally prodded me away from the shore and we retreated beneath the cover of the stilted house.

I felt a tickle in the back of my nose, then a familiar drowning warmth. Nosebleed. I lifted my hand to catch the first drop, then untucked the hem of my T-shirt and used it to pinch my nose. Cool night air drafted across my bared stomach.

"Oh, Cady. Not again."

"I didn't mean to," I said, my voice muffled inside my shirt. My eyes brimmed with prickly tears.

Lon offered me a waded up paper napkin from

his coat pocket. "I meant the nosebleeds. Of course you didn't mean to—"

Kill the second most powerful person in the Hellfire Club? I thought back to him in response.

"Just because he was Number Two doesn't mean he was second in charge," Lon said. "You know that. He just got the second slot when my father died. Dumb luck."

Dumb luck or not, Merrimoth had been a fixture in the club for twenty years. Dare wasn't going to be happy. *If I hadn't bound him . . .*

"He might've broken his neck instead of his back. He was seventy-two, Cady, not seventeen."

He was in good shape.

"I'm not sure if a cat with nine lives would've survived a fall from that height. Damn sure thought I was a goner until you saved me. What the hell kind of spell was that?"

It wasn't a spell, exactly. I just wanted to stop you from falling and it happened.

Lon's eyes tightened into slits. "No spell?"

I shook my head.

"That's —"

Scary as shit?

"Amazing."

A slow, salt-tinged wind blew rain beneath the stilted house. Lon pulled his coat closed and began fastening a row of oversized buttons. His next question was spoken in a low, quiet voice. "Why were you thinking about your mother?"

Ugh. Trying to control my thoughts when he was transmutated was impossible. It took me a few moments to answer. *I saw an image of her, or something. Over there,* I said internally, and nodded my head to my left.

Lon glanced at the sand. A flat patch of evening primrose grew around the stilt where I'd seen her standing. His brow knitted as he dug around inside my thoughts. "She looked solid but disappeared when you dropped the moon magick."

It was probably nothing. Just a memory. I tried to push her image out of my head and failed. *Maybe my brain's broken. I don't know why I'd be thinking of her. She can't be alive. That albino demon took her— She just can't, Lon. She can't,* I repeated, as if saying it made it true.

"You're right, she can't," Lon agreed, but the way his eyes drifted made me wonder if he was lying to make me feel better. And though he surely heard me thinking this, he dropped the subject and shifted down to his human form. Horns spiraled and disappeared, fiery halo receded to his usual gold-speckled green, and our telepathic connection was severed.

After my nosebleed slowed, we made our way to the front of Merrimoth's house and waited for Dare under a wide porch bordered by a grove of Monterey cypress trees. The rain ended as two SUVs finally arrived. A few bulky Earthbounds exited the first vehicle—people on Dare's security team—then, from the second car, Dare himself.

Dressed in a tuxedo, the elderly Hellfire leader

shoved fisted hands inside his coat pockets as he marched up the driveway. A green halo trailed as he nodded his bald head in greeting. Dare was easily the most powerful Earthbound in the area, not to mention the wealthiest. He owned a successful energy company, was invested in half the businesses in La Sirena, and put the mayor in office. Forty-some years ago, he started the Hellfire Club with Lon's father. After the senior Butler died, Dare became Lon's de facto father figure.

When Lon and I started dating, Dare did some digging into my background and discovered my true identity. He knew my most dangerous secret: that Arcadia Bell was just an alias. No one else but Lon and a few people in my former magical order knew that I was Sélène Duval, daughter of the Black Lodge Slayers. If he chose, Dare could use that information to ruin the independent life I'd struggled to build as Arcadia. And that's how I ended up working two jobs: bartending at Tambuku Tiki Lounge, and being on-call for Hellfire magical work.

Dare stopped in front of us, a grave look on his face. "Show me."

"Back here," Lon said.

Dare signaled his men to follow and we hiked around the house to the beach. Lon pointed to the rock where Merrimoth's broken body lay, now just a dark shape being battered by the surf. Dare requested a flashlight from one of his men and shined it over the outcropping. He made a despondent noise when the beam found its mark. We stepped closer, until the tide broke around our shoes. Dare held the flashlight on the body. "He wasn't transmutated?" Dare asked. "You're certain?"

"He wasn't," Lon said.

"No horns or fiery halo," I agreed. "We didn't see him every time he set the fires, but I watched him create ice right in front of me. No transmutation."

Dare stared out at the sea for a moment. "Ever seen anything like that before?"

"Never."

"I worry this isn't an isolated case."

Lon perked up. "Why?"

"Have you been paying attention to the news back in Morella? The robberies?" Dare swept a palm over his bald head. "A glut of them over the last couple of weeks. Home invasions. Burglaries. Stick-ups."

"Not that unusual around the holidays," I argued. "People get desperate."

"This is different. Reporters haven't noticed, but they will. The robberies are all being committed by Earthbounds."

"Are you sure?" Lon asked.

Dare nodded. "Earthbounds using strange knacks."

"Like Merrimoth."

Dare nodded. "You couldn't pick out anything from his thoughts that indicated what caused this?" Dare asked Lon as he pointed the flashlight beam across the burnt-out second-story window frame where Merrimoth had blown fire at us. "Anything at all? A spell? A person? A name?"

Lon squinted into the surf. "I almost caught an image of another person when he was bragging. Think it was a male, not sure. He blocked me out of his thoughts before I could fully catch it."

Dare flicked off the flashlight and handed it to one of his henchmen. "Retrieve the body before it floats away and I'm forced to pay a boat and a crew to drag the water for it later. Have Caine comb the house and dump anything remotely incriminating into garbage bags. He can load them up in one of the SUVs and take them to Swan Drive until I can sort through it tomorrow. Then call the police."

His man nodded and began following orders as Lon and I trekked to the front of the house with Dare. "Are you just going to wait and see how all this plays out?" I asked.

"Right now most of the crimes are happening in Morella, but if it spreads here to La Sirena, then everyone's going to be looking to me for answers. So what do you think, Ms. Bell?"

"I think you're going to ask me to start poking around Morella."

He gave me a tight smile. "Why would I want you to do that when you couldn't even handle the simple task I gave you tonight? All you had to do was bind Merrimoth." He looked at Lon. "And all *you* had to do was read the man's mind. Instead, you not only fail to get the information I wanted, but you also managed to kill the target. My grandson could've done a better job. You're both worthless."

"Excuse me?" Lon was pissed—*really* pissed. So was I.

Dare ignored Lon's stare and looked at me. "I'll find someone else to do the job you couldn't. Consider yourself temporarily relieved from your Hellfire duties. When I need you for something less important, I'll call." Dare pointed a gloved finger at Lon and me. "Regardless, appearances are important, so you're both coming to David's funeral. He wouldn't have wanted you there, of course. But he should've thought of that before he decided to jump into the ocean. Goodnight."

And with a half-hearted wave, he began marching back to one of the waiting cars.

Lon was seconds away from doing something he'd regret later; I could practically feel the anger radiating from him. But this was my fight—not his.

My fight, and what was I going to do about it?

I don't know if I felt empowered by the magick I'd done, or stressed over the vision of my mother, or upset over the fact that I'd just accidently killed a man. But I did know that at that moment, I wasn't going to just stand there and take any more shit from the jackass walking away from us.

I was finally ready to do what I should've done the first time Dare threatened me.

"No."

Dare stopped and turned around. "What?"

I shook my head in annoyance. "Forget it. I'm done."

"Fine," Dare said. "I don't give a damn if you come to the funeral or not."

"I'm not talking about the funeral." I strode to meet him, everything suddenly clear to me. There were a lot of things I couldn't control, but this was one I could. "I'm done being your slave."

"Slaves don't get paid."

"I never asked for the job. You bullied me—no, you *blackmailed* me into working for you."

"It's not my fault you're living a lie."

"No, but you're a dick for taking advantage of it. And I'm done with you. Don't wire me any more money, don't ask me to do anything else for you." Surging anger heated my chest and loosened my tongue. "If it weren't for me, seven of your club's children would be dead by now and Central California would be overrun with Æthyric demons." I stuck a finger in his chest. "You should be kissing my feet. You have *no idea* what I could do to you, demon. No fucking idea. If you did, you'd be sending me roses everyday, begging for my forgiveness."

He didn't look like he was about to fall on his knees and ask for said forgiveness any time soon. But he did look surprised. Probably because no one ever stood up to him.

"I—"

"What? What are you going to do? Have your lackeys shove a gun in my face and force me on another job? Go on, I dare you."

Now he was angry, too. "If you want to negotiate

more agreeable terms, I'm open to that. But you seem to be forgetting that I could bring down your matchstick framework of an existence with a couple of phone calls."

I stepped closer. Close enough to smell the expensive aftershave clinging to his leathery skin. Close enough to see a muscle jump in his jaw. "Go right ahead," I goaded. "Tell the whole world. I'm not going to pay for my parents' crimes for the rest of my life. If I end up in jail for living under a stolen identity or aiding and abetting my parents' disappearance, then you're just going to have to bail me right back out, because I can't charge your damned Hellfire summoning circles from prison. And if you even think about using Lon to get to me, or threatening anyone I care about, you and I will be enemies. And you'd do well to remember all my enemies are dead. Including the man you're about to fish out of the water."

Dare stood stock-still, measuring me. Strategizing. Then he flicked his gaze over my shoulder.

"Lon."

Oh, that was it. If he wouldn't listen to my words, he'd listen to the hum of electricity I was going to shove inside his chest. I reached inside my inner coat pocket and whipped out a miniature caduceus—a graphite-cored staff I used for directing kindled Heka into spells. Half-crazed with fury, I prepared to siphon electrical current and raised the caduceus like a dagger, ready to strike.

Dare lurched backward and stuck his hand in his jacket like he was reaching for a gun.

"Enough!" Lon jumped between us, and roughly shoved Dare's arm away. They stared at each other for a long moment.

"I'm done being ashamed of my past," I shouted at Dare over Lon's shoulder. "And I'm not paying for it anymore."

The Hellfire leader blinked at both of us, looking old and weary in the shadowed light.

Nobody said anything else, so I just crossed my arms over my chest and started walking up the driveway. After a few moments, I heard footsteps following. I was pretty sure they were Lon's. He has a certain loose way of walking, as if nothing in the world could ever hurry him along. I knew for sure it was him when he de-alarmed the car and reached around my side to open my door.

I was still angry. Shaking a little, even, as I hoisted myself into Lon's SUV. His valrivia cigarette dangled from his lips as he started the engine. He cracked the window then pulled out of Merrimoth's drive onto a winding coastal road. We sped around a curve, sitting in silence. My anger bled into a slow-moving anxiety. Lon still hadn't said a word.

Was he upset at me for mouthing off at Dare? He often told me to stand up to the man, but admittedly, it might not have been the best time to rebel. Dare just lost one of his oldest friends. At least, I guess Dare and Merrimoth were friends. Associates.

Colleagues. Fellow club members. Whatever the hell they were to each other, it was decades old.

Maybe I should've thought of that before I told Dare to go to hell. Maybe I should've thought of how this would affect Lon. Then it dawned on me that this wasn't the reason for his silence.

I'd never told Lon that Dare had uncovered my family secret.

Crap.

"I don't know how he found out," I said. "But he knows who my parents were. He knows about my order. Everything."

"Figured that out from your rant," he said quietly. "How long?"

"Since the Halloween parade."

He made a small noise.

"I don't know why I didn't tell you. I guess I was . . . I don't know, ashamed. Stupid, I know. But you can't understand what's it like to keep a secret like that hidden for so many years—I built my life around keeping that secret. I just . . ."

My words trailed into a groan. I was frustrated with myself. And sick of all of it. "We're not supposed to have secrets between us, and I should've told you. I'm sorry. But I mean what I said. I'm done with him. I'm tired of hiding."

And in a weird way, I was glad I came to that realization on my own. If I had told Lon, he likely would've gotten in Dare's face for me. I know he would have. But it felt good to do it myself.

Lon was silent for several moments.

"Are you mad at me?" I asked.

"I'm not happy."

That was fair. "You wouldn't do anything stupid to Dare, right?"

"If I would've known he was holding that over you—"

"I'm really sorry I didn't tell you. But this is my bone to pick with him. I don't want you going Neanderthal."

It took him awhile to respond. "You haven't called me that in a while. I sort of miss it."

Relief washed over me. He wasn't too mad. I gave him a soft smile. He squeezed the back of my neck and steered the car down another road.

"You think Dare will tip off the FBI or police about my identity?" I asked after a few minutes.

Lon grunted. "No. He's not that stupid. No matter how he postures, he's afraid of you."

"Still, I better go ahead and tell Kar Yee."

"It's probably time."

"I'm not telling Jupe, though."

"When you're ready, I think he can handle it."

"I'm not ready yet."

Maybe after the holidays. Lon's former in-laws—Jupe's grandmother and aunt on his mother's side—were coming for Christmas and that was enough family drama to worry about right now.

Lon slowed the SUV as we approached a red light. "We'll worry about it later. Right now, let's just go home. We'll have some wine, reheat our dinner, watch a movie."

It sounded glorious. And, for the most part, we *did* salvage the remainder of the evening.

I got one night of peace and quiet. One night to relish my liberation from Dare. To ignore the feeling of dread that settled into my bones with the unexplained expansion of my moon powers. To block out the vision of my mother standing outside Merrimoth's house. To forget about the demonic crime wave that was spreading across the city.

One single, enjoyable night before everything turned to shit.

3

My shift at Tambuku Tiki Lounge the following night was busy early in the evening, but the crowd tapered off before midnight. Not unusual for the Yuletide season. The Earthbounds that patronized our demon-friendly bar came in for happy hour drinks, then headed off to office parties, family functions, and shopping. By Christmas Eve, only hardcore alcoholics would walk though the neon-crowned Moai statues flanking our door.

Though I was still feeling resolute about my decision to stand up to Dare, I tried not to think about my expanding magical abilities while I worked, and I especially avoided any stray thoughts about my mother. After sleeping on the whole incident, I'd almost convinced myself that I hadn't seen her. Almost. Before I came into work, Lon reminded me that even if she were alive—and how could she be?—she'd be alive in the Æthyr. I wasn't going to bump into her on the street. This gave me enough peace of mind to make it through my shift.

Lately I'd been working less—only three days a week, and just one of those shifts kept me until closing time at two. When Kar Yee and I first opened Tambuku two years back, I'd bartended six nights a week, usually working twelve-hour days. Then I met Lon. The drive from Tambuku to my house in Morella was fifteen minutes; the drive from Tambuku to Lon's house in La Sirena was half an hour, or longer, depending on traffic.

I hadn't slept at my own house in weeks—not since the demon Lord Chora disabled my house wards. But walking into the Butler home at three in the morning wasn't working for any of us; Lon was a walking zombie on photo shoots and I sometimes went days without seeing Jupe, since I was sleeping when he was getting ready for school and already at work when he came home.

Lon never complained or asked me to change my schedule. But Jupe was vocal enough for the both of them, griping that his fourteen-year-old self was turning into a "latchkey kid." I'm not sure where he heard that phrase, but it made me feel guilty enough to change my work schedule. After all, I was half-owner, and the bar was successful. We could afford another bartender. Kar Yee wasn't working more than three shifts a week after recently promoting our lead server Amanda to assistant manager. Amanda liked closing and Kar Yee was starting to trust her with the Holy Bank Deposit, miracle of miracles. Everyone was happy.

One of those happy people marched down Tambuku's cement steps into our basement entrance. With an aqua-blue halo and a fuck-off stare that could make Dirty Harry flinch, Kar Yee was my best friend and co-owner of Tambuku.

The Chinese expat nodded at a couple of regulars who were playing the vintage Tahiti Tropicana pinball machine that Jupe had found online. The boy had a major crush on Kar Yee and went to extravagant lengths to hatch excuses to talk to her. His latest ploy was scouring eBay and other sites for Tiki-themed junk. The Tahiti Tropicana was from the seventies and showcased two half-undressed island babes; one flipper stuck whenever you tried to hit one of the chipped silver balls. The old machine was an eyesore, but Kar Yee loved the damn thing: it averaged twenty dollars of quarters every day.

Kar Yee plopped down on a spinning stool and propped her elbows on the bamboo bar top. "It's dead already?"

"Been dead for an hour." Which is exactly how long ago I'd shut off the canned music. Only so many times you can hear "Mele Kalikimaka," the so-called Hawaiian Christmas song, before wanting to stab sharp objects into your ear. "However, we did have an office party earlier that dropped several hundred."

She twisted one of the two pointy locks of hair that extended past the severe line of her bob. "I'll start on the receipts in a minute."

I eyed two guys who walked into the bar. Their

faces were covered in stage makeup: one was painted to look like a reindeer with a red nose and the other was either supposed to be an elf . . . or a robot wearing an elf hat. Either way, his ears stuck out comically beneath it. I couldn't tell if they'd been at some lame holiday party or if they'd been part of a stage production of *The Nutcracker Suite,* but I could tell from the slight build of their bodies that they had a fifty-fifty chance of being legal.

And if they thought they were going to pass off fake IDs, they could think again.

"Where's Doctor Feelgood?" Kar Yee asked.

Her nickname for Bob, a thirty-something Hawaiian shirt–wearing Earthbound who'd spent most of his nights at Tambuku since the first day we opened. Bob's father was a popular Earthbound doctor here in Morella before he passed away, and Bob inherited a milder version of the man's healing knack.

"He was in here a second ago," I said, then gestured toward the arched hallway at the back of the bar, where our TV hung under a net of twinkling white lights. "Maybe in the restroom."

"I pulled a muscle," Kar Yee complained, rubbing her shoulder.

"Oh, I'm sure he'll be more than happy to put his hands on you."

Kar Yee's kohl-rimmed eyes narrowed. "Bob needs a girlfriend. Hell, I need somebody, too. Looks like you're the only lucky one for a change. By the way, I know a secret you don't know."

I stared at her. "What secret?"

"Just a little something," she said enigmatically, with a teasing lilt to her voice. "A surprise. My future boyfriend told me."

"Oh, that reminds me . . ." I leaned down beneath the bar and rummaged around for a small package. "Someone asked me to give this to you."

Kar Yee reluctantly accepted the gift. It was bundled in Cthulhu print wrapping paper, complete with green tentacles—and *way* too much tape. Her face relaxed when she read the sloppy, hand-printed label. "A present from Jupe?"

"He says you can't open it before Christmas."

She shook it near her ear and grinned. "What is it?"

"Not telling, but it's pretty sweet."

"I have to know. Don't tell him I opened it early." She tore into the wrapping and pulled out a small wooden box. Inside sat a small figurine carved from wood: a beautiful but strange female with long robes and a gold and silver mask painted over her face. "It's a traditional Chinese opera character," she said in small voice. "My mother loves the opera."

"Jupe said gold and silver would be someone supernatural. A demon."

She turned it in her hands, seeing the green disk that had been placed over the crown of the figure's head. "It represents me." As she grinned, two deep dimples appeared in her cheeks.

"He ordered it from someone in San Francisco who makes them."

"I love it! What a nice gift." Her smile faltered. "Now I have to get him something?"

"It would be the polite thing to do, yes."

"What do I know about teenage boys?"

"Enough to encourage this stupid infatuation, apparently," I complained.

"He realizes I'm teasing about the 'boyfriend' comments."

"You know he's using one of those pictures he took of you on the boat last month as the screensaver on his laptop? God only knows what else he's done with it. Probably photoshopped your head onto some porn star's body."

Her thin lips tilted in a slow smile.

"It's not funny," I said. "Get him a movie gift card. His feelings are going to be crushed if you don't do something."

She dropped Jupe's present inside the pocket of her gold and black coat. "Technically, my dad is Jewish, you know. I am under no obligation to participate in this holiday."

"I thought Judaism was passed down through the mother."

"Well, my mother is a Taoist, so I'm covered either way."

"You said your mother always puts up a Christmas tree in Hong Kong!"

She sighed heavily. "Can't you just put my name on a gift you've already bought? I'll pay you back."

"Maybe if you tell me more about this 'surprise.'"

"No can do. I'm the official secret-keeper. Jupiter trusts me."

I muttered to myself, but was reminded about a certain secret of my own that I needed to spill. I had no idea how she was going to react; even if Lon thought she'd accept my real history, I wasn't completely convinced. I'd been lying to her for years. Had plenty of chances to come clean, but never did. I was worried that she'd hate me for keeping the lie alive so long, but I was terrified that she'd be so disgusted by the truth that she'd want nothing more to do with me.

But I couldn't risk Dare telling her first. And, you know, since I'd conjured that vision of my mother on the beach—if it really was a just a figment of my Heka-soaked brain—maybe my subconscious was trying to tell me to stop running.

To move on.

"Hey, I need to talk to you about something," I said, a little nervous.

"Oh?"

"Maybe after closing, we can go grab some food at Black Cherry . . ." I began, but my words trailed away when I noticed the Santa's Village rejects had stopped at the end of the bar. The big-eared elf boy had a pale green halo and was anxiously looking around while his reindeer friend—who sported a military buzz cut under fuzzy antler head boppers—hoisted his backpack onto a barstool and unzipped it. Looked like he had a big metal can inside.

"What the hell is that smell?" Kar Yee said. "Is something burning?"

Shit. My new protective wards around the door. The sigils were glowing like embers. Not exactly a blaring warning. Guess that's what I got for experimenting with unknown magick.

My focus flew to the costumed kids. Reindeer Boy stuck a small metal bar at the edge of the can. He was prying a lid off.

A paint can? Panic raced down my spine.

"Hey!" I shouted, striding toward him. "What the hell are you doing?"

"Hurry!" the elf said as he unzipped his coat and pulled up a pair of bulky black goggles hanging around his neck.

The silver can floated up from the open backpack into the air. Telekinesis. I saw it all the time in the bar, but most Earthbounds who possessed this knack were only able to lift the toothpick umbrellas out of their Mai Tais—not heavy cans of paint.

Reindeer Boy made a motion with his hand and the can tilted in midair. A thick wave of red paint sloshed across the floor in front of the barstools. Kar Yee shouted incoherently as it sprayed across the bottom of her pants.

I acted on instinct. My hand reached for the winged caduceus I kept behind the bar—a full-size one, several feet long—but Reindeer flicked a hand in my direction and the carved staff flew out of my reach, sailing across the bar before crash-landing against an empty high-top table.

I'd never seen that kind of telekinetic range. Never!

"Now, idiot!" Reindeer Boy shouted to his gangly blond companion as he snapped on his own pair of goggles.

The elf-painted Earthbound shut his eyes. A disconcerting *pop!* crackled through the room. The TV went black, along with the nets of white lights and the Easter Island lamps at the booths.

He'd shorted out the electricity. All of it. The bar was pitch black, except for the soft unearthly glow of green and blue halos, and a patch of dull street light that filtered in through the stained glass window by the door.

Panicked shouts rang around the black room.

"Everyone stay where you are and you won't get hurt," a voice said. Reindeer Boy. His halo gave him away. Three red dots switched on around his googles—around his friend's, too. Night vision goggles.

"You. Bartender." Something slid across the bar top. I thought it was his backpack, but I wasn't sure. "Open up the register and put everything inside that."

A fierce rage caught fire inside my chest.

"They covered up the binding traps with the paint!" Kar Yee shouted.

Bold. And stupid. I didn't need the damn binding traps anymore. Without electricity, they were no good to me anyway. I could just summon up the Moonchild power. But then I thought of my mom's appearance at Merrimoth's beach house . . . and hesitated. Only for a moment, but it must've been too long for Kar Yee, who didn't know about my extracurricular talents. In her mind, my caduceus staff was across the room, and the binding triangles were compromised with paint.

A horrible, throat-closing fear hit my body, vibrating me like a struck gong. I heard myself whimper. Heard screams of the bar patrons bouncing off the carved tiki masks and kitschy tropical decor. But it wasn't until I'd ducked behind the bar, retracting as if I were a frightened turtle, that I remembered the intensely piquant feeling of Kar Yee's knack.

Kar Yee had the ability to cause everyone within a few yards to quake in their shoes: her knack was known simply as fear. Problem was, she had no control over it. All or nothing. She couldn't direct it to a specific person.

I knew this. Knew exactly what was happening to me.

But I still couldn't move.

Gods above, I'd never been so frightened. Terror clouded my thoughts and hijacked my body. My heart stuttered inside my chest and goose bumps spread over my arms. My gaze jumped around the darkened bar, searching.

A metallic rattling drew my attention to the low counter lining the back wall of the bar. The register shook like an airplane taking off from a runway. It rose into the air. The attached monitor slipped, then crashed onto the floor near my feet, cords dangling. I lurched sideways as the black, boxy metal till sailed through the air.

That piece of shit Reindeer.

I couldn't see him, but I heard a crash and his pained grunt.

"Come on, come on!" The elfy one said, his voice squeaking with fear.

More grunting. Rubber-soled sneakers slapped against the floorboards, as coins jingled inside the till like sleigh bells. They were robbing us, and I was cowering behind the bar like a small child.

"Stop!" Kar Yee commanded, forceful as an army sergeant. On the heels of that shout came a sharp sound. The floor shook with the thump of flesh, crack of bone—too similar to the sound of Merrimoth being impaled. Kar Yee screamed and a wrenching, pained sound that stabbed through my heart. The fog of fear lifted immediately.

I leapt to my feet and zoomed around the bar. When I turned the corner, my feet slid in thick paint. I flew sideways, grabbing the corner of the bar top just in time to stop myself from landing on my ass.

The thieves were silhouetted inside the open door, red lights from their goggles making them look like dark aliens. "You're both fucking dead!" I shouted in their direction.

I reached out for the Moonchild magick. Saw the Tambuku door slam shut as my already-dim surroundings blackened to nothingness. The pinpoint of blue light glowed. With my mind, I began shaping it into a standard binding triangle bordered with sigils, but instead of the numbing silence that usually accompanied the moon magick, I heard . . . voices? Whispering voices. The blue light began fading. I blocked out the whispers and concentrating on the binding—

Until something slithered down my left leg of my jeans.

The moon magick snapped away like a broken rubber band.

Alarmed and shocked, I reached for my pant leg. Nothing. The sensation disappeared. The whispers were gone. A strange dizziness stole over me. I didn't get dizzy from using the Moonchild power. That only happened when I kindled Heka with electricity. What the hell was going on with me?

My mind jumped to my mother's image. Christ, at least I hadn't seen her again.

A horrific sob rent the air. My heart twisted. I'd never heard that sound, not in all the years I'd known Kar Yee.

I scrambled toward the sound, slipping in slick paint.

My foot kicked something. I dropped to my knees and crawled on all fours on the paint-coated floor. A noxious scent of latex filled my nostrils. "Kar Yee!" I reached out a sticky hand and touched her—where, exactly, I couldn't tell. It was too dark. But I felt the puffy gold lamé of her jacket.

She whimpered and said something in Cantonese. Her voice was small and fragile.

"Where are you hurt?"

"I slipped. I'm broken up here."

Broken. I slid a hand up her coat, searching. She lay on her back—I could tell that much from the feel of the coat's zipper and the direction of her voice. My fingers touched warm skin. Her neck? She cried out. I snatched my hand away.

"Broken where?" I asked. "Your shoulders? Arms? Ribs?"

"My collarbones," she said between sobs. "Can't move!"

"Don't try. Be still. Stay calm." The last instruction was for myself as much as her.

"Cady!"

I glanced up. Electronic white light floated in the air. Bob jogged toward us, using his cell phone like a flashlight.

"She says her collarbones are broken," I told Bob as he wobbled on his feet and began slipping. "Careful!" I wrapped a steadying hand around his shin, leaving a wet splotch of paint on his pants. He righted himself and knelt down with me, shining his phone over Kar Yee. Her eyes were shut tight. Kohl-tinged tears tracked down her cheeks. Her teeth were gritted. Red paint soaked her clothes; skin, and her razor-straight black hair.

"I'm here, Kar Yee," Bob said.

"Help me," she pleaded.

He leaned closer, gingerly pulling open one side of her coat. His slicked-back dark hair gleamed in the light of the cell phone. "I can't heal bone until I know where the break is. We need an x ray first."

"Someone call 911—now!" I shouted behind me. "Tell them we've been robbed and someone's injured." When a couple of voices replied in consent, I turned to Bob. "Sacred Heart's a few minutes away."

"A lot of Earthbounds on staff there," he agreed. "Maybe someone knew my dad. I'll ride with her in the ambulance."

She sobbed again.

"It's going to be fine," Bob assured her in a calm voice. "You aren't bleeding?"

She said no, but who could tell with all the damned red paint everywhere? Assholes. They ruined my binding traps, stole from us, and hurt Kar Yee.

Then it hit me: this was part of the crime spree Dare had been talking about last night.

Like Merrimoth's out-of-control temperature knack, the telekinesis and electricity-zapping I'd just witnessed were not normal, but the boys hadn't been transmutated. No horns. No fiery halos. Just teenage Earthbounds with enhanced preternatural powers. How the hell was this happening?

A distant crash sounded from somewhere beyond the door.

"Stay here with her," I told Bob. "I'm going after those jackasses." I pushed myself up, careful not to jostle her.

"Get them," Kar Yee bit out.

I shuffled past the bar, asking if everyone was

okay, recognizing a few voices that called back in response. The light was better here, near the window. Stupid ineffectual wards. All they'd done was scorch the doorframe. I threw open the door and took the steps two at time, a black rage pulsing in my veins. When I got to the top step, my gaze fell to the cement. Silver and copper coins fanned out over the sidewalk like ocean spray over rocks. A few scattered green bills fluttered in the wind, dancing when a car on Diablo Avenue zipped past. The empty till sat broken and dented against the brick wall of our building.

I ran down the sidewalk, scanning both sides of the street, then abruptly turned around and looked behind me. A few Earthbounds ambled out of a late-night diner. A homeless man huddled under a dirty blanket on a bench. But nowhere did I spy a thieving Reindeer or his elfin cohort.

They'd gotten away.

4

A devastating feeling of loss and disappointment washed over me as angry tears welled in my eyes. Defeated by two scraggly punks, all because I'd used the wrong magical wards and gotten lazy. I should've pounced on those kids the second they walked in the bar. After all the shit I'd been through, you think I'd know better than to let my guard down.

I'd failed Tambuku. Failed Kar Yee.

Failed myself.

But while Bob rode with Kar Yee to the emergency room, I pushed away these nagging feelings of incompetence, donned my Responsible Business-Owner cap, and stayed behind to handle everything.

Dealing with police always made me twitchy. Living under an alias did that to a girl. The two officers who responded to the robbery were both savages—humans who didn't believe in anything supernatural—so I couldn't exactly tell them that the hoodlums who robbed us were Earthbounds with crazy, amped-up knacks. I did my best to gloss over the paranormal details. They couldn't understand how the fuse box had been blown—and I do mean blown, as the thing was smoking and the connected wires melted—but a forensic examiner dusted it for fingerprints anyway and bagged up the dented till.

While she did, I made a phone call to an electrician to replace the fuse box and get our lights back on, but the soonest he could make it was tomorrow afternoon.

What a mess. The red paint under the barstools had already dried in spots. The barstool legs were going to have to be stripped, the binding sigils repainted. The floor refinished. Once the cops had taken statements from some of the customers and told me they'd be in touch, I put a sign on the door that said Tambuku would be closed several days for repair. Then I locked up the bar and headed to the Metropark.

Bob called. The ER was slammed. A local overpass had inexplicably collapsed, causing a multi-car pileup that closed down the highway and brought in dozens of critically injured passengers. He talked to an Earthbound doctor who'd told him that the recent slew of petty crimes around the city was becoming a nightmare for the hospital. Patients arrived with fatal burns, unexplainable plague-like diseases, internal bleeding, and more broken bones than the man had ever seen in his career. I was starting to think that Dare was right to be worried about all this. Not that I was going to change my mind about working for him, but Jesus. There was definitely something weird going on.

A nurse examined Kar Yee, gave her ice packs and pain meds, and told her it'd be two hours before she could get an x ray. Bob was taking her back to his place, so I hopped in my old Jetta and sped to meet him there.

Bob lived in his parents' old house in one of the nicer neighborhoods of Morella. At one time, it was probably a grand, lovely house, but Bob's inheritance was dwindling, and home-maintenance was not his top priority. I'm sure all his über-successful doctor and lawyer neighbors loved the fact that his gutters were overflowing and his lawn was overgrown, but they were probably all jerks anyway, so I told him he shouldn't care.

Ever since the night he'd saved Lon's life, he'd been going to an alcoholic support group twice a week. I tried to tag along with him every other meeting. I couldn't be his sponsor, as I'd never had a substance abuse problem, but I figured since I was the one who'd served most of his drinks over the last couple of years, I could take the time to help him stop. He still came to Tambuku every night—which was totally against the support group's rules—but I made him virgin drinks. And, with his permission, I'd been adding a small dosage of a medicinal tonic I'd brewed up with milk thistle and kudzu root, which was purported to cleanse the liver and reduce his cravings for alcohol. He said it helped; he'd been sober for five weeks now.

I knocked on the front door and opened it. "Hey, it's me."

"Back here," Bob called out.

His house was messy and always smelled like a combination of spoiled picnic basket and elderly shut-in. I suspected he had something dead inside one of the walls—a rat, bat, or cat—and told him to call an exterminator, but he said I was imagining it. (I wasn't.)

A long hallway led past the living room to his deceased father's home office. A desk sat in front of a wall of anatomy books and medical periodicals, and at the far end of the room was an examination table, a glass cabinet filled with half-empty pharmaceutical drug bottles, and some random medical equipment, including a portable x-ray machine. Bob stood in front of a computer screen. Kar Yee reclined on the examination table, which had been adjusted so that she was almost sitting.

Dried red paint clung to her hair, hands, jeans. It was spattered over her gold coat, which was draped over a nearby chair. She stared straight ahead, unmoving, her arms flopping at her sides. She looked awful. I swallowed hard and tamped down worry.

"Hey," I said, padding across the room to stand next to her.

"I'm never going to the emergency room again," Kar Yee answered, her voice weary and cracking. "They are all assholes. 'Put some ice on it,' that's what they told me. And the ambulance ride was worse than Bob's car. A waste of insurance money."

"They were understaffed," Bob said, his focus remaining on the computer screen. "But it's fine. I've already x-rayed her. Pulling the image up now."

"I probably have radiation poisoning," Kar Yee said, blinking lazily.

I forced a smile. "You sound like Amanda. Before you know it, you'll be drinking green protein smoothies and riding a bike to work."

"Bikes are for schoolchildren and poor people," she said tartly. "I will saw off my legs before these feet touch pedals." Her sarcastic snobbery lifted a small weight from my chest. I'd take that over tears any day. "So, did you bring it?" she asked.

I tugged a brown vial out of my jean pocket— a magical medicinal, fairly strong if unpredictable. "What did they give you at the ER?"

"Something that should wear off in about an hour," Bob said. "Let's wait, to play it safe. If she overdoses right now, she'll have to spend all night in the waiting room before they can pump her stomach."

"I'll take the risk," Kar Yee said. "Dope me up, Cadybell."

She *never* called me that. No way was I giving her the medicinal now. I leaned against the examination table and ran my fingers over the long lock of hair at the front of her bob, now tipped in red. "I think you can use WD-40 to get latex paint out of your hair."

Her gaze tilted up to mine. "Really?"

Pity and guilt knotted my stomach. "I'm sorry I

didn't get them," I said. "Your knack caught me off-guard, and when you fell . . ."

"They'd destroyed your binding triangles," she said.

"I know, but I've been experimenting with a different kind of magick. Something that doesn't require—" I hesitated, wanting to tell her more than I should in front of Bob. "It doesn't matter," I finally said. "I should've been able to stop them. I'm sorry I didn't. And I'm sorry you got hurt."

"Don't blame yourself," Bob said. "It's like I told you on the phone—these robberies are happening everywhere. I've never known an Earthbound who could short out electricity like that. I thought that was something only *you* could do, Cady."

"Me too," I admitted.

"You think it could be magick?" Kar Yee said. "A talisman?"

I brushed a paint-tipped lock of hair off her cheek. "Something that boosts the potency of the wearer's knack?"

"Is that possible?"

Not that I knew. I mean, there was the Hellfire Club's transmutation magick. But even if it wasn't a closely guarded secret only doled out to select members, even if it didn't bring out the horns and the fiery halos, that kind of magick—a permanent spell cast on a person's body—couldn't be replicated in a temporary sigil worn around someone's neck.

"I seriously doubt it," I told Kar Yee. "But something weird's going on."

"And Tambuku's not the only business on the block to get hit," Bob said. "Right before we left the ER, I heard someone saying that the corner shop two blocks away got robbed earlier today."

"Diablo Market?" I said.

"Ooh, they carry that cantaloupe-flavored gum from Hong Kong I like," Kar Yee said. Yeah, she was definitely doped up, missing the point.

"Did you hear any details about their robbery?" I asked Bob. "Maybe it was the same kids."

"The woman didn't say. I just know they're closed for a few days. A lot of broken glass."

"Not us. We'll be open tomorrow," Kar Yee said.

Like hell we were. "Let's not worry about that right now," I told her.

A loud knock rapped three times on Bob's front door. The door slammed shut and heavy footfalls sounded. I peeped my head out into the hallway. Lon's honey-brown head bobbed in out of shadows. *Oh, thank God.* Just the sight of him filled me with relief.

"Hey," I called out as he approached.

"You all right?" he said as he reached for me.

"I'm fine."

He held my face in his hands and tilted it up for his inspection, then pulled me against him. I hugged him briefly then led him into the room. "She's in here."

"Hello, Lon."

Lon nodded a polite greeting. "Bob."

"Hey," Lon said to Kar Yee, towering over her. "Hanging in there?"

"This? Pfft. It's nothing," Kar Yee said with a silly grin. "How's my favorite pirate captain? Did you come to give me something nice to look at? A little pirate booty?" She snorted a laugh at her own joke.

Lon stared at her in horror for a moment then said, "What's she on?"

"Dilaudid," Bob answered from the computer. "She's just experiencing a mild euphoria. It should wear off soon."

"Where's my future boyfriend?" she asked Lon. "Did you leave him at home?"

"He's got school tomorrow."

"Sorry to interrupt, but here it is," Bob said, looking at the x ray of Kar Yee's chest on his flickering computer screen. On the wall above, several framed certificates hung in black frames. Universities and state licenses . . . all belonging to his father, Hector Hernandez. Bob had gone to medical school when he was younger—he was in his thirties now—and dropped out. My guess was that he had a good deal more medical knowledge than the average person, but healing surface wounds or simple bone breaks was one thing. Messing around with hearts and brains and complicated diseases was another matter altogether.

Lon and I looked at the screen over his shoulder. "Find anything?"

"Look, right here. Clean fractures"—his fingernail

tapped the screen twice—"one and two. You were right, Kar Yee. Both clavicles."

"Can you heal them?" she asked.

Bob's mouth twisted to one side as he smoothed a palm over his dark hair. "I healed Tamille Jackson's broken toe two weeks ago."

"So, that's a yes?"

"Doesn't look like any bones shifted," he mumbled to himself, squinting at the computer screen. "And I think it usually takes two or three months for this kind of fracture to heal naturally. I might be able to cut that down to a few weeks."

"Weeks?" She sounded horrified.

Bob's brow furrowed. "I don't know. You could feel back to normal in a few days, but you certainly aren't going to be able to unload a truck at the bar."

"Cady unloads the trucks," she said, all matter-of-fact. "How long before I can move my arms?"

Bob looked at me and shrugged, the grinning Tiki masks on his Hawaiian shirt moving up, then dropping.

"Probably a few days, yeah, Bob?" I said, rolling my hand in an encouraging gesture out of Kar Yee's sight.

"Definitely," he said, shaking his head with a panicked look on his face.

Didn't matter if it was true or not. It was just what she wanted to hear.

"Let's get to it, then," she said. "I've got to work tomorrow."

The only work she'd be doing was sleeping. I wondered if I could pay Bob to sit with her and make sure she didn't leave her apartment—I certainly couldn't babysit her *and* take care of all the crap at the bar. I still had to call the employees who were scheduled to work and tell them what happened. Find someone to clean up the red latex pool on the floor. Contact the artist who originally painted the binding traps. And as Bob cracked his knuckles and prepared to work his healing mojo on Kar Yee, I added another line to tomorrow's ever-expanding to-do list: talk to the owners of the convenience store down the street.

I sat on a rickety examination stool, Lon's hands on my shoulders as we watched Bob leaning over Kar Yee. And even with everything going on, all I could think about was the eerie whispering I'd heard when I used the Moonchild power in the bar . . . and the terrifying feeling that something had jumped through the Æthyr and crawled down my leg.

5

Bob did his healing mojo on Kar Yee, then we knocked her out with some oxycodone he found in his father's prescription drug stash. We figured that was more stable than my home-brewed medicinal. And though Lon offered to hire a nurse to sit with Kar Yee for a few days, Bob volunteered before I even had a chance to ask.

The next day, I woke thinking about my mother and the last time I'd seen her, when I was handing her over to Nivella, the albino demon who took her and my father to the Æthyr. If anyone could confirm my mother had died after she'd crossed the veil, it would be the demon who killed them. And, since I was a talented magician, I could simply summon up Nivella by using her glass talon, now sitting in a safe in Lon's library.

Easy peasy.

But when Lon swung open the heavy door to the wall safe, he spotted a problem I hadn't anticipated: the glass talon no longer had a soft pink glow of Æthyric Heka surrounding it.

"This doesn't look good," I said, hefting the crystal claw in my hand. "Why would the Heka disappear?"

Lon stared at it for several moments. "Only one reason I know of."

Me too, but I tried anyway, just in case. I spent half an hour constructing a strong binding inside a summoning circle. I had Nivella's name, class, and her talon—everything that should've been needed to call her from the Æthyr. But the albino demon did not come when I called.

Nivella was dead.

Anxious and stressed, I rode back to Morella with Lon that afternoon in his black pickup. In the back was a generator he had in storage, just to help me get some temporary lighting in the bar. I spent most of the ride thinking about my mother. Just because Nivella was dead didn't mean that my mother was necessarily alive. The demon could've tortured my parents to death and died later of something unrelated.

That's what I told myself, several times, until Lon turned on the radio to distract me. A local news station was reporting Tambuku's robbery, along with several others in the area. It pissed me off, to be honest. Why couldn't we make the news for winning some award or hosting a noteworthy event? Seemed like my failure to catch the robbers was being broadcast for the world to hear. *Look at the mighty magician: she couldn't stop two douchebags from maiming her business partner and making off with the register!*

After we set up the generator in the alley, I left Amanda and one of our busboys to wait for the electrician to show up and fix our fuse box. Lon and I walked two blocks over to the corner shop that had been robbed.

Like many of the businesses in this area of the city, Diablo Market had a small Nox symbol on its sign, indicating it was demon-friendly. It had once been a run-of-the-mill place to buy Cokes and candy bars, and beneath the counter, cheap valrivia and the latest issue of *Savage Shemales*. Last year it remodeled and started carrying overpriced organic juice and Brazilian chocolate. I liked it better when it was trashy.

We waited in front of a coffee house for the walk signal to flash so we could cross the street to the market. One of the baristas waved at me through the front window. Davey. He was a couple years younger than me and cute in a starving-artist, nice-guy kind of way.

Lon made a small noise. Passing cars kicked up a wind that blew open his thin, brown leather jacket, revealing a taupe T-shirt tucked into jeans. My eyes dropped to his fly. This particular pair of jeans, though pricy enough to be hanging around the hips of a male model, had a permanent, whirlpool-shaped dark mark below his belt buckle, caused by developer chemicals in his darkroom. I swear he wore them on purpose to distract me.

"Who's that?"

"Huh?" I tore my eyes away from Lon's hypnotic

dark spot to see him jerking his head toward the coffee shop window, his gold-and-green halo trailing. "Oh, that's nobody."

"Well, *nobody* sure is staring pretty hard at you."

"I highly doubt that."

Green eyes squinted down at me. "Then why are you embarrassed?"

"I'm not embarrassed," I protested, but I totally was.

"And why is he jealous?"

I glanced at Davey through the glass and gave him a tight smile while speaking to Lon. "You can't possibly read his feelings this far away . . . can you?" We were a good twenty feet from Davey. No way his empathic knack worked from this distance.

"He's got a jealous look on his face," Lon explained.

"Oh," I said, a little relieved. For a moment, I wondered if Lon's knack was getting stronger. If this enhanced-knack phenomenon was affecting *all* Earthbounds, I'd be in some major trouble. "Davey and I went out once. It wasn't a big deal."

"He's a kid," Lon grumbled. "Probably doesn't even have to shave."

And a year ago, I would've laughed at the idea of dating a man Lon's age, but now . . . well, I couldn't disagree: Davey seemed like a kid to me, too. "I said we went out once. There was a reason for that."

"Which was?"

I glanced down at his dark swirl again, then met his gaze. "No chemistry."

Lon tried—and failed—to suppress a cocky look while the streetlight turned yellow. I pulled his jacket closed, then jumped when he cupped two bossy palms around my ass.

"Hey," I protested weakly.

He gave my cheeks a slow squeeze. "Just want to show the scrawny barista what he's missing."

"If I knew you were so fond of PDA, I'd have never taken up with you."

"Liar."

I chuckled.

"Hey," he said. "Stop worrying about things you can't control. If your mother is alive, we'll deal with it."

I gave him a soft smile. "You're my favorite person, you know."

"You're my favorite person, too."

Our private code. A normal couple would've already exchanged the L-word, but Lon was uncomfortable expressing emotions. Being constantly bombarded with everyone else's feelings made him apprehensive about wearing his heart on his sleeve. I also wondered if his failed marriage made him guarded. Understandable, if it did. But no way was I saying it first, regardless of how I felt. Besides, this worked just fine for us.

"Light's changing," he said, letting his fingers trail over my back as he released his grip on me. "Come on."

Holding his hand, I matched his stride, ponytail swinging across my shoulders, and stuffed my free hand inside the pocket of my black hoodie. It had an embroidered dragon on the back and the word KOREA curved over it in big block letters—something Jupe and I found in a Morella thrift store a couple weeks back.

The handwritten sign on the market's door looked similar to the one I'd stuck on my bar's: CLOSED TEMPORARILY FOR REPAIRS. WILL REOPEN NEXT WEEK. Yet, the lights were on inside, unlike at Tambuku. I rapped on the door until a stooped-over elderly Latino man with a dark green halo peeped from behind a rack of freeze-dried fruit snacks. I waved and smiled.

"We're closed," he shouted through the glass. He was dressed in a loose pink panama shirt and khakis. No shoes.

"I'm the owner of Tambuku Tiki Lounge down the street," I yelled back.

He looked at me as if to say "So?"

"We got robbed last night, too."

That got his attention. He clicked open a lock and cracked the door, tossing a wary glance over my shoulder at Lon. "You got robbed, you say?"

"Yeah. Around midnight. I was wondering if I could talk to you and compare notes. Maybe it was the same people."

He glanced up and down the block, then waved us inside and locked the door behind. I winced at the smell. Rotten milk? A large plastic bin on casters was filled with leaking melted gourmet ice cream and boxes of no-cheese gluten-free frozen pizza. A couple of young boys were emptying their freezer display.

"Our electricity was out for too long," the man

explained, waving a grizzled hand toward the boys. "We lost everything perishable."

"Us, too. My lights aren't back on yet. I've got a guy replacing the fuse box. My name's Cady, by the way, and this is my boyfriend, Lon."

"Andrew," he answered, glancing up at Lon's strangely gilded halo, then at my silver one—clearly he was curious, but not enough to straight-up ask. That was my general experience, anyway. Many Earthbounds even assumed I was one of them, just . . . different. "They did a number on us, as you can see." He pointed toward the checkout counter. The entire area looked as if a tornado had ripped through it. The glossy wood countertop was splintered and tilted into an upside-down *V*. The register was missing, and a big black safe jutted up out of the middle of the destruction.

"Christ," Lon muttered.

Andrew settled both hands on his hips and sighed dramatically. "My wife and I have owned this store for twenty years. We've been robbed at gunpoint twice. Thought we were done with that after the remodel." He turned to me. "How did yours happen— your robbery? Guns?"

"No guns," I said.

He gestured to my halo, finally acknowledging it. "You're the magician who binds Earthbounds."

I gave him a soft smile. "I am."

"People talk," he said by way of explanation, turning his attention to re-stacking a fallen display of all-natural beeswax lip balms. "Tell me about your robbery."

"Two Earthbound kids. Late teens, maybe. One blond, one dark-headed. Both faces were painted in theater makeup. A reindeer and an elf."

"A horse and some sort of frog," he said in agreement, referring to his robbers.

Could've been the same get-ups. It was, after all, *really* bad makeup.

Andrew's mouth twisted briefly. "Did the blond boy *poof!* your electricity?"

"Yep. I've never seen a knack that powerful. The other boy used telekinesis to lift my till drawer across the room."

The shop owner nodded slowly. "He tried to lift the damn safe straight up through the counter."

Thank God we kept Tambuku's safe in the back office. Those punks might've made it out of the bar with a thousand dollars or so, but they missed five grand in the safe. Idiots.

Andrew continued, saying, "He nearly killed one of my girls who was stuck behind the register when he was trying to lift that thing. Thank God she had the sense to crawl away."

"He slopped paint all over our floor and my partner slipped and broke her collarbones."

Two thick gray eyebrows shot up. "The pretty Chinese gal?"

I nodded.

He made a sympathetic noise.

"She'll be okay," I assured him. "A healer is helping knit her bones back together. She's at home resting right now."

"Poor thing. What's wrong with kids these days? No respect. No caution." He waved an angry hand, gesticulating wildly. "In my day, we were taught to hide our knacks at all cost. You start flaunting it, you draw attention. No one cares anymore."

"I don't think these are normal knacks," Lon said. "I've never seen anyone lift anything that heavy."

Andrew grunted an acknowledgment as I squatted near the splintered countertop, inspecting the damage. "Korea, huh? Ever been?"

I glanced over my shoulder. "Oh, that. No. Just liked the dragon."

Andrew nodded as a strange look pinched his face.

"Not a dragon fan?" Lon squinted at him with his Emotion Detective face, like he sometimes does when he's trying to suss out the source of my bad mood.

"No, it's not that." Andrew shook his head. "It's probably nothing."

"You sure?" I said, suddenly interested in what Lon was sensing.

"It's silly."

"Maybe not," I encouraged.

"It's just . . ." Andrew scratched his ear. "The blond boy dressed like a frog . . . it's hard to be sure, but he sounded like . . ." Andrew shook his head. "Ah, never mind. My wife says old age is ruining my hearing. Have to turn up the TV to hear the news."

"Go on," I encouraged. "The blond boy sounded like what?"

"Not a 'what.' Λ *who*." Andrew squinted one eye shut as he studied my face, then looked away. "I didn't realize this until now, but he sounded like a boy who used to come in here after school. Been a few months since I last saw him. Think he might've started college. Don't know his name. Only know that his father drives a beautiful old Plymouth Road Runner."

I gave him a blank look, but Lon was grunting in appreciation.

"An old racing car from the seventies," Andrew explained. "Prettiest shade of sky blue you've ever seen with a black stripe down the center of the hood. The kid sometimes drove it here—parked it outside by the curb. Had a dragon bumper sticker on the fender. The dragon on your jacket reminded me." He shook his head. "I don't know. Maybe I'm wrong."

"And you don't know his name?" Lon asked.

"Sorry." Andrew said.

I looked at Lon. "Unusual car. Can't be that many of them in the city."

"I don't know," Lon said. "A lot of car collectors in Morella."

"Especially the old muscle cars," Andrew agreed. "They race them every month."

"Where?"

"Speed Demon Rally. Down at the Morella Racetrack, on the highway going out toward La Sirena. I go sometimes. Next one's tomorrow night."

"Have you ever seen that boy there?" Lon asked.

"Saw the car there a few weeks ago, but not the boy."

Couldn't hurt to check it out. At the very least, one of the collectors might know the name of the kid's father.

I thanked Andrew and told him I'd let him know if I found out anything. On my way out, I paused at the door. A dark sedan was parked across the street where we'd seen Davey through the window. The driver was staring at the corner store, but ducked when he saw me through the glass. Huh.

"Hold on," Andrew called out from behind me.

I pulled my attention away from the car and watched him hurry down the candy aisle. He returned with a white plastic tub that fit inside my palm and rattled when he handed it to me. "For the Chinese girl," he said.

I looked at the label. It was the cantaloupe gum from Hong Kong that Kar Yee loved.

"On the house," he said. "Tell her Mr. Andrew says to get better. And if you find that boy and it *was* him who robbed us, you bring him here to me." He lifted the hem of his pink panama shirt to reveal a giant jeweled belt buckle shaped like a cobra head. "My kids are too old to get a whipping, but he's not."

I grinned. "Sure, I'll let you have him, but I want the telekinetic boy."

Lon and I exited the corner shop. As we discussed tracking down the Road Runner at the racetrack, I glanced across the street. The dark sedan was gone.

6

"This place is bananas!" Jupe shouted over the rumble and roar of muscle car engines. His spiral-curled, bushy dark hair was limned in both the lime-green of his halo and the megawatt halide lamps lighting up the night sky inside the Morella Racetrack.

Jupe was tall for his age, only a few inches shorter than his dad, and though he was skinny as hell—all legs and arms and slender fingers—a masculine build was blooming beneath his lankiness. He had Lon's green eyes and his African-American mother's alluring mouth—well, as best as I could tell from photos; I hadn't actually met the woman. Yvonne used to be a model when she was younger. And though she'd pretty much given up her visitation rights (it had been a couple of years since she'd bothered coming to see Jupe), her mother and sister remained close—they were the ones coming to spend Christmas with Jupe and Lon.

Jupe, Lon, and I made our way past half-empty grandstands and a massive warehouse-like building that housed a retail shop and a long aisle lined with food vendors. There, we stood for a moment, watching the track. Old, rusted muscle cars sat near the starting line.

"So they don't race the restored cars?" Jupe asked.

"Too much money and time in the restorations to risk wrecking them. The race cars are beaters with souped-up engines," Lon said. "It doesn't matter. We're not here to watch races. We're here to find the ass who robbed Cady."

Jupe zipped up a green army surplus field jacket covered with old horror movie patches. "I know, but what's wrong with multitasking? Oh man, I think I smell nachos."

Funny, because all I smelled was burnt engine oil and stale valrivia smoke. "Help me find a sky-blue Road Runner in that side lot over there," I said, pointing to rows of restored cars that filled a curving strip of asphalt, hoods propped open to showcase gleaming engines. "And if you do, I'll buy you nachos with extra cheese."

"Throw in some jalapeños and you've got yourself a deal," Jupe said, waggling his brows.

Lon snorted. "So I can listen to you moan and bitch when you've got a stomachache later? Forget it."

"Jalapeños are barely even hot going in," Jupe noted. "Why do they hurt so much coming back out?"

"God moves in mysterious ways."

"Hoof it," I said, planting my hands on the kid's shoulders and pushing him into motion.

Jupe loves cars. Jupe loves old things. So a couple of months ago Lon and I gave him a busted-up

1967 GTO for his fourteenth birthday. Lon thought it would be a good experience for his son to learn how to rebuild a car in the two years he had until the dreaded sweet-sixteen driver's license—otherwise known in the Butler residence as the first day of the apocalypse. Neither of us expected Jupe to actually do all the work by himself. I personally thought he'd remove a few rusted bolts and call it a day. Surprise, surprise: Jupe had managed, with a little help, to strip out half of the parts under the hood. The kid was smart. And determined. Lon might've made a huge mistake giving him that thing.

We strolled down the first aisle of vintage cars, stopping every few feet so Jupe could ooh and ah. The fourth car we came to was a red convertible GTO. "Look, Dad! It's just like my car!"

"I see."

Jupe leaned over the engine, craning his neck to peer inside as the owner, a middle-aged Indian man with a light blue halo and matching blue-framed glasses, walked up. "Did all the work myself," the man said, proudly.

"Cool. I've got one, too!" Jupe blurted. "Mine's a '67. What year is this? '70?"

"You're close. '71."

Jupe backed up to look at the grille. "Wire mesh. I should've known."

"Ah, very sharp. I'm Nihal, by the way," he said, offering his hand to Jupe.

"Jupiter."

"You restoring yours, too?" the man asked.

"Sure am. It's a hunk of junk right now, but I'm going to get it in shape like yours. Hey, how long did this take you, Nihal?"

"Eight years, I—"

"Eight?" Jupe's horror-striken eyes were big, green grapes. "Man, it better not take me *that* long. How much did it cost you?"

"Jupe," Lon chided. "That's rude."

Nihal grinned. "No, that's okay. He's a fellow GTO-lover." He walked with Jupe, who was now checking out the driver's seat. "I bought it for $18,000 and put about $15,000 into it."

Jupe mouthed the amount to Lon.

"But I've insured it for $55,000. That's how much it's worth."

"Holy sh—"

"Crap," Lon and I both spoke over his response.

Jupe frowned at us. "I was going to say 'shamrock.' Geez, give me some credit."

Nihal grinned.

"He was raised by wolves," Lon said to the car owner.

"Oh, *please*," Jupe said. "Don't flatter yourself." While Lon shook his head and slowly inhaled, Jupe ran a slender finger over the leather headrest. "Hey, Nihal. You wouldn't happen to know about a blue Road Runner that shows here?"

Nihal's eyes tightened briefly, then his brows shot up. "Sky blue? Black stripe on the hood?"

"That's the one," I said.

"Sure, I've seen that here before. I think someone bought it at last month's rally."

Dammit. "Do you know the owner's name?"

"His first name was Dan, I think. But I never knew his last name. Ask Freddie—he's the guy at the end of the row standing next to the white Barracuda. Freddie's a Plymouth man. I'll bet he knows."

"Thanks, man!" Jupe said.

"No problem. Good luck with your restoration. If you need any pointers, I usually come here every month. Stop by and see me again."

"I will, thanks."

We strolled away from Nihal, heading toward the man he'd pointed out, but stopped a few cars away for Jupe to inspect another Ford.

"So Nihal was being honest?" I asked Lon.

"Completely," Lon said as Jupe ran a hand over white-walled tires.

Kinda figured he was, but you never knew. Lon often busted my bubble when it came to trusting people—not that I need much help in that department. But because of his knack, I no longer ate at the sweet little fish-and-chips restaurant near Tambuku with its nicer-than-pie elderly owners. Lon informed me that they were lying about their spotless food safety inspection scores; the grade A posted in the window, much like my own birth certificate, had been falsified.

We made our way down to the Plymouth expert,

Freddie. He was in the middle of a conversation with someone. Jupe wandered off, chatting up another muscle car expert, while Lon took a work phone call.

I glanced toward the racetrack and felt the ground-shaking rumble of rusty old beaters steering into place behind the starting line. It was almost eight. About time for the races. I wanted to have the name of the Plymouth owner before they started. Feeling antsy, I swung my attention back to Freddie, who was facing the other way. As he laughed, he leaned against a shiny yellow car, allowing me to see the person with whom he'd been conversing. Not a man, but a boy. A blond boy with a pale green halo. He adjusted the fit of his crimson Speed Demon baseball cap, pulling it down tighter . . . which made his ears fan out like two pale seashells glued to the side of his head.

Well, well, well. Theater makeup or not, it was the blond elf who robbed me.

The boy laughed at Freddie. As he did, his gaze drifted to mine. His eyes widened for a moment. *Yeah, that's right. Recognize me, don't you?* He spun on his heels and took off.

"You little pig fucker," I mumbled as I bolted after him.

The boy was young, skinny, and fast. He wove in and out of the crowds mingling near the cars on display, heading toward the back of the lot. Adrenaline spiked through my body as I pushed myself to catch up. I heard Lon yelling my name, but I didn't look back.

He made it to the end of the lot. Towering in front of him was a wall of cement bricks painted with the Morella Racetrack logo. Beyond it was a garage for the racecars. No way he could scale the thing. Either he could head to the left behind the grandstands, or turn around and try to make his way past me, back through the lot.

He did neither.

Instead, he made a sharp right turn, heading for a rusty chain-link fence that separated the showcase lot from the main dirt parking lot outside the racetrack. With feline grace, he jumped several feet and grabbed the top of the fence, then pushed himself over it.

Dammit!

Chain-link fences and I don't mix. The last time I went over one was at the abandoned putt-putt course outside of La Sirena with Lon. I nearly cleaved myself in two in the worst possible way. But I'd be damned before I let this little ratfink get away from me. Mentally girding my loins, I climbed the fence as best I could. Rust bit into my fingers as I groaned and swung a leg over the top. It felt all wrong. In trying to keep the prized parts between my legs safe, I overshot and tumbled over the fence. The air whooshed out of my lungs when my shoulder hit the dirt.

I ignored the pain and scrambled to my feet.

The kid's red cap danced in the distance. I

bounded between two parked cars and skirted a sign identifying the color-coded parking area. He was two rows away from me. A car backed up in front of him, causing him to skid. Maybe it was just the break I needed. For a moment, I had a vision of how crazy I must've looked, chasing after a skinny little boy like he was the devil. But what did I care? They'd all do the same thing if they knew what he'd done to me and Kar Yee.

Zigzagging through unevenly parked cars, I halved the distance between us while he sidestepped the moving car. He glanced back at me, looking like a frightened rabbit. I wanted to shout something cool and intimidating, like "you're dead!" but frankly, I was huffing and puffing too hard to spit out the words.

Maybe I should have tried.

To my surprise, the boy pitched to the side, then leapt onto the hood of a parked leopard-spotted van and sprinted over the top of it, jumping off to land in a cloud of dust in the next row. Showoff. But a few seconds later I saw why: the cars were parked too close together here. I mentally grumbled and followed suit.

The leopard-print hood creaked with my weight. Just as I leapt to the roof, I heard a loud grunt from the boy. An oh-too-familiar noise followed: the buzz and pop of electric current being overloaded. Multiple explosions cracked through the parking lot before everything went dark. White sparks showered the air above me . . . in front of me . . . they fell from every light pole in the parking lot. Glass tinkled across the tops of cars. A few random shouts echoed around the lot. The lights inside the racetrack were still on. Must've been wired separately. At least I knew the kid's knack had some limits.

As I teetered on top of the van, I caught sight of his red cap. He was picking his way around a damaged light pole. No night vision goggles. He was hindered like I was. Glass crunched under my feet as I jumped to the ground. I dashed across the dirt lot, weaving through parked cars until I saw the boy skid to a stop in front of a car. He bent low, struggling with keys.

My lungs burned as I picked up speed, trying to catch him. He got the door open. I wasn't going to make it.

No way in hell was I letting him get away again.

I stopped short in the middle of the aisle and called up the Moonchild power. The grays and blues of the parking lot shadows turned black as my pinpoint of blue light appeared . . . and along with it, those same strange whispers I'd heard before. No discernible language or voice. It struck fear in me, but at least it didn't catch me off-guard like it had when I tried to use the power during the robbery. I ignored the whispering and focused on the task at hand.

No screwing around this time. I didn't bother concentrating on the binding symbols, nor trying to shape the blue light as I had in the past. Like I had at Merrimoth's, I just poured all my willpower into one singular thought—

Trap.

The boy made a choking sound as my immediate environment snapped back into view. The whispering hushed. And there was nothing foreign slithering down my leg. So far, so good.

Silver fog shrouded the air in front of me, creating a tunnel of swirling ethereal light that led to the blond boy. He was trapped inside it, sprawled on the front seat of his car, one leg dangling over the doorframe, gasping for breath.

What the hell kind of trap was this? It was as if I was radiating some sort of noxious silver gas. Then I noticed the point of origin: above my head. My hand flew to my hair. I jerked my head back and looked upward at my silver halo. Impossible! It was growing and spreading—like the silver fog from the night I slowed time at Merrimoth's house.

An intense nausea made the ground below my feet seem to buckle. I stumbled, panicking, as the boy began crying for help, pleading for me to stop. Lon's voice bellowed in the distance, entwining with the boy's pleas. But it was the third voice, a lighter-than-air feminine voice that stabbed me like a dagger to the chest.

"Ma petite lune."

I jumped back in surprise, lost my footing, and

fell on my ass. The silver fog funneled back into me, rushing toward my face like a vortex was centered above my head, sucking it all back in. It happened so fast it made me dizzy. Every muscle contracted at once. I cringed, biting down on my tongue until it bled. I felt sick. Exhausted. And scared out of my mind.

An engine rumbled. Tires spun and squealed, kicking up a small cloud of dust that went up my nose as the blond boy drove away. I coughed, tasting blood. When the dust cleared, I spotted a dark figure huddled between two cars across the aisle. A man. Something about the way he was standing made me thing he was hiding. And the way he retreated deeper into shadow as I tried to focus on him made me think he was trying to slip away unseen.

As he moved out of sight, I thought of the dark sedan I'd seen outside the corner shop, though God only knew if there really was a connection. My head was so rattled at the moment, I was probably half-crazy. I tried to push myself up, but I was too weak.

"Cady!" Lon's deep voice vibrated through me. "What happened? Talk to me."

But I couldn't talk. Intense, jumbled emotions flooded my senses. And when he gathered me up, pulling me against his chest, all I could do was wilt inside his arms as he mumbled, "I've got you. It's okay."

But it wasn't. As much as I didn't want to admit it

to myself, it was all kinds of *not* okay. Something was wrong with my powers and it was getting worse.

Ma petite lune. My little moon. Only two people ever called me that, and both of them were supposed to be dead.

7

Jupe stuck his head between the front seats of the SUV on the ride back to their house, touching me with little pokes and prods, trying to get my attention. Trying to make me smile. I finally gave in—there was really no other option with him, as he'd mastered the art of pestering—and turned sideways in my seat, letting him hold my hand. His skin was soft and he smelled nice, like the coconut in his shampoo.

"At least we got the name of that punk," Jupe said.

Noel Saint-Hill. Lon had tracked down the Plymouth guy, Freddie, before we left the racetrack. He didn't know where the Saint-Hills lived, but we could probably do some Internet sleuthing and figure it out. Something positive came out of all of it, but I couldn't shake the sound of my mother's voice, repeating in my head like a bad song.

"I wish you'd tell me what's wrong," Jupe said as we sped along the dark highway that connected Morella with La Sirena. "Maybe I can help."

"I wish you could," I said. My tongue was fat in my mouth, swollen from me biting it.

"If I were you, I'd be bragging to everybody. You need a comic book hero name, like Silver Fog, or something. That was insane!" he said enthusiastically.

"Yeah, it was pretty crazy." It was the *other* crazy thing I was more concerned about at the moment.

"And you didn't know you could do that?"

"Can't say I did."

Lon grunted. His eyes were on the road in front of us, lost in his own thoughts. Probably wondering the same thing that was floating through my mind: *how was my mother still alive in the Æthyr, and what the hell was I going to do about it?*

"Well, you shouldn't be upset," Jupe was saying. "Because that fog spell was one hundred percent bad*ass*. When you jumped up on that van, I was all, holy shit! I thought—"

"Shut it, Jupe," Lon warned.

"I'm just sayin', maybe she should be happy about it. Who knows what she could do if she tried." He poked me on my elbow. "Besides, you told me magick is unpredictable."

"I told you that the results are unpredictable. And that talent is varied."

"Oh, please. Don't quote semantics to me."

"You mean 'argue' and '*with* me.'"

He chuckled sheepishly. "I don't really know what it means."

"Well, you used it right, by some miracle."

He made a pleased clucking sound with his tongue. "Because I'm smarter than I have any right to be. That's what Mr. Ross says every time I prove him wrong in class."

Lon made an exasperated noise and knocked the back of his head against the headrest.

"You aren't supposed to prove your teachers wrong," I said. "You're supposed to listen and do what they tell you."

Lon's phone rang. He looked at the screen and answered in his usual terse manner, grunting and mmm-hmming his way through the call.

"What-ev," Jupe whispered, eyeing his father as he conspired with me. "Mr. Ross is wrong, like, twenty times a week. He said yesterday that if I was so sure about myself, maybe I should be teaching the class. And I said, 'Hand me the chalk!' And I think he was *this* close to sending me to—" He glanced at Lon, then silently mouthed *detention* to me.

I almost laughed. He was making me feel better, despite everything swirling in my head. It was hard to be upset with all his energetic mile-a-minute chatter.

"Oh!" he said, suddenly changing gears. "Lemme read your palm. I read a book today in the library that teaches you how."

Like that.

As Lon hung up the phone, I let Jupe spread open my palm and squint over the armrest, studying the intersecting lines in my skin by the soft blue glow of the dashboard and the brighter bud-green emana-tions from his halo. Skinny fingers traced flowing patterns as his spring-loaded, flouncy curls tickled my cheek.

"I hate to be the one to tell you this, but you're going to die, like, whoa! Three times. Wait, wait, wait. Hold on." He squinted harder, peering an inch away from my hand. I was tempted to smack him in the face, Three Stooges style. "That's not your life line. What the hell kind of line is this? I can't tell jack about any of these lines. That palmistry book was junk."

He continued to mumble to himself, exasper-ated but fully intent on solving the mystery inside my palm. I nibbled the back of his neck playfully. He giggled and shoved me back with the side of his head. We were laughing. It was all good. Then, out of abso-lutely nowhere, I started crying.

What the hell was wrong with me?

Jupe dropped my hand in alarm. "I didn't mean it. You're not going to die three times."

I covered my face with my hands and slouched in my seat. "I don't even . . . know why I'm . . ." I grit-ted my teeth and groaned, forcing back tears. I felt so out of control, like I could lose it completely at any moment.

I couldn't just break down like this. I mean, so what if my mom really was alive? She was on an-other plane. She couldn't touch me here. And if we shared some sort of connection through the stupid

Moonchild power—God only knew what sort of ritual magick she'd conjured up when conceiving me—then I'd either find a way to sever it, or just stop using it completely.

I took a few deep breaths. Lon and Jupe were staring at me in that *Oh-Shit, Female-Is-Crying* sort of way. "I'm fine," I said, sniffing and brushing tears off my cheeks. "I'm fine.

"Maybe you're, you know." Jupe squinted at me knowingly.

"Know what?"

He gave me a superior look. "Oh, you know. '*That* time.'" He made air quotations with one hand. "Women get weird then. I've noticed a lot of girls crying at school on the same days. Kiya said it's because when girls spend a lot of time around each other, they start to, *you know*, on the same schedule."

"Well, right now I'm not, 'you know-ing,'" I air quoted him back. "But thanks for teaching me about my own body."

"You're welcome," he said seriously. "See. I'm learning all kinds of things at school. Last year none of the girls were crying. But this year? *Whew*! Watch out, buddy."

"Why does God hate me?" Lon murmured.

The SUV began its familiar ascent up the dark roads that led to Lon's secluded cliff-top property. Soft moonlight filtered through pines and redwoods. I blew out a breath and relaxed in my seat as a mind-numbing exhaustion settled over me. I wasn't going to think about my mom anymore. Tomorrow we'd track down this Noel Saint-Hill in Morella. Maybe I'd even just do the normal thing and file charges against him. Let the police handle it. Not try to fix things with magick for once.

Two roads led to Lon's house: a zigzag death-trap of a road that visitors used—and on which I'd once wrecked my car and been chased down by an Æthyric demon sent to kill me—and a hidden side road that only family used. Both roads led to locked gates that required either a key code or a remote to enter. But the side road gate's auto-open feature had broken last week. You had to get out and open the gate manually, then shut it behind you once you drove inside; the guy who installed it was supposed to fix it soon.

Jupe had closed it when we left for the racetrack, but it was now open.

"Lon," I said, sitting up straighter. My galloping pulse cleared the emotional fuzz from my brain. "The gate."

"It's fine."

The only other people who used it were the housekeepers who lived on Lon's property, Mr. and Mrs. Holiday. And they were more anal about security than Lon.

"I *know* I latched it," Jupe protested. "You think a wild animal knocked it open? Maybe an Imp?" A circular magical ward kept the acre around Lon's house safe from intruders and Imps: small transparent demons that have the ability to pop back and forth between the planes—the only known entity with a free pass to travel at will. They were like ghostly cockroaches, irritating but harmless.

But we'd just crossed over the house ward, so it couldn't be Imps.

"Maybe it was Foxglove," Jupe suggested.

"Dogs can't open gates," Lon said as he stopped the car. "Go shut it."

"What if something's out there?"

Hey, I didn't blame the kid. These cliffs were heavily wooded, and Lon owned ten acres of property. The only other souls up here were the Holidays. It was peaceful, but kind of creepy at moments like this. "I'll shut it," I said, jumping out of the SUV.

I scoured the dark woods around me as I walked. It was quiet and serene. A biting wind whispered through the brush and scattered the scent of cypress and dead leaves. If I stopped to listen, I'd hear the surf crashing against the rocks half a mile down the cliff below. But I didn't want to try, not when I felt this creeped out. I thought of the man hiding in the shadows of the racetrack parking lot and moved faster. The gate screeched as I swung it shut and latched the handle. I hurried back to the yellow-lit interior of the SUV and slowed when I heard Jupe make a joyous noise. Lon shushed him.

"Okay, okay," Jupe protested.

I stopped in front of my open door. Both of them stared back at me, wide-eyed, like they'd been caught with their hands in the cookie jar. "What the hell is going on?" I asked.

"Get in," Lon said.

"Not until you tell me what's going on."

"It's nothing. Just get in."

A horrible worry cramped my stomach, but I got inside and shut the door.

Lon shifted into gear and drove toward the house, a modern long-lined construction of stack stone and plate glass. Very Frank Lloyd Wright. Expensive but not showy. It sprawled on a section of cleared land that overlooked the Pacific, with stunning views. But right now it was the house itself that was worrying me. I could see movement inside the golden light outlining the oversized windows. I'd usually assume it was just the Holidays. They came and went freely, and their snug cabin-style house was only a short walk down another side road.

But when I spotted the strange white Mercedes parked behind Lon's dusty pickup truck in the circular driveway in front of the house, I started to sweat.

"Whose car is that? Is that a rental? That's a rental. Is that car from the airport?"

Lon pulled up behind it. "Now listen. I didn't know. Mrs. Holiday just called me."

Jupe squealed in delight. "Cady, you are going to love them!" He opened his door before the SUV came to a complete stop and leapt out, then ran up the path to the dark red front doors.

"What's going on?" I was close to sobbing again. Could this night get any worse?

Jupe's voice carried to the SUV as he flung the double doors open. "Gramma!"

"Oh, God," I said. "Why are they early? Why didn't you tell me?"

"Rose didn't warn me. She does this sometimes."

Rose Giovanni, aka Gramma. Lon's ex-wife's mother. And she was with Yvonne's sister, Adella. Lon's in-laws. Jupe's real family. *Send me back to the racetrack.* I could deal with a supernatural fight. I could *not* deal with interpersonal family relations. Not yet. I needed more time to prepare.

I stepped out of the car in a daze. Lon walked around to my side. "I didn't know," he insisted, forcing me to look at him. "Hey. Stop worrying."

"But I'm the enemy," I whispered. "I'm Yvonne's replacement. I'm young. I'm a dirty stinking magician."

He lifted my chin up. "You'll win them over."

"Ugh."

"Give them time to get to know you. They'll accept you."

I grunted.

"If you need time to go upstairs and get cleaned up, I'll go in first. Come down when you're ready, okay?"

"Okay."

"Just remember, Rose can hear through walls."

Clairaudient. Worst knack ever. I feigned a small weeping noise.

Lon pulled me close. "We'll figure out what's going on with your Moonchild power. And we'll hunt down the rat who robbed you tomorrow. Can't do much tonight anyway." He kissed me softly, first on the lips, then on the tip of my nose. "Mmm?"

I nodded, and we made our way to the front door.

Giddy talk and laughter rang though the house as we stepped inside the foyer. My gaze swept over the living room as Lon walked toward the commotion.

The Butler home was minimally decorated, lots of pale wood and long, low seating. White lights covered the branches of the World's Biggest Christmas Tree. It was heavy with Jupe's ornaments (some were made in elementary school, some were miniature plastic models of comic book characters he collected) and took up half a floor-to-ceiling window.

Sliding doors led to an expansive deck in back. I could see figures reflected in the glass there. And as Lon rounded the foyer hallway wall, I paused, scoping out the visitors before they saw me.

At first, all I saw were the twin white-bobbed heads of Mr. and Mrs. Holiday. They weren't actually a Mr. and Mrs.—that was just what Jupe had called them since he was a kid, and the names stuck. In actuality, they were two women in their late sixties. They looked like Martha Stewart stand-ins. They treated Jupe as if he were their own grandchild, and I was pretty fond of them and their no-bullshit attitudes. Right now, they were laughing with the

Giovannis as if they were all best of friends. Mrs. Holiday moved out of the way, and I caught my first glimpse of the in-laws.

Yvonne's younger sister Adella was as I imagined: tall and willowy, with a dark mass of curls very similar to Jupe's restrained by a wide purple scarf. Pretty in an understated way. She wore a sheath dress the color of wine, and a long string of mismatched metallic beads. Her complexion was darker than Yvonne's, a deep cinnamon-warmed brown. Round cheeks shone under the living room lights as she laughed. Jupe was flexing his barely-there arm muscles for her. "Feel that!"

She pinched his upper arm. "Here? Or here? Tell me when you're ready to flex."

"I'm flexing!" He gave up and tackled her around the waist, trying to lift her off the ground. "Urgggh! Damn, Auntie. Have you gained weight?"

She reached across his back and slapped him playfully. "Let go of me, fool, and give me a proper kiss, or you're not getting any of Gramma's blackberry bars."

His head shot up as he turned to look over his shoulder. "Youmadeblackberrybars?"

"Kiss. Now." Adella pulled his face to hers and kissed him loudly on the lips, their green halos and springy curls briefly mingling.

He hugged her tight, grunting with the effort. "I'm so glad you're here."

A funny feeling fluttered inside my chest. And as if she sensed this, Jupe's black lab, Foxglove, trotted around the corner and jumped up on my legs, panting in my face happily as she greeted me. I scratched her behind one floppy ear and peeped around the corner, watching Lon strolling over to his ex-mother-in-law.

"I told you not to bring a shitload of sugar in this house, Rose."

"And I told you to stop swearing in front of my precious grandbaby, so I guess it all equals out."

Cropped, silver-white hair fanned around Rose Giovanni's slim face. The woman may have been in her sixties, but she was stunning. It was easy to see where Yvonne got her supermodel looks.

She wore stylish glasses and was dressed in a pale green pantsuit that matched her halo. Adella's halo. Jupe's halo. And even from across the room, I could see Jupe's green eyes beneath her glasses—which were even more startling paired with her darker skin. I always assumed Jupe inherited Lon's eyes, just a lighter shade, but now I wasn't so sure. Lon once told me that Rose's parents were from the Caribbean. Puzzle pieces fitted into place.

Lon dipped his head and kissed Rose on the check. She wound an arm around him and rubbed his back. "Not mad we came early, are you?"

"Are you joking?" Jupe answered for him. "It's an awesome surprise, Gramma. Winter break starts tomorrow, so I'm all yours. And now we have three days before Christmas Eve, and there's all kinds of junk we can do."

"Anything you want."

"Anything? I'll make a list. And the number one thing will be for me to demonstrate my persuasion knack for you." Jupe squinted one eye shut and wiggled his fingers dramatically, like he was a stage magician using fake mind powers.

"Absolutely not," Lon said.

"But they've only heard about it. I want to show them."

"No, you want to show *off*," Adella said. "Plenty of time for that later."

"Listen to your auntie." Lon smiled at Adella and reached to hug her, arms loosely encircling her. She mumbled something against his ear; he kissed her on the forehead in response. They were casual and comfortable around each other. Affectionate. I never saw Lon act that way with anyone but me and Jupe. Never. It made me wonder how Lon and Yvonne acted when they were together. And that thought made me a little nauseous.

"Wait, where's—" Jupe's gaze found mine before I could sneak upstairs. "Cady! Com'ere, com'ere!"

All faces looked my way. My stomach dropped three stories. Nothing I could do now.

Jupe strode to my side and tugged me into the middle of everything. My hair was sweaty around my nape. My jacket had dirty streaks on the sleeve from rolling around on the ground at the racetrack. And my eyes were red and puffy from crying. I'm sure I made a great first impression.

"Everybody, this . . . is Cady."

8

Jupe said my name like it was fifty feet high and studded in lights, but the reception was decidedly mixed. Rose stared at me without saying a word. Adella stepped forward and offered her hand. "So good to finally meet you." She sandwiched my hand between both of hers and gave me a sweet smile.

"You, too," I said. "Jupe talks about you—"

"Constantly?" she guessed. "Because I get weekly updates about you. 'Cady this. Cady that.'"

Jupe almost looked embarrassed, but he really didn't have it in him to be shy. "You told me I talk about movies too much, so what else am I going to say? Geez."

She winked at him. "Anything you tell me, I'm happy to hear. Besides, I talk about art all the time."

I remembered that Adella taught art history at the University of Portland. "Is the semester done? All your classes, I mean."

"Yes, thank goodness. Finals graded, and all my meetings finished. The students fled the campus yesterday like they were outrunning a tornado."

At thirty-five, Adella was ten years older than me, and a handful of years younger than her sister, Yvonne (who was in her early forties, like Lon). She had a kind face. In other circumstances, I would've liked her immediately. And I did, but it was tainted with self-doubt and worry that she wouldn't accept me, despite how nice she was being. Looking at her mother, that worrisome feeling intensified.

"And this is my Gramma," Jupe said proudly.

Rose Giovanni didn't offer her hand. Just coolly looked me over, eyes blinking rapidly. For every inch of my body she examined, I think I shrank two. She might be the demon, but I certainly felt like the devil in the room.

"It's nice to meet you," I said, wondering if I should add "ma'am." Or would that be insulting? Better play it safe and keep my mouth shut.

She stared above my head. "There's that silver halo we've heard about."

"Yes."

"A real live witch, huh?"

"Magician," I corrected.

She made a little I'm-not-impressed noise, then glanced at the dirt streaks on my sleeve.

I looked down at them as well. "It's . . . been a bad night."

"Oh?" She pushed metal-rimmed glasses up

the bridge of her nose with one polished nail, then turned to Lon and lifted a brow. "What happened?"

Great. She'd officially cut me out of the conversation.

"Cady's bar got robbed earlier this week," Lon said.

"Oh dear," she said. "A dangerous business, I'm sure. Open all night, attracting the wrong element. Like owning a liquor store."

A mild spark of irritation pushed away my initial self-consciousness. "We're open until two, and we've never been robbed before."

"Tambuku is the most awesome bar in Morella, Gramma," Jupe said.

"I'd love to see it," Adella said. "I teach a class on Polynesian art every summer."

I didn't think our Tahiti Tropicana pinball machine was going to impress her, but at least she was being nice. I started to answer her, but Rose cut me off. "There's nothing 'awesome' about a bar, Jupiter. Drinking leads to misery."

Somewhere behind me Lon mumbled, "Christ, I think *I* need a drink right now."

"It's not like that," Jupe protested. "Right Cady?"

"Bartending isn't a respectable profession," Rose said.

I'd never felt ashamed about what I did for a living, and I wasn't about to start now. If this woman was trying to take me down a few notches, she'd have to try a little harder. "I'm a good bartender. I police my bar and stay aware of how much I'm serving people. When a patron's crossed the line, I cut them off and call a cab."

"But you still serve them, don't you? And just because they get in a cab doesn't mean they don't go somewhere else and do stupid things. No good comes from drink."

I suddenly realized what she was getting at. Yvonne's stints in rehab—her public struggle with drugs and alcohol. Car accidents and gambling debts, all of it fueling tabloid headlines back when she was still working as a model. I didn't know if she'd sobered up recently; Lon and Jupe didn't talk about her. And the media had lost interest in an aging supermodel that hadn't worked for years.

The Giovanni family had disowned Yvonne. Rose had bonded with Lon over Jupe and chosen them over her own daughter. I knew this was a sensitive subject. I didn't want to upset Jupe, but I didn't want to back down, either.

I straightened and locked gazes with her. "I can make a good guess as to why you feel that way, but don't make the mistake of confusing me with your daughter."

She flinched in surprise before staring me down like she could will me to burst into flames. The room was uncomfortably quiet for several beats.

"Now, if you'll please excuse me," I finally said, "I need to wash up."

I turned to head upstairs. Lon tried to follow, but

I put a firm hand on his arm to tell him no. And as I climbed the first few stairs, I heard Rose say behind me, as if nothing had just happened, "Who wants oatmeal blackberry bars?"

The evening got better. An unexpected introduction to Mr. Piggy helped liven things up. Who could resist a pygmy hedgehog that could climb up the Christmas tree and leap onto your shoulder when you least expected, like some kind of little psychotic, quilled monkey?

I avoided speaking to Rose directly, except to say "thank you" and "excuse me" and "sorry my pet hedgehog jumped on your shoulder." And she avoided speaking to me as well, but wasn't antagonistic. After the hedgehog incident, Lon put on music, a Stax Records compilation he sometimes played on Waffle Day, otherwise known as Sunday outside the Butler household. It was hard to be upset while listening to Issac Hayes and Otis Redding. He knew this; he'd played it on purpose. And when Jupe and Adella began telling a long story about the origin of a handmade Christmas ornament on the tree—a clay disk that on first glance was Jupe's handprint, but on second, was actually the impression of Foxglove's foot—Lon slid beside me on the couch and pulled me close, almost into his lap, wrapping his arms around me. Out of the corner of my eye, I saw Rose darting the occasional glance our way, but she made no comment.

Adella and Jupe finished their story. They both made big, sweeping hand movements when they talked. What else had he inherited from his mother's side? It was as if the mysteries of his dynamic personality were being revealed, layer by layer.

And, dammit, I really liked Adella. She was smart and witty, and she snorted when she laughed, just like Jupe. I tried so hard not to be jealous when Jupe begged her to come up to his room and watch late-night TV. But, you know, that was *my* job. *I* got to turn off the TV when Jupe fell asleep on my arm.

Dear God, what a pity party I was having. I wanted to slap myself. Instead, I excused myself and ate another blackberry bar in the kitchen. As I was licking the last sticky crumb off my finger, Rose walked through the doorway. Alone.

"I'd have made more if I knew they'd go so fast," she said, staring down the nearly empty plastic-wrapped pan.

They were pretty freaking divine, though I wasn't about to tell her that. And I wasn't sure if she was trying to tell me to keep my grimy hands off her baked goods, or if she was acknowledging that she was pleased I liked them. Maybe she somehow knew this was my third one, even though I'd tried to be stealthy.

I really didn't know her intentions at all, so I just didn't say anything.

She'd taken her jacket off and was walking around in her stocking feet. She had firm, slender arms and incredible legs, which wasn't fair. She was in her sixties. Her legs should be . . . well, I don't know, but they shouldn't look like that. Mine didn't. I was sort of relieved when she put the blackberry bars in the fridge and moved her too-good legs out of my sight, standing behind the curved kitchen island as I washed my hands in the sink.

"I don't believe in couples living together outside the bonds of marriage."

My hand slipped on the soap pump. A streak of green gel sprayed against the white subway tile behind Lon's sink. "Is there somewhere you're going with this?" I said as I aggressively lathered my hands. "Or is that just a general comment?"

"Lon told me it was none of my business when I asked if you were living here, which is probably true. But Adella told me that Jupe said you rent a house in Morella."

"I *own* a house in Morella," I corrected.

"Well, regardless of whatever arrangement you and Lon normally have, I'd like you to stay at your own house while I'm visiting."

I slammed the faucet handle off and spun around halfway, flinging droplets of water into the sink. "Let me get this straight. Are you telling me—"

She held up both hands. "It's not a demand, but a request. I don't like Jupiter thinking that couples living together without strings is okay. And if I consent to stay here while you're living in sin with Lon, then that sends a signal to Jupiter than I approve of this. And I don't. I'd like you to respect that."

"Well, I think that's pretty ballsy of you to ask."

She took off her glasses and wiped them on the corner of her striped, sleeveless shirt. "No one's ever accused me of being timid about speaking my mind." Without looking at me, she fit her glasses back in place. "Regardless, it's either you or me. If you stay, I'll go to a hotel in town. But I'd appreciate it if you decide soon, because it's half-past nine. That may not mean much to someone who works the graveyard shift at a bar, but I've spent the afternoon standing in security lines at the airport. I'm tired. I'd like to go to bed. And I'd also like for Christmas to be a happy time. His mother ruined one too many holidays for all of us. I hope you don't do the same."

And as I stood there with my mouth hanging open, she turned and walked out of the kitchen.

Dear God, that was some nerve she had.

First, it was none of her damn business what arrangement Lon and I had. And what did she think my leaving would accomplish? If I left for a few days like she wanted me to, I'd just be back when she went home after Christmas, shoving my wanton ways in her grandkid's impressionable face. It made no sense. I wasn't leaving. Forget it. Decision made. I had other things to worry about than her moral compass. Like stupid punks with impossible knacks and whether my serial killer mother was trying to make my life miserable again.

Putting a lid on my anger, I exited the kitchen and headed to Lon's photography studio.

My fingers found the light switch and flipped it on. Bright white light illuminated an expansive room ringed on three sides by wide windows. In the daytime, it was warm and golden in here, lit up by natural sunlight. But at night, the glass made a dark, constricting bracelet around the white walls.

Various light stands, diffusion umbrellas, and scrims stood in a corner next to loops of cord hanging on the wall. Long, pale wood tables bordered by rolling stools held multiple computers and screens, a large format photo printer, and some other equipment that was lost on me. A couple of areas of the room were staged for shoots.

I liked it in here. It was both organized and messy at the same time. Quiet. My gaze flicked over a wall of recent photographs, some of them for work, some personal. One was of me, asleep on the couch with Jupe. When I'd first seen it, I was embarrassed: I looked half-dead, mouth open and lax. Seeing it now pinched at my heart. I forced myself to look away and headed to an area where Lon stored photography paper and framing supplies. He strolled into the studio behind me.

"I need some sketch paper," I said, all business-like.

He didn't ask me why, just bent to reach an over-sized pad. "Like this?"

"Perfect. I need a couple sheets."

He tore out two. When he handed them over, he gave me a look that was all Cool Hand Luke and dismissive. "You live here. She's family. No one has to leave."

I stared at him.

"She just told me," he explained. "No one's going anywhere."

All the emotions I'd been keeping in check flew out like a swarm of bees released from an apiary. "Apparently one of us is." I knew she could probably hear me with her stupid clairaudient knack. I just didn't care.

"This is silliness."

"I agree."

"You were right earlier," Lon said, obviously not concerned if Rose could hear us, either. "This is about Yvonne."

Clearly. But I still stood by what I said: I was not Yvonne. And Jupe wasn't going to follow in his mother's footsteps just because his father's girlfriend worked in a bar or lived in his house without getting a ring on her finger first.

Rose was trying to push my buttons. Testing me. Maybe she wanted to see how far she could shove me until I broke and caused a huge scene. Then I would be the bad guy. I would be the one who ruined Christmas.

If I stayed, she'd leave, and Jupe would be upset. On the other hand, if I was the one who left, Jupe might just be confused. Better confused than caught in the middle of a family fight. As jealous as I was of these two women, and obviously I was—but, come on! How could I not be?—there was no way I was going to fight Rose Giovanni to prove a point.

Dammit.

I found a clean space on one of his photography tables next to the door to the darkroom and laid down the sketch paper there. After lining them up, I carefully folded and creased the papers together into a neat square, which looked a little like the white flag I was now ready to wave. "I'll leave," I said, turning around to face him.

Towering over me, Lon placed one hand on the edge of the table near the right side of my hip, then the other on the left, trapping me inside his arms. He shook his head slowly, then leaned down and dragged his mouth over my cheek. "No," he whispered in my ear.

He kissed me, softly, deliberately slow. My resolve liquefied. His hips pushed against my lower stomach. Was there anything better than this?

"No," he repeated against my lips.

Sure, he was using sex against me. And as far as arguments went, it was a good one. Just sex with Lon on its own was enough to sway me, but now his head dipped and he was inhaling deeply against my neck, his expanding lungs pushing his stony chest into my breasts as he sucked in the scent of my skin. His loose, honey-colored hair fell over my face, and I was overwhelmed by the urge to beg him to hold me. To give me a refuge. To allow me an unguarded moment. Because of all the things he could do to me, do *for* me, this particular ability was high up on the list. No one else, not a single living, breathing soul on this plane or the next, could I trust like I trusted Lon.

I didn't always understand him. His motivations were often half-hidden, and the quiet strength he commanded, especially when he was transmutated, was sometimes frightening and alien to me.

Yet I trusted him. Utterly. And after what I'd been through with my parents, this was no small feat.

"Let me handle this. I'll convince her to stay," he murmured. "No one's leaving."

But an insistent thought danced in the back of my mind and wouldn't leave, dousing my body's revving heat. Even if Lon could convince Rose to stay, even if he changed her mind, what was I going to do? Go to bed with Lon, knowing she could hear the sheets rustle? She could probably hear the shiver-inducing scrape of his mustache against my neck right now.

I was afraid to use the bathroom, for the love of Pete, knowing that she could hear me peeing.

Everything about this stunk. Stink. Stank. Stunk.

Pushing him away was soul-crushing. "I'm going."

His eyes darkened. "You can't spend the night in your house. It's unprotected."

"I'll go to Kar Yee's place," I reasoned. "Bob can't stay there forever. She'll end up killing him. I'll give him a break. It's good for everyone."

"We haven't spent a night apart in weeks."

"Every time you go on a photo shoot we spend the night apart."

"And I despise every damn second of it."

"I hate it too, but I'm not going to Yoko your family. If anyone's going to ruin Christmas, it's gonna be her, not me. Because when I'm not here in the morning, she can damn well tell Jupe that she was the one who made me leave."

I hadn't known it until I said it, but that was it, wasn't it? I wasn't interested in playing the martyr. I *wanted* her to lose. And the way that Lon's eyes crinkled at the corners, I knew he'd picked up on this, too.

"Besides," I said, picking up the folded sheets of sketch paper. "I have to track down that Noel Saint-Hill punk in Morella tomorrow. It'll save me a drive."

Which was true, but I had something else I wanted to do. Because at some point during the hedgehog attack and Rose's insistence that I leave, I realized there was someone who could tell me if my mother was still alive and kicking on another plane.

9

Kar Yee's apartment smelled like microwave popcorn. I surveyed the pristine white-and-gold living room and kitchen, and smiled when I spotted her lone tribute to the holidays: a tabletop white Christmas tree wrapped in red lights sat on the glass table in the dining room, and beneath it, a pile of presents, including Jupe's tiny opera figurine, now spattered in drops of dried red paint. Kar Yee's bah-humbug protests in the bar were such a crock.

I dumped a duffel bag of clothes in the foyer near a low wooden rack made for visitor's shoes. Kar Yee was a shoe-phobe. She was convinced that footwear was invented by Satan himself—or, at best, carried the plague. It was almost one of those obsessive-compulsive things. She often walked around Tambuku's office in socks or silky slip-on dance things. It was kind of ridiculous, but it was worse when we lived together in college—God help the person who dared to put their disgusting shoes on her dorm bed.

But I guess we all had hang-ups. I slipped off my boots, placing them next to a pair of men's brown lace-ups, and padded down the hall.

Like every other room in her compact apartment, the decor in her bedroom looked as if it belonged in some swank Far East hotel. Gold leaf-patterned curtains draped the window, blocking out her view of midtown Morella. A muted, oversized painting of Hong Kong's Victoria Harbor hung over the bed. She was sitting in bed, propped up against gilded pillows, wearing her collarbone brace over yellow silk pajamas. Her normally super-shiny black hair looked dull and limp, pulled back into a bun atop her head. A mostly empty snack bowl was wedged between her legs.

Bob sat in a stuffed chair next to her, his feet on an ottoman. He appeared quite comfortable, lounging in a light blue Hawaiian shirt, white pants, and no shoes. A taupe blanket with a woven cherry blossom pattern lay across his legs. I wondered if this is where he'd been sleeping instead of the couch in the living room.

As I stepped through the doorway, they looked up from what they'd been watching on TV. They were both smiling goofy grins.

Clearly, I'd walked into some sort of apocalyptic nightmare.

"What are you watching?" I asked.

"A *Three's Company* marathon," Kar Yee said in a lazy voice. "Bob says the three of us should move in together and recreate episodes. What do you think? Tambuku could be the Regal Beagle."

"Are you *both* on painkillers now?"

This was too weird for me. I'd be glad when the bar was open again and Kar Yee was in the back office being her normal ruthless self.

"Are you okay?" Bob asked me.

Kar Yee feigned a pouty face. "Never mind little miss killjoy. She's sad. She doesn't get to sleep with her big-handed boyfriend tonight. Boo-hoo."

"Big-handed?"

A lock of Kar Yee's hair slipped out of its sloppy topknot. We'd managed to get most of the paint out, but not all, so she'd had her hair stylist come by and chop off an inch of her bob. Now it was too short to stay in its binding. "His hands are veiny and muscular," she explained.

"You make it sound like he's got gigantic ham hands." They were like the rest of him: strong and lean. He was in perfect shape. It was almost criminal. Muscular, but not showy or beefcake-y. Fabulous arms. And a beautiful stomach with the most perfect ridge of dipping muscle right above his hipbones and—

"His fingers are long, but they sure aren't skinny," Kar Yee noted. "Pressing all those camera buttons must give them a regular workout."

And taking all these pain pills must be rotting soft spots right through her brainpan.

"They are very tan fingers," she added, the beginnings of a slow smile lifting her lips.

"So's the rest of him. He spends a lot of time outdoors."

"Is he tan below the waistband?"

"Please stop fantasizing about Lon."

Bob squirmed uncomfortably beneath the cherry blossom blanket. He looked as if he might hack up all the popcorn they'd been chowing down. "Is this what you two talk about after work?"

I said "no" at the same time Kar Yee said "yes." Then she threw a piece of popcorn at me.

"Seriously, Bob," I pleaded, bending to pick it up and toss it back in her bowl. "Wean her off the meds. You said she could take the brace off tomorrow."

"She *can*," he insisted, then mumbled, "You try to wean her off."

Kar Yee was laughing at the TV, oblivious to our conversation. Once Bob left, I was going to swap out all her pills with Tylenol. "Hey," I said, snapping my fingers in front of her face. "If you even care, I got the name of one of the guys who robbed us."

Her languid gaze sharpened immediately. "Don't tease me."

"Noel Saint-Hill. The one who used his knack to cut the lights."

"The wimpy elf?"

Bob threw off the blanket. "Are you serious? How did you find this out? The Morella Racetrack thing?"

I gave them a brief account, leaving out the parts about the silver fog and my dead mother's voice. Though I did tell them about biting my tongue, which still hurt like hell. Kar Yee offered me one of her painkillers; Bob quickly shook his head while she wasn't looking.

Part of me wished Bob wasn't here. It might've given me a chance to talk to Kar Yee about my identity. Confessing while she was doped up might make things easier. Then again, that was pretty chickenshit. I guessed I'd wait until after she was healed up, but it was starting to make me antsy. Once I decide to do something, I prefer to get it over with.

"By the way, I need two favors," I said.

Bob looked up. "Yes?"

"Can you start searching for Noel Saint-Hill's address online?" I'd already done some poking around on my phone during a short break in the Giovanni-Butler reunion and found what could very well be a couple of his social network profiles—it was hard to tell from the photos, but it didn't matter, because they were protected.

"On it," Bob said, whipping out his laptop.

I thanked him, then spoke to Kar Yee. "I also need the key to the rooftop access stairs."

"Why?"

"Magick. I have to do a spell."

"On the roof?" she complained. "It's past midnight."

"It's important. Will take me thirty minutes, tops. No one will see."

She raised a slim, dark brow and puckered her lips, as if she might say no, then blew out a spacey, drug-blissed breath. "Ehhh, all right. As long as you're not painting pig's blood on anything, the key is hanging over the phone in the kitchen. But if any of the other tenants catch you, I have no idea who you are."

Kar Yee's apartment building stood ten stories high on the edge of midtown, surrounded by Morella's twinkling high-rises. Behind me, twenty miles in the black distance, lay La Sirena and the Pacific coast . . . and the bed I normally shared with Lon. I wondered if he'd have trouble sleeping without me. He said he did when he was on business trips.

I made my way to a sheltered area behind a line of air conditioning units. Tenants often used the cement-topped roof for parties. A low brick wall kept drunken guests from falling to their death onto the busy city street below. And even now, when most people back in sleepy La Sirena were in bed, I could hear a steady, speeding rumble of traffic all around me. Somehow this was comforting.

When I first met Lon, I had a link to the Æythr. A witch's familiar, of sorts—or perhaps a better description would be a magical lookout, a being that could be called upon for information or help. Priya.

After being my eyes and ears on the Æthyric plane for most of my adult life, Priya died a horrible death trying to defend me against demonic attack.

Priya was what magicians call a Hermeneus spirit, an asexual messenger entity that looks sort of like a humanoid bird-person. They are highly coveted, hard to wrangle, and not every magician successfully manages to snare one. To petition their help, you have to lure them in a special ritual. If one of them likes the cut of your jib, it might offer up a lifetime of service. They form a link to your Heka signature—something as unique to each magician as a fingerprint.

Like other Hermeneus spirits, Priya didn't physically cross over from the Æthyr to my plane when I called. Instead, it used my Heka to transmit a kind of hologram of itself. All they could really do here was relay information, so they weren't much use for earthly tasks, but they were invaluable Æthyric spies.

And they also had the unique ability to reincarnate.

The last thing Priya relayed to me before dying was a plea to wait for its return. That it would find me. I had no idea how long that would take. Years, maybe? But it had been months, and maybe that was long enough. I didn't really want to try to bond with another Hermeneus. Sure, Priya and I never had a *friendship* kind of relationship—these creatures were notoriously aloof. But it was hard to imagine linking up with someone new.

Still, I wasn't sure if I could afford to wait much longer. I needed an ally who could confirm or deny my parents' deaths in the Æthyr. I needed someone to tell me exactly what this Moonchild power was, and find out what the hell my parents had called down into me when I was conceived.

A cool night breeze fluttered my hair as I set down the things I'd scrounged from Lon's for the calling ritual: a zip-top bag of salt, a paring knife, the folded sheets of sketch paper from his photography studio, my pocket-sized caduceus staff, and a nub of my trusty red ochre chalk.

I set to work with the chalk, sketching out a generic beacon sigil for Hermeneus spirits on the paper Lon gave me. A companion symbol was tattooed on my inner arm in white ink, along with several others inside an ancient Egyptian style cartouche that could be activated with a smear of Heka-rich body fluids like spit or blood. When Priya and I were linked, I used the tattoo to call it. But Priya's death severed this link, and to reestablish it, I was going to have to do some creative spellwork.

In my magical order, calling a Hermeneus spirit would be a big to-do, a temple ritual that would be witnessed by the congregation. Sort of like a Bar Mitzvah. The magician calling the spirit would be in ritual robes. There'd be an energy-raising ceremony beforehand, a lot of chanting. The whole shebang would be presided over by the leader of the order, the Caliph—my godfather. And afterward, depending on the success of the ritual, which had a fifty-fifty chance of working, depending on the magician, there would be a celebratory round of wine or consolatory round of "it just wasn't in the stars" and "maybe next time" speeches.

I would no sooner don a ritual robe than stick a

knitting needle in my ear, and I didn't need a crowd of chanting occultists to cheer me on. It felt good just to be doing magick the old-fashioned way, chalk in hand, caduceus by my side, whistling "Breaking the Law" while I worked.

Once finished with the beacon, I used the second piece of paper to write Priya's name inside a cartouche with my personal sigil as a magician—a moon cradling a flat three-tiered rose—and connected the two sketches with a series of linking symbols. I didn't really know for sure that this would work. I hadn't actually known any magicians who'd tried to re-link themselves to reincarnated guardians. On the rare occasion that a guardian died, most magicians would just try to call a new one.

But I didn't want a new guardian. I wanted Priya.

In the center of the calling sigil, I poured a small pile of the salt I'd stolen from Lon's kitchen—some sort of fancy gourmet sea salt I liked to tease him about, because Morton's table salt was too crude for his superstar palate. For a brief moment, I idly wondered if better ingredients, as in cooking, made for better magick.

His hundred-dollar paring knife was certainly sharper than the dime-store utility knife in my kitchen drawer. And it damn sure made a sizable nick on the pad of my pinkie finger. Kneeling on the cement, I pressed the edges of the cut together and watched as dark drops of my gourmet Heka-rich blood plopped onto the white salt pile.

A soft gust of wind sifted through my hair and caused a few grains of salt to scatter. Better get this done before the whole pile blew away.

One good thing about living in a big city was that there was such a wealth of electrical current. I barely had to reach out for it. A bright stream of electricity jumped into my body, latching onto my Heka, mixing with it, charging it. My nerve endings fizzled with raw energy. The roots of my hair swelled and lifted. Cells bounced around, dancing deliriously.

I was alert. Strong. In charge. And *damn* if it didn't feel good!

But as I kindled Heka, somewhere in the horizon of my mind I spotted the now-dreaded flicker of blue light.

10

No fucking way. I definitely did *not* want to screw around with wild magick while I was trying to do something so specific and technical. And I damn sure didn't want to hear my mom's treacherous voice again.

It was all I could do to hold on to my kindled energy while I pushed back the Moonchild magic. I wasn't sure how long I could keep it at bay, but I had it under control for the moment. Maybe I could learn to pick and choose what I want to use for kindling: electricity or moon power. The best of both worlds. That thought gave me a little thrill.

Breathless and shaking, I sputtered the words to the spell, a phrase of rough commands in classical Hebrew. Then I slammed the graphite tip of the winged caduceus onto the outer edge of the calling sigil.

"Priya, come!" I shouted into the wind and released the kindled Heka. It poured into the caduceus, coursed through it, and spread across my red ochre marks—all the way through the line that connected the calling sigil to Priya's name. The marks lit up with a pulsing white light.

Reflected energy ran back up my arm and hit me like the kick of shotgun. My shoulder jerked back as the caduceus overloaded and flew out of my hand. It streaked across the cement roof and struck the low brick wall, exploding into a shower of wood splinters and golden sparks.

And before I had a tenth of a second to be surprised, the post-magick nausea lashed up and slapped me silly. My stomach clenched, my chest heaved. The sharp, acrid stench of the vomit that followed mixed with something sickly sweet. I really wish I hadn't eaten all those stupid blackberry bars.

Lesson number one when doing any big spell-work involving a lot of kindled Heka: bring tissue and water . . . which I did not. As I swayed on my knees, I spit twice in disgust, then wiped my mouth on the sleeve of my jacket, making a mental note to shove it in Kar Yee's washer later.

A mass of crackling white light appeared in front of my face.

"Shit!"

I instinctually scrambled backward, struggling to pull my legs out from under me. The light flickered like a TV set with a bad connection, then a human-sized boy lunged out of the sky.

A boy with a head of black hair that stuck out straight in all directions like a sooty nest.

Flying.

With wings.

His body was human, mostly. His nails were glossy, black, a little longer than they should be—almost talon-like. His skin had a silver gray cast to it. He was wearing loose pants that fell below his hips.

A massive pair of black, feathered wings fanned over his bare shoulders.

What the hell was going on? Because unlike Priya—who used to appear to me as diffused, soft translucent being, neither man nor woman, stoic and cold—this creature flying in front of me was solid flesh. Very male flesh.

He gazed at me with enormous black eyes.

Bird-boy had a dusky gray halo, which rose like smoke above his punked-out, anime hero, Robert-Smith-meets-Sandman mop of hair. He also had a handsome face with sunken cheeks and high cheekbones, and an aquiline nose that was prominent and curved and beaky, but definitely still a human nose.

His wings flapped madly, stirring up the air and whipping my hair across my face. He floated closer and reached out a hand. I jerked away and fell back against the concrete roof. Undeterred, he shifted his wings—Jesus, they were huge!—and his body tilted. He flew over me, inches above, mimicking my prone position.

My heart galloped. I sucked in a strangled breath and tried to unscramble my thoughts.

What had I done? Was this an Æthyric demon? Had I just summoned a damn Æthyric demon with a binding triangle? Couldn't have. No way. That wasn't a summoning circle. And Hermeneus spirits didn't actually cross the veil to our plane: they were just projections—magical holograms.

But they had birdlike features. Priya had birdlike features. Just not quite like this . . .

The flying boy studied my face with his big, black eyes. Tiny feathers framed his eyelids instead of lashes. And I stared back, his mouth widened into a disarming grin.

His teeth weren't human teeth, but tiny, silver points! Dozens of them.

I flinched. The back of my head smacked the cement. He flew closer and touched my cheek with long, cool fingers.

"My mistress. It is I, your loyal guardian." His voice was low and crackly. Rougher than rough. He cupped my face in both hands, long fingers grazing my scalp. "It is Priya."

My heart stopped.

"Priya?"

His dark eyes went all squinty as he smiled and touched the tip of his nose to mine.

"Mistress!"

I pulled away from him and scooted across the cement into a sitting position. He squatted down in front of me, flapping furiously, and folded his wings into two black compact shapes against his back.

My voice stuttered along with my panicked heartbeat. "It can't be—you're . . ."

"Changed," he said with great pride. "I am reincarnated into a new body."

"You're a boy," I said dumbly.

"A beautiful boy," he agreed. His chest plumped with pride. "Do you find me pleasing?"

"Uh . . ." I blinked rapidly, my eyes darting over his bare silverfish skin, ripped with muscle. "Sure. You're something, all right."

He smiled with that mouth full of sharp, metal teeth. It was freaky. And kind of cool. "Are you as happy to see me as I am to see you?"

"I . . . umm, Jesus! How are you here on Earth? In the flesh, I mean?"

"I am as surprised as you. My species does not travel corporeally between the planes. Perhaps your magick is stronger. Or perhaps my new body is special. I have only had it a short time."

"If it's really you—"

"Of course it is. How could you not know me? I died saving you."

I grimaced. A terrible pang of guilt clinched my roiling stomach. But I still wasn't convinced. This could be the Æthyric equivalent of an Internet stalker. Maybe bird-boy had hijacked Priya's identity.

"How did you die, exactly?" I asked. "I need proof."

"I was eaten alive by hundreds of lichen insects that a Pareba demon sent after me."

My pulse pounded in my temples. "Anyone might know that," I said shakily. "Tell me something no one would know but us. Priya and me."

"You sent me to find a spell to change your hair color when you were young and vain. I told you it was a waste of my skills, but you insisted."

"I wasn't vain."

"You were vain," he insisted.

"You never found the spell."

"It doesn't exist. But that didn't stop you from stripping the color from your hair anyway, did it?" He reached out with one arm, silver-skinned and corded with wiry muscle, to snag a lock of the bleached section of hair behind my ears.

A small sob escaped my lips. "Priya."

"Yes." He touched my cheek again, and this time I placed my hand over his. I was astounded. Shocked. Reeling. And totally, completely humbled. It felt like I'd just brought an old friend back from the dead.

And in a way, maybe I had.

It felt strange to touch him. *Him*—I still couldn't believe it. He looked young. Maybe twenty, maybe older. It was hard to tell with Æthyric creatures. They tended to age slower than humans. I let go of his hand and swallowed hard, trying to hold back tears.

"I heard your call," he said. His feathery eyelashes fanned as he blinked. "I knew it was your Heka. Unmistakable. And the magick was so strong. It made a tunnel of light through the sky. I stepped in the tunnel and your Heka pulled me right through the veil." He made a descriptive gesture with his hands and blew out a *whoosh!* sound.

"Holy shit," I murmured.

He glanced around us for a few moments, surveying the twinkling city all around us, as if he just noticed where he was. He lifted his face and inhaled, breathing in the night air, then turned back to me and smiled. "I am so happy that you did not call another guardian to replace me while I was gone."

"You told me to wait for you."

"And you did."

"Well, I waited as long as I could. I wasn't sure you were alive yet."

He nodded thoughtfully. "You called me because you need me. You are in trouble?"

I shifted my legs and glanced at his wings, the tips of which were softly bent where they met the roof behind him. "Umm, yes. Maybe. I'm—my Moonchild power is changing."

"You are getting stronger," he agreed. "I could tell that from your call. And your Heka smells rich."

I made a face. Maybe he was smelling the blackberry bar vomit. "Anyway, I've been able to do crazy things with it. Slow time, make a weird silver fog trap out of my halo—"

"And pull your guardian through the veil. You are powerful," he agreed. His lips quirked up. "It is exciting."

"Anyway," I said, "I'm worried about my power getting stronger, but I'm mostly worried because I saw a projection of my mother."

His dark brows lifted. "And that is strange because . . . ?"

Oh. Right. Priya died before I found out my parents were guilty of all the ritual killings, handed them over to the White Ice Demon, and let her whisk them away to the Æthyr as her war prize. It took me several minutes to tell the story, but Priya listened intently, crouching before me with his silver arms wrapped around his legs, his chin resting on his knees. He was barefoot, I noticed. And his toenails, though not as long as the talon-like nails on his fingers, were glossy black.

"I will admit, I never liked your family," he said when I was done.

"Why didn't you say anything? Did you know they were guilty?"

He shook his head rapidly. "Of course not. If I thought you were in danger, I would have warned you. But I did not understand the workings of this world, and it was not my place to give opinions about your personal life."

"You don't seem to have a problem with it now," I noted.

He shrugged, black eyes gleaming. "I am different now. But let us return to your problem. You thought the White Demon would kill your mother and father in the Æthyr."

"My parents tricked her. Used her. I just assumed she would take their lives."

"But now you are worried that she didn't."

"I heard my mother whispering to me. I saw her—it was like a projection, you know, how you used to appear to me. I'm worried. I want to use the Moonchild power. But if she's alive, could she find a link through my Heka signature?"

Priya's face drew up as he thought about this. "It is unlikely, but there is only one way to find out. I will hunt her in the Æthyr."

A heavy relief sank through my bones. "Would you, please?"

"I am yours to command."

"Don't say that. I don't want to *command* you. I'm asking a favor."

"I was made to serve you. When I was reborn into this body, the first thing I remembered was your face." The way he said this made me equal parts flattered and uncomfortable. And he was staring at me intently, though it could be because his gigantic black owl eyes make every glance intense. It was hard to tell.

I decided to play it safe and offered a logical reason. "We were linked for so long." From the time I was sixteen until a few months ago, to be exact. Nine years. Yet this was the longest, most personal conversation we'd ever had.

He began to respond, but as soon as his mouth opened, his body seemed to crackle with unseen energy. We both stared at each other for a long moment. "My strength is fading. The Æthyr seems to be pulling me back. I feel ungrounded."

It made sense. Æthyric demons couldn't stick around on this plane for long without a host.

"I will hunt down news of your mother," he said, and quickly jumped to his feet.

I followed. "Wait! What about our link? Can you reestablish it?" I could call him using this ritual again, I supposed, but it was much easier—and less vomit-causing—to be able to use the homing sigil on my arm.

Strong, indefinable emotion slackened his facial features. Then he said in a low voice, "It would be my greatest honor." He held out his hand, requesting mine. "We can do this directly now," he said, noticing my hesitation. A wave of crackling energy made his neck muscles strain.

We didn't have much time. I nodded my head quickly and gave him my hand.

Foreign and lush, Æthyric words tumbled from his lips in a low chant as he held his palm over mine. This certainly was a lot more direct than the gigantic Heka burst I had to send through the planes to link us the first time around. After a few moments, a nebulous cloud of sooty black light floated out between our palms—a light that matched his halo. I felt a sharp pinch. He made a noise, then things felt . . . different between us. I felt the link.

I pulled my hand away, half expecting it to be marked somehow. But it wasn't mine that was marked, it was his: my personal sigil, black as ink, was etched into his palm. A whisper-thin spider web line floated from my palm and his.

That was new, too.

I ran my other hand between, and it went through the line as if it were a laser beam. Not solid. Just like the line that had connected me to Jupe's tattoo when he was in trouble.

Priya grabbed my hand and peered down at it. "There is another link here," he said, startled. "You have another servant?" He said it like I was cheating on him.

"It's someone under my protection. A demon child."

Priya's face lifted. "Ah. I understand now." His body crackled again, and this time he almost completely disappeared. "I must leave. I will come to you when I have information. I will not fail you again."

"You didn't fail me." For the love of Pete.

Black wings snapped open to reveal an impressive span. Rather intimidating. Not an everyday sight, that's for damn sure. Holding his marked hand over his stomach, he canted his head, then gave me another smile before both he and the black line connecting us disappeared completely.

And before I could process everything that just happened, my phone chimed inside my jeans pocket. I looked at the screen.

MSG FROM JUPE, 3:05 AM: DAD SAID YOU HAD EMERGENCY AT KAR YEE'S. ARE YOU BOTH OK? TELL HER I SAID HI. NEXT TIME YOU SHOULD TAKE ME WITH YOU. I CAN SLEEP ON HER COUCH.

Dammit. Lon managed to remove the blame from the whole "you leave or I leave" situation. That was . . . the right thing to do. And he went against his big honesty-or-death policy, telling a little white lie to make the peace. Just like that, I felt tender and weepy again. I sent Jupe a response.

SENT 3:05 AM: EVERYTHING OK. WHY R YOU STILL AWAKE?

MSG FROM JUPE, 3:06 AM: I FELL ASLEEP AND WOKE BACK UP. HEY, GRAMMA IS TAKING US ALL OUT TO EAT TOMORROW NIGHT SO BE SURE TO GET BACK HOME BY 5 EXACTLY. SHE'S A FREAK-A-DEAK ABOUT BEING ON TIME BUT I WON'T LET HER LEAVE WITHOUT U.

SENT 3:06 AM: PROMISE TO BE ON TIME. NOW GO TO BED, MOTORMOUTH.

MSG FROM JUPE, 3:06 AM: GOING! G'NIGHT!!! <3 YOU!!!!!!!!!!!!

Heart you, too, kid.

11

That wasn't the only text I received. Before I went to sleep, Lon let me know that he'd found Noel Saint-Hill's address—which was good, because Bob's online search was fruitless. Lon volunteered to pick me up at Kar Yee's the next day so we could check it out. I told him not to bring his gun. He told me I was awfully bossy.

Around noon, I got ready to meet him. I was worried the T-shirt I'd packed was too casual for Rose's dinner plans, so I dressed in jeans and one of Kar Yee's tops, a long sleeve striped blouse that cost a small fortune. It was sort of tight around my chest, but Kar Yee was a couple of sizes smaller. Normally she wouldn't let me borrow clothes—no way, no how. But at the moment she was too hopped up on Bob's happy pills to care.

I took the elevator down and stood outside the stoop of her building, scanning my surroundings. No dark sedan across the street, and no dark figure slinking in the shadows. No shadows at all, actually. It was one of those sunny days in California where the sky is so clear and big, it makes everything around you seem a little less crowded. I lifted my face up, soaking in rays and wishing the temperature was just a few degrees warmer as traffic whizzed by on Kar Yee's street. After a couple of minutes, a luxury SUV slowed to a stop in front of me. The dark-tinted driver's window lowered. A gorgeous Earthbound with a gold-flaked green halo and a dead-sexy smile draped his arm out the window.

"Need a ride, little girl?"

"Depends," I said, stepping up to the car. "Where you going?"

His lazy gaze slid down my body. "Probably to hell. Wanna come?"

Why, yes—yes I did. And I was certain he could hear the zing of desire that went through me. "Sorry, my boyfriend doesn't like sharing."

"Is that so?"

"Besides, aren't you kind of old for me? I'm not sure you could handle all this."

"I have a feeling I could." A breeze from his open sunroof lifted strands of golden brown hair. Good God, he was hot. Just beautiful, all golden and rugged, with those deep crescent hollows in his cheeks and his perpetually narrowed eyes. "And I don't think I need permission to take what's already mine."

Goose bumps blossomed over my arms. "Did you miss me last night?"

"Get in the car."

"In the front or back?"

He seemed to consider that for a moment as his gaze dropped to my breasts. They immediately felt swollen and overripe under his perusal. If he didn't stop looking at me like that, I might bust a few seams in my borrowed top.

Then he said, "My seat goes all the way down."

"What a coincidence. So do I."

"Get in the car, Cady." Oh, he was mad now. Not mad-mad, but impatient-mad, like he gets when I tease him too much.

I stood on tiptoes and leaned through the window to kiss him. It was just going to be a peck, but he tasted like the cinnamon gum he always chews, and I really did miss spending the night with him. Before I knew it, he was urging my lips apart—or maybe I was doing the urging, hard to tell—and his tongue was hot in my mouth, and I pretty much melted on the spot.

I didn't care that pedestrians were doing double-takes as they strolled past on the sidewalk. I was ready to pull him through the window. But just when it started to get good, Lon pulled away. I moaned a complaint.

"That's all you get," he said, grasping my chin firmly with one hand. His voice was all deep and rough. "You think about it tonight when you're trying to decide whether you want to sleep in your own bed or play nursemaid to Kar Yee."

"No one at Kar Yee's place is demanding I leave on account of my whorishness."

"I like your whorishness. And that's all taken care of. Situation fixed."

I stared at him for a moment, waiting for him to tell me how. Did he have a talk with her? What was his idea of "fixed," exactly? Probably not the same as mine. If she hated me even more now, I was going to be pissed at him. "What did you do?"

"Nothing you need to know about."

"Try again."

He sighed. "I had a little talk with her. Gave her some information that changed her mind. End of story."

"What information? You didn't use your trans-mutated knack on her, did you?"

"Nope."

"Magick?"

"No magick. Can we drop it? I'll tell you in good time."

"Why not now?"

"Cady," he pleaded.

"I know, I know. Get in the car." He clearly wasn't ready to share, so I dropped the subject for the time being and headed around the SUV to hop inside. He was wearing a jacket I loved, a fitted, softer-than-butter hazel-colored leather deal that was almost more green than brown in the sunlight. I could make out every bump and dip of arm muscle. The inside of the car was warm, the breeze from the sunroof cool. He turned down Thin Lizzy on the radio and offered me some valrivia, which I waved away.

"How is she?" he asked as he pulled out into traffic.

"Kar Yee? Much better. Bob's healed her bones three times now. He says the brace can come off and she can do non-strenuous stuff, like actually leave her apartment. I think he's going to try to take her somewhere today. He's up there arguing with her now."

"Bob spent the night?"

"Yeah, in a chair next to her bed. But after sleeping on her couch, I understand why. I've got a massive crick in my neck. Then again, that could be from my rooftop adventures. Guess what I did?"

He looked askance at me through squinty eyes. "Does it have to do with the paring knife you stole?"

"I can't steal what's already mine," I said.

That got a slow smile out of him.

I sighed and gave him the lowdown about Priya, leaving out the whole *first thing I remembered was your face* remark. Having no experience dealing with a Hermeneus spirit, Lon wouldn't understand their desire to serve. Even so, his reaction was less happy, more alarmed than I expected.

"Are you certain it was Priya and not some sort of demonic trickery?"

"Pretty positive."

"I wish I could've been there to hear his emotions."

"Maybe you can meet him when he reports back."

Lon didn't comment.

Noel Saint-Hill's address was a half hour drive from Kar Yee's place. The neighborhood was Richie Rich.

Brand-new McMansions were squeezed into tiny plots of land between older homes. I hated when people did that—bought a house for the location and tore it down to build something that didn't fit the neighborhood. What kind of person needs six bedrooms, a home gym, and a three-car garage? Apparently the Saint-Hills, as their four-story home was one of the new ones.

And it was surround by two police cars and an ambulance.

A crowd of onlookers was gathered on the front lawn of the neighboring house, and when Lon slowed the car, I saw why.

A sky-blue restored vintage car with a Road Runner logo on the trunk and a dragon sticker on the bumper was sitting askew across the shallow driveway. A bloody body lay on the cement beneath it, crushed under its rear left wheel.

Lon parked farther down the street, away from the cop cars. We trotted over to the crowd as a police tow truck was pulling up. Two officers were talking to the driver, and another officer was holding the crowd back. Lon pushed his way to the front of the crowd, tugging me along. And from where we stood, we got a pretty good view—or bad, considering.

The body was quite literally crushed. The wheel sat on what was once a chest. Bone and flesh spread out beneath it, looking like something that should be in a butcher's shop. Bright red blood pooled around the carnage, seeping into the driveway. My stomach lurched. Then I spotted the lock of blond hair. I craned my neck to peer around the wheel.

It was Noel Saint-Hill.

I grabbed Lon's jacket sleeve.

"What happened?" Lon asked a middle-aged man nearby. Another Earthbound.

He hesitated for a moment, looking at Lon's gilded halo, while a woman who could've been his wife spoke up. "It wasn't an accident. People are saying that it was a hit and run, but they're wrong. I saw the car lift off the ground. Saw it through my living room window."

"Brenda," the man said warningly. "It's none of our business."

"Look at the grass," she said, ignoring him. "No tire tracks. If someone drove the car up on the lawn like that and hit him, there'd be tire marks. That car was dropped on top of him."

The cop handling the crowd was calling for witnesses and telling everyone else to go home. Brenda's husband dragged her away, telling her to stay out of things. I wanted to talk to her, to ask her more about what she saw, but her husband was quick and the crowd was shifting.

Lon pulled me aside to the edge of the throng and spoke in a low, agitated voice near my ear. "You know damn well what happened, don't you? Remember the safe in Diablo Market?"

I did. Nearly lifted through the counter by the other robber, the telekinetic kid who floated

Tambuku's register through the air. "A safe is a hell of a lot smaller than a car."

"Maybe his knack got a little stronger."

"Shit. You think that Brenda woman saw the telekinetic kid do it?"

Lon swiped a thumb over one side of his mustache. "Don't know, but Brenda is an Earthbound." He glanced over his shoulder. "The police aren't. And based on what I heard of her husband's feelings, he's worried the cops might overhear his busybody wife telling a 'crazy,' unexplainable story about a boy lifting a car with his knack."

And if the boy was deranged enough to kill his own friend, what else was he capable of?

"We need to talk to her . . . without her husband," I said.

Lon nodded. We marched around the crowd. Lon's healthy six-foot frame gave him a better view. After a few seconds of shuffling, he spotted them striding across the street. We trailed them, hoofing it to catch up. "You distract him," I told Lon, then shouted the woman's name. They both turned around. "Can I ask you one more thing?"

Her face lifted, as if she was more than happy to talk, then her husband said something I couldn't hear. Whatever it was, it annoyed her. Lon stepped up immediately, asking the man for directions to the civic center. As soon as the husband began spouting off streets and pointing, I pulled Brenda aside.

"I know this sounds weird, but I think I've seen

a kid who has a knack strong enough to lift that car," I said conspiratorially. "He was buddies with Noel. Dark hair—"

"Telly," she confirmed, nodding her head quickly. "I don't know his real name, but that's what Noel called him." Telly was a common nickname for Earthbounds with telekinetic knacks. I heard it around the bar all the time. "That boy's been hanging around here a lot over the past few months, showing off, lifting things in the driveway where anyone could see him. Humans live on this block, too," she complained. Yep, biggest gripe that older Earthbounds had against the younger generation, just like Andrew, the owner of Diablo Market. Don't show off your knack around humans: it only leads to trouble.

"Did you see him lift the car?" I asked.

"No. It all happened so fast. I saw it in the air, then the crash shook the floor in my house. But I thought I saw someone running. I wouldn't put it past Telly do something like this. That kid is bad news." She leaned closer and spoke in a lower voice. "A couple of months ago, someone broke into Noel's school and stole computers, money from the cafeteria registers. Wrecked the principal's office and the teacher's lounge. Did over a hundred thousand dollars in damage."

Jesus. I remembered hearing about that in the news. "They never arrested anyone, but someone hacked into the school's security system. Deleted school files."

"That had to be Telly. Noel's bragged about Telly's computer hacking skills. Noel's mother grounded him a few weeks ago for stealing credit card numbers and using them to buy things online. Noel said it was Telly's idea. At least, that's the rumor around the neighborhood."

"Any idea how his knack is able to do something like that?" I said, nodding to the gruesome scene across the street. "I've never known a telekenetic to be able to lift that much weight."

She shook her head. "No telling with that kid."

"Do you know where he lives?"

"He doesn't live in town," she said. "He's from the suburbs, or somewhere on the coast. La Sirena, maybe."

Damn. Finding a telekenetic teenage Earthbound in La Sirena . . . well, needle in haystack, and all that. But maybe Brenda saw the disappointment in my face, because she quickly added, "Wherever he lives, he spends a lot of time hanging out under the railroad bridge at the end of Monterrey Street with some other delinquents. I called the cops on them once to chase them out, but they all came back after a few days."

"Brenda!" Her husband was Mr. Frowny Face again. If Lon shushed me like that all the time, I'd have to tell him where to stick it. Thank God for Lon's quiet, laid-back ways and his ability to keep the husband occupied long enough for me to get what I needed.

Turning back to Brenda, I mouthed a thank-you

right before her testy husband escorted her away. Monterrey Street. Didn't know where that was, but GPS could find it. I started to tell Lon all about my discovery and suggest we try our luck hunting Telly when a car pulled up, brakes squealing. A blonde Earthbound jumped out. Police tried to stop her from running onto the crime scene.

"This is my house!" she yelled. And when she pushed the officer out of the way and saw the Road Runner, she made a horrible keening wail.

Lon grabbed my arm and tugged me from the chaos. "I can't be here," he said sharply as he marched me back to his parked car. It took me a few moments to realize from the pained look on his face that he was trying to disengage his knack. Sometimes when he's steamrolled with a lot of strong emotions coming from too many people at once, he gets overwhelmed and has trouble tuning it all out. I could only imagine what he could hear right now—the confusion and anxiety of the crowd, the amped up intensity of the police, the mother's grief. . . .

When we got back inside the SUV, he seemed to have put enough distance between his knack and the scene. "You okay?" I asked.

He shook his head and didn't say anything more about it. Just started the engine and drove away.

12

Monterrey Street was a few blocks away, where the rich neighborhood petered off into middle-class, then suddenly connected to one of those sketchy, vaguely ominous pockets of the city that had been neglected for years. Lon slowed the SUV as I peered out my window, eyes following the old, disused railroad tracks that crept along the bridge in the distance. Couldn't see much from here. It spanned what was once Monterrey Creek, according to GPS, but now looked like nothing more than a weed-infested ditch.

Lon stopped the car a half-block away. "I'm parking here," he explained. "If this kid can lift cars, I don't think I want to give him any weapons."

I glanced around, doing my best to push down rising anxiety, wondering how much time we had before someone busted one of Lon's windows to perform a little hot-wire surgery.

He patted the dash in answer to my worries. "Fort Knox."

"What about Telly? What if he's hanging out with some other Earthbounds who have amped-up knacks? We could be walking into a hornet's nest."

"Good thing you've got an early detection system." Yeah, I did feel safer knowing he could sense sudden changes in emotion. He reached across my lap and stuck his hand between my knees.

"Hey!" I said, but it came out a little too hopeful to be a proper protest.

"You wish. Move." His hand dove beneath my seat and surfaced with the sawed-off vintage Lupara.

"I distinctly remember telling you not to bring that thing," I complained.

"Felt like you were daring me." The thin lines around the outer corners of his squinty eyes tightened as his mouth quivered.

"Better than your full-sized shotgun, I suppose. At least you can hide this one."

"You're welcome. Come on."

We trekked down a sidewalk webbed with cracks, my jeans brushing brittle, dead grass. The bridge running parallel had seen better days. Its concrete was marred and crumbling, girders rusted. The underbelly arching over the dry creek bed was hidden in shadow. If someone was down there, we couldn't see them . . . but they couldn't see us, either.

Lon stopped me where the sidewalk ended and the dusty slopes of the creek bed began. After a few moments, he glanced around and removed the Lupara from the inside of his jacket. He held up two fingers and nodded toward the shadow under the bridge. Okay, two against two. Hopefully it wasn't two gigantic lunkheads with Merrimoth's amped-up temperature knack. But as we took quiet, careful steps down the steep grade, following a well-worn path through dry grass, we didn't see muscle-bound fire-breathers, or monsterific trolls waiting to collect a toll. Just three tattered camping tents lining the creek bed, a few lawn chairs, and two boys, shooting the shit and laughing.

One was dark-headed, but his back was facing us. The other was maybe sixteen, seventeen. Hard to tell. I could only see his profile. But he was husky and animated and begging the dark-haired one for something.

"Come on, let me just see it."

The thought crossed my mind that we were about to break up some seedy yet kinda hot street punk blowjob exchange. In that case, maybe we should, you know, just wait until it was over. No sense in ruining a good show. Lon looked askance at me. I shrugged. Guess I was the only filthy-minded person, because the boy wasn't trying to get in the other guy's pants, he was tugging on a bag.

"You can't have any. Forget it."

"One drop."

"You got three hundred bucks buried under the tent? I don't think so. But if you wanna be my wing-man, you can earn it."

While the boy hesitated, the other one, the boy

in charge, shifted the bag out of reach. It could've been any old backpack. And it was hard to tell if his hair was merely short or if he had a buzz cut, but he *did* have a blue halo. I homed in on his voice as Lon and I crept closer.

"You want me to help you sell it?"

"My supplies are running lower than I'd like, so I need to replenish. I want you to help me get a little more cash."

"I thought you took it. Why don't you just steal some more?"

"There are only two places I can get this, and the person I ganked it from . . . I just can't go back there. Besides, he only had a little more, and I'm not interested in small-time stuff. I want to go straight to the source this time, and this guy's got major security. So I'm gonna need money for some new equipment to get around it. I'm talking James Bond shit—plasma cutters, C-4 plastic, hacking software. All that costs. So I want you to help me clean out a few safes and registers."

"I thought you and Noel were done with that."

Mother trucker.

"Noel was a pussy. You want to help me, or not?" He reached inside his backpack and retrieved something. After peeling off a cuff of bubble wrap, he held it up for the other kid's inspection. It was a small, clear bottle with a cork stopper, filled with bright red liquid. It looked exactly like some of my medicinal jars.

"Whoa," the boy cooed, practically salivating. "How much is that worth?"

He wound the bubble wrap around the bottle and stuck it back in the backpack. "Five grand. Twenty-five doses of bionic juice," he said proudly as he zipped the bag closed and set it on the ground behind his chair. As if he wanted to put just a little more distance between it and the chubby boy with the greedy eyes. "Enough to amp up twenty-five ordinary knacks."

Bionic juice.

I glanced at Lon. It was a fucking medicinal. An elixir. Had to be. The old-fashioned bottle screamed *I-was-brewed-by-an-occult-magician!* My blood was boiling. I was done being stealthy.

A cloud of dust rose around my feet as I charged down the embankment, not giving a shit whether they heard me or not. There wasn't much of anything with enough heft to be worth tossing our way—tents, cardboard, lawn chairs? No cars in the immediate vicinity. My blood practically sang with the urge to draw a shit-ton of current and zap him in the balls.

The boys looked up, startled, when I came barreling toward them. Both leapt from their chairs. Lon's Lupara clicked beside me.

"Where's my money, you little prick?" I shouted.

Telly leveled a look at me that was wholly unafraid.

"You have it stashed in a hole under one of these tents? Or was Noel Saint-Hill holding it for you when you smashed him under a fucking car?"

The second boy made a noise. His gaze flicked nervously to Telly's.

"Was he the first person you've killed with your new trumped-up knack? Does injuring women not do it for you anymore? Because you fucking broke my partner's bones with that stupid paint stunt you pulled in my bar."

"If you wanted to take me down, maybe you should've brought her out here," Telly said in an even, taunting voice. "Because you'd have a better chance with her fear knack than some long-haired beach bum with a gun."

A shot exploded. The boys lunged to the side as a mushroom cloud of dust flew up from the cracked dirt near Telly's feet.

"Holy fuck!" the second boy shouted as he backed into a lawn chair that overturned.

"Bullet trumps knack," Lon said as my ear rang from the blast.

Telly's face flashed deep red. He was pissed. He flicked his hand to the side and Lon's arm followed the motion. He clung to the gun even as Telly was trying his damnedest to pull the thing away—the same thing the boy had done to me in the bar with my caduceus, only Lon wasn't caught off guard like I was. He strained to keep his grip on it as Telly grunted in frustration. The whole thing looked like a bad mime act.

But just when I thought Lon was going to win the tug-o-war, the Lupara flew across the riverbed and landed in a pile of weeds on the opposite embankment. Why did he give it up? A second later, I had my answer. A familiar unearthly sensation went through me like a herd of stampeding horses. Light burst around Lon's shoulders as his halo doubled in size and flamed up into a fiery golden oval that covered his shoulders. Twin, ruddy horns spiraled out of his hairline above his temples, curling around his ears.

Both boys froze, eyes bugging. A dark spot spread over the crotch of the husky kid's jeans. Telly's mouth fell open.

"Wiped that cocky smile off your telekinetic face, didn't it?" I said. "No juice required."

Before he could reply, the boy who'd pissed his pants whipped around and booked it, racing up the opposite embankment. I briefly considered running him down, but we didn't need him. Right now I wanted to focus my attention on the main problem.

"Your friend bailed on you, Telly," I said. The sound of his name in my mouth made him flinch, just barely. "Maybe you'll just kill him, too, when you catch up with him later."

He ran a jerky hand over his buzzed hair.

"What's in the bag?" I asked. The backpack lay on the ground a few feet away from Telly.

"Seems you already know," he answered.

"Who'd you steal it from?" Lon asked.

Nervous eyes darted in Lon's direction, but Telly didn't answer. Stupid piece of shit didn't know Lon could read his mind at this point. He spoke to me instead. "I'll give you your money back."

"Yes, you will. But what are you going to do about the damages to my bar? The lost income? And you broke my partner's bones."

"I didn't do anything. Not my fault she was clumsy."

Fury and adrenalin rushed through my chest. "You're going to pay for that, you little shit."

Reaching out for electricity, I marched toward him, closing the distance between us. He was a twitchy trapped rabbit, muscles tense, wanting to bolt. But he couldn't leave the backpack. It lay between us, and I saw the desperate longing in his face when he glanced at it. I tapped into current somewhere above the bridge and pulled. Prickly heat blossomed inside my cells.

I heard Lon bark my name behind me, but I was so close. Telly and I lunged for the backpack at the same time. We both got our hands on it. Only, my hands were a little more dangerous than his. I pushed kindled Heka through them, sending a lash of it through the metal zipper I was white-knuckling.

Like many other gifted magicians, my body was resistant to electrical voltage. At least, coming in. Going back out was another story. I needed graphite to even out the release, because once it bonded with Heka, it went a little haywire.

I had no graphite.

The shock sent Telly flying. With a yelp of pain,

he slammed into the ground and skidded. Exactly the result I wanted. Only, the kickback from the release hit me, too. I knew the moment it happened. Knew I was in for pain and some hair singeing.

My fingers froze around the zipper. Hot pain buzzed through my cells as my body made a closed circuit with the metal. For a moment, the pain was so excruciating, so jarring, that all I could see was white light. My mind emptied. The world dropped away. Everything just . . . rebooted.

I'd done this before. Just had to let it happen and survive it. Wait for the nightmare to end. Would only take a few seconds, though they seemed an eternity. And as the shock lessened, I felt a weird, silent rumble. Like I was standing in the middle of an earthquake. We were in California. It was possible. And I knew the rumbling wasn't coming from me.

The muscles in my hand were nearly at the point of unclenching. I felt the change when it happened. When the pain shifted. Electric Heka still coursed through me. It was a horrible feeling, but not bright and debilitating like the actual shock. My bones turned to jelly. And as I felt my legs begin to buckle, I smelled Lon. How funny was that? I smelled him. Not his shampoo or his cinnamon gum or his leather jacket. Just him. The scent I could identify underneath all the other stuff. The one I smelled when I woke up in bed and his arm was curled around my waist.

And that's where his arm was now. He yanked me against him as the world roared back.

Not more than a yard away, an enormous black shape fell from the underbelly of the bridge. When it hit the ground, it sounded like a bomb exploding. My bones rattled. Teeth clacked together. An enormous cloud of dust and dirt shot into the air. A tidal wave. Lon shoved my face into his chest and covered me with his body.

We coughed up dust. It stung my eyes, coated my lips. And after a few moments, when it began to settle and clear, I was able to see what caused it all: a thick plate of steel, maybe twenty feet long, five feet high, lay across the creek bed, crushing one of the tents and two lawn chairs, whose bent pipe legs jutted out from beneath it like the legs of a dead roach under a boot.

I shielded my eyes with my hand and looked up. A huge section of the outer girder lining the railroad bridge was missing. That telekinetic asshole had used his magically enhanced knack to somehow pull the side of the bridge loose.

I surveyed the area. No sign of Telly. He'd pulled a tidy smash-and-run. If I wasn't hacking up dirt, I might've cried in frustration. But then I smelled something burnt and glanced down at my hand. Scorched from my Heka unload and streaked with a line of red paint, his bionic-juice-filled backpack dangled from a strap looped around my wrist.

13

In the distance, a couple of people were gravitating toward the bridge, looking for the source of the horrific crash that had echoed around the dying neighborhood. We took the backpack and hustled back to where we parked. For a moment, I freaked out when a dark sedan sped past us. The windows were too dark to make out anything inside; it could've been anyone. I was being paranoid. No one was following me. I couldn't start suspecting every dark car I saw or I'd go insane.

Once we got back to the SUV, we slammed the doors shut and stared at each other.

"I'll tell you what," Lon said, "the boy who wasn't able to get a safe through the Diablo Market counter a few days ago has sure acquired some strength."

"No joke."

"You okay?" He'd already asked me that twice. "You're shaking."

"Electrocution by Heka can't be good for my heart. Almost worse than being struck by lightning."

He swiped his thumb over my eyebrow, brushing dirt away. I patted dirt out of his hair. And after we'd cleaned each other like monkeys, I rifled through the backpack. Inside, I found: a single bottle of red liquid, a box of sugar cubes, a glass dropper, a high school chemistry book, and a zip top bag filled with quarters. I wouldn't have been surprised if they were quarters from Tambuku's register. But of course there was no identification. Nothing of interest but the medicinal.

We took turns holding it up to the light, peering through the glass.

Lon said, "I wonder if the kid was taking multiples doses to increase his knack to that point, or if one dose is progressive?"

"In my experience, a dose is just going to wear off. My bet is that Telly's been dosing regularly to build his strength."

"Ever seen a medicinal this color?"

"Can't say I have. Probably a few books back at my place I could thumb through, see if I could cross-reference it. But, you know, if I'd seen a recipe for 'Bionic Knack Juice,' I think I might've remembered."

"I probably have all the same books in my library," he mumbled, shaking the liquid around.

No doubt. I glanced out the window, warily watching the street. "Telly said his supply of the potion was running out, so maybe his strength will start waning and he won't be so out of control."

"If this bottle is all he's got, he'll try to get it back from you."

Oh. I hadn't considered this.

"He knows who you are," Lon said. "He knows the bar. He's killed someone already. Would've damn well killed us if we were a standing a few feet north."

"Maybe it's a good thing the bar's closed."

"When is your artist coming to repaint the binding triangles?"

"She's in Colorado for the holidays, so not until after New Year's. I thought about opening for a few days before then, but maybe that's not smart. If it were just me—"

"But it's not just you. You need to think about the rest of your staff. Customers." He handed the potion back to me and drummed his fingers on the steering wheel. "What's your best guess on how long the potion lasts?"

"Most of my medicinals only last a few hours—a day, max. Never seen anything that stretched beyond that."

"So he'll be looking for more," Lon said.

"He said there are only two sources of this: one big, one small."

Lon nodded. "The maker and the distributor."

"Would make sense. And if Telly needs money to break into the maker's stash—"

"He might rethink his plans and go for the smaller source after all," Lon finished.

"The nosey neighbor said Telly didn't live here

in the city—said he might be from La Sirena or somewhere on the coast. If that's true, the distributor might be, too. After all, Merrimoth got it from someone."

"But the crime spree's been happening here," Lon countered. "And Telly couldn't have committed every robbery. Too many of them happening the same night, too many different knacks."

I nodded. "More dealers in Morella."

"Easiest way to find a normal drug dealer is to track down people who use and learn where they bought it."

"Follow stories about bionic knacks. See if someone will tell us where they bought it."

"Exactly," Lon said.

"And in the meantime, maybe I can find out more about the potion. How long the effects last, and all that."

"I can help you research potions."

"Sure, we could do that. . . . Or, we could try something a little more direct. I *do* know a drug dealer."

Lon turned his head to the side and mumbled a string of curses.

"Now, now. Hajo's been on his best behavior since we took the vassal potion back from him. I could call him. Maybe get him to meet me somewhere."

Lon grunted. He may not like it, but he knew I was right. If anyone was dealing the bionic drug in Morella, Hajo would be get us a name.

"I'll call him after dinner tonight," I said, hearing cop sirens in the distance. "Right now, we better get out of here."

I got my Jetta out of Kar Yee's parking garage and followed Lon's SUV back to Chez Butler, pulling in right at five. "Don't be late," Jupe had insisted, and we barely made it.

Ugh. Family dinner with Rose.

Lon said he took care of everything with her. Guess I was about to find out how true that really was. I could do this. Yes, I could. My chin was up, I was ready, and everything was going to be fine.

As I shut my car door, the troops filed out of the door: Adella, Rose, Mr. and Mrs. Holiday, all led by Jupe.

"You made it!" he said as he strode to meet me, corkscrew curls bobbing.

"Told you I would."

He flashed me a humungous, toothy grin and tackled me in a hug.

"Jeez, I've only been gone one night," I said into his hair. But I was secretly pleased that he was so glad to see me. It bolstered my shaky nerves. "Really only a few hours."

"Seventeen hours," he corrected with his usual mathematical precision. As he pulled away from me, his gaze fell to my chest, then leapt back up. His eyes were moons. He bit the inside of his mouth and made some weird noise before turning away to shoo Foxglove back inside the house.

Heat blazed across my face.

Why did I wear Kar Yee's shirt? It was way too tight. I considered running inside to change. Maybe I was underdressed anyway. But when I quickly surveyed everyone, I found that they were all pretty casual. Adella was even wearing jeans. She was not, however, wearing a top that made her breasts look like beach balls.

I slapped on a smile and greeted everyone with a weak "hello."

Rose's gaze swept over me as she studied me through glasses perched low on her nose. I braced myself.

"Good afternoon, Cady. You're looking better today."

Uhh . . . was that a dig? She smiled at me. Pleasantly. Was it fake? Was she trying to tell me that my boobs were a salacious spectacle, further proof to her theory that I was unfit to be in Jupe's life?

"No chasing down robbers, I take it." She pressed two fingers into her silvery cropped hair and fussed it into place.

"Actually—"

"Did you catch them?"

"Not yet."

She smiled again. "I'm sure you will. Do you like seafood?"

Still waiting for the punch line, I answered hesitantly. "Umm, yes?"

"Good. We're going to Cypress House, out on the water. Ever been?"

"No."

"We have standing reservations," Mrs. Holiday said. "We go every year."

"Maybe I should just run in and change—"

"It's casual, don't worry," Mr. Holiday assured me.

"The kind of place that gives you wooden hammers to crack crabs on the table," Lon added.

"Which is *awesome*," Jupe piped up, now over the fact that I flaunted my dirty pillows in his face. "Crab guts everywhere. I once got crab brain in my eye. But, Cady, listen—"

"Listening."

"—they have these things called spot prawns. They are the biggest shrimp you've *ever* seen, and they're only available certain times of the year. And they grill them in the shell. Oh, and they normally come three on a plate, but I can eat a dozen."

"That's impressive," I mumbled.

"They're good, but I'm with Lon. Dungeness crab all the way," Adella said, waggling her eyebrows like Jupe always does.

"Why choose?" Jupe said with a slow shrug. "Gramma's paying."

The Giovanni matriarch smiled the sweetest smile at him and tousled his hair. "That's right. You order whatever you want, baby. Now how are we getting there, Lon? You think we'll fit in your SUV?"

"If we don't, we'll just tie Motormouth to the roof."

"Oh, yeah! Dare me! I'll do it," Jupe said brightly. "You think we'd get arrested?"

"I think you'd get splattered in bugs," Adella said. "You can sit on my lap."

"No way! You'll tickle me."

And while they continued to argue about seating, piling into the SUV one by one, Rose patted me on the shoulder as she was going by. That's when it really hit me: she was being genuine. Not judge-y. Not accusatory. Had I just been accepted? I glanced at Lon in disbelief as he helped her into the front passenger seat. What in the world had he told Rose to change her mind? He gave me a little wink, as if to say "told ya—I got this."

It was all I could do not to break down and weep.

14

Two hours later, we were all slumped in our chairs, full and groaning. Cypress House put us on an enclosed outdoor patio twinkling with white lights. It overlooked the dark ocean and a winding, lit walkway leading to a cluster of Cypress trees growing on a bluff above the water. It was really nice, but casual, just as they said. And I was surprised how easy it was to feel comfortable around the Giovannis.

Imagine that.

I laughed at family stories. Jupe and I even told a few of our own. I felt like I was part of something. Like I was welcome, and things were going to be okay after all. It was pathetic, really, how much I craved their acceptance. Rationally, I knew if I was sprawled on some doctor's couch, delving into the deep, dark workings of my brain, I'd come to the realization that this was because of my fucked-up relationship with my fucked-up parents. Of course it was. But knowing something and *experiencing* it were not the same.

Lon flashed me a small, approving smile when no one was paying attention. I think I might've actually sighed with happiness at that smile. And as the dinner progressed, that smile changed to something bolder. He gave me pornographic looks from across the table, heavy gaze sliding to my breasts, squished inside the too-tight shirt. One of those looks gave me goose bumps, and his oh-so-smug look told me he knew. It was kind of romantic for a moment, minus being surrounded by in-laws and Jupe merrily mutilating the steaming corpses of several crabs with his wooden mallet. Though he never managed the dozen spot prawns, he made up for it in crab, and now sat between Adella and me, bellyaching.

"I think I'm going to explode," he moaned.

"Are you really?" Adella's hair wasn't tied back with a scarf tonight; the shape of her poofy mass of curls was exactly the same size as Jupe's. She poked a finger into his ribs, making him jump in his seat.

"Don't do it, Auntie," he pleaded. "I might throw up."

"He might do worse than that," Lon said after swigging the last of a beer.

"It's true," Jupe admitted, stifling a soft belch. "Don't say you weren't warned."

A commotion somewhere inside the restaurant dragged my attention to the patio door. It swung open, and a tall African-American woman strolled onto the patio with a protesting waiter in tow. Dark glossy hair cascaded around her bare shoulders, swaying with the flowing hem of her gold and black dress. Towering on clicking, spindly heels, she came to a stop in the middle of the patio and surveyed the room. After a moment, her long, regal face turned our way to reveal almond shaped brown eyes framed by miles of lashes, and flawless nutmeg skin.

She looked like a supermodel. A supermodel with a green halo crowning her head. A green halo flecked with gold.

Yvonne Giovanni.

No no no no no.

Her eyes found Lon's. I saw it all unfold in slow motion, as if I'd used my moon magick to slow time. Shock stretched his facial features. With a shrill pop, the neck of the brown beer bottle shattered in his hands. He didn't even notice. His nostrils flared as he pushed to his feet, and then—

And then his face just turned to putty. His eyes went all liquid and adoring. He looked as if he'd just seen the face of God. Rapturous.

My heart stuttered inside my chest, turned black, and shriveled.

If I hadn't been consumed by a jealous rage, I might've realized that what I was seeing in Lon's face was her knack being turned on full-blast. And if I realized that, I might've had sense enough not to look back up at her.

But I didn't have sense, and I did look up. And my world tilted.

I was awestruck. Reeling. I knew how Cupid

must've felt when he looked upon Psyche after prick- ing himself with his own arrow. The woman who'd strolled onto the restaurant patio moments before was beautiful, but this woman—this version of Yvonne— was brighter than a star. Ravishing, beautiful, perfect. I wanted to stare at her for hours.

How could one person be so . . . divine?

For a moment, just a moment, I heard a chorus of murmurs around the table, murmurs of awe con- firming the same feelings I had. Then a single, sharp voice broke through the haze.

"Yvonne Grace Giovanni! Switch that off before I come over there and knock you into the middle of next week."

All the shiny, shiny brilliance and the beauty and the overwhelming goodness just . . . dimmed. The goddess disappeared. And a retired forty-something supermodel stood in her place. Still stunning. Still regal. But just a person.

How had Rose resisted Yvonne's knack? Was she immune, being her mother? Or just accustomed to it? Whatever it was, Yvonne didn't seem surprised—she just took a deep breath and spoke to her.

"Hello, Mama."

"What in blazes are you doing here?" her mother snapped.

"It's Christmas. I came to see my child."

"I told you not to come!" Jupe said in a desperate voice.

Lon stepped between Yvonne and the table, as if

he meant to defend all of us from some fire-breathing dragon. "You've been talking to him?" His brows knitted. An angry, deep line creased the middle of his forehead as he got in her face. She moved her head to the side, trying to avoid his gaze, but he moved with her, not touching her, but close. She finally gave in and stared back at him, a little defiant, a little fearful.

"She called last week," Jupe mumbled next to me. "I should've told you, Dad. I'm sorry. But I told her not to come—I swear! She was asking about dinner, and—"

Lon whipped around and stared daggers at Jupe. "And you told her?"

"He didn't have to," Yvonne said sourly. "You all eat at the same place every year."

"I told her not to come," Jupe repeated again, and started to offer some other protest, but Lon shot him a warning look that shut Jupe down—they'd definitely be discussing the kid's secret-keeping later.

Lon swung back to Yvonne. "The court says you get to see him from noon until five, Christmas Day, as long as you notify me first. You've known this for years. Nothing's changed."

"Well, what if *I* have?"

"If I had a fucking nickel every time I've heard that."

She sniffled, affronted, then squared her shoulders. "That's fair, I suppose." Her eyes roamed over him, curious. Her shoulders dropped. She swallowed. "You look good, Lon." She reached out to touch his hair, but he jerked his head back. Her arm fell against her hip. She blinked a few times and awkwardly tried to make light of the rebuff. "It's not fair you aren't going gray. I have a regular appointment at the stylist to keep mine covered." She gave him a soft smile. When he didn't return it, she stepped out of his path and glanced around the table.

"No hello from you?" she said to Adella. "I've left messages the last couple weeks."

Adella stared her sister down for a few minutes, then simply said, "Been busy."

Yvonne nervously rattled her clutch handbag against her thigh. She nodded at Mr. and Mrs. Holiday. "Good to see you, both."

They didn't answer.

Finally, Yvonne's eyes flicked to mine. Then my halo. She flinched as some sort of recognition sparked. Oh, yes, she knew who I was. At least, she knew *what* I was: the girlfriend. A thousand expressions passed over her face. At first I thought she might laugh—some vaguely cruel, laughter-like sound got stuck in her throat. Then she looked confused. Or maybe it was disbelief. She slanted a glance at Lon, shook her head, and said, "I see."

In my head, I'd imagined Yvonne as an evil villain. Someone who abandoned her son for parties and a cocaine addiction that survived five stints in some of the country's most exclusive rehabilitation centers. Who unashamedly cheated on Lon with countless other men. Who slashed Lon with a knife in front of the county courthouse on the day of their divorce. Who the judge decreed wasn't fit to see her own child without another adult present.

Someone her own family had given up on years ago.

But now that she was standing in front of me, looking less like a monster and more like someone who'd fucked up their life beyond repair, I didn't know what to say to her. She didn't have my sympathy, exactly, but I felt sorry for her, nonetheless.

She cleared her throat and spoke to me. "I'm Jupe's mother."

It took me a few moments to recognize the remark as laying claim. Some weird feral part of me bristled. For a brief moment, I had visions of jumping on Yvonne and scratching her eyes out. Maybe calling up the moon power and binding the shit out of her until she begged me to release her.

Then Jupe's hand slipped into mine under the table. He was shaking. And that melted my heart a little. I folded my fingers around his. This was about *him*—not about me or my insecurities. He was looking up to me. I had to be the bigger person. So I simply replied, "I'm here now."

He squeezed my fingers. I squeezed back.

Gold bracelets clinked on her wrist as she lifted her hand to flip her hair away from her shoulder. "I'm sure you've heard stories," she said to me. "Remember, not everything you read in tabloids is true. I've had to sue over some of those articles."

Did she think I really sat around looking up old stories about her online? I hated to break it to her, but beyond a couple of browsing sessions when I first met Lon, her name wasn't in my search history. I didn't need to torture myself viewing photos of her perfect body posed in exotic locales, wondering if Lon took those photos, or what they'd done together when the shoot was finished.

"What are you really here for, Yvonne?" Lon asked. "You're not getting any more money out of me. I don't care if they've foreclosed on your house again."

"Why do you have to embarrass me in front of our son? My house is fine. And I'll have you know that I'm working. I have a new modeling contract. I've also been sober for six months, going to recovery meetings. You would know these things if you'd answer the phone." She glanced around the table. "If *any* of you besides Jupiter would answer the damn phone!"

The table fell into silence, then Adella shot Yvonne a dark, wilting look. "I'll answer the phone when it's the coroner's office calling, asking me to identify your body."

Dear *God*.

"Adella!" Rose snapped.

Adella glanced at Jupe and mumbled an apology.

"Addy—" Yvonne pleaded.

"Don't 'Addy' me. Don't waltz in here like you deserve pity. The things you've done to this family are unforgivable."

"That's enough," Rose said in a sharp voice. "Jupe, why don't you and Cady and your Auntie go outside while your dad and I talk to your mother."

But Adella was fired up, and didn't pay any attention to this request. "Mama might forgive you one day. Lon and Jupe might forgive you. But I will *never* forgive you for what you did to me."

What in the world had she done to Adella? Jupe seemed just as surprised by the outburst, so whatever it was, he didn't know either.

Yvonne's nostrils flared. Arms went rigid at her sides as her eyes brimmed with tears. "I can't change the past. I can't keep saying I'm sorry. But I'm trying to get my life together now. It would be easier if you'd all be supportive. I'm staying at the Landmark Hotel in the Village if you want to contact me. Otherwise, I'll see you at noon on Christmas Day—this is me officially notifying you, Lon." She glanced at Jupe. "I've got presents for you. I want this to be a nice holiday. I hope at least you'll give me a chance, baby. I want to be part of your life again."

As his face contorted with warring emotions, Yvonne brushed a tear away, straightened her shoulders, and strode out of the restaurant.

15

The ride back to Lon's house was pretty damn awkward. Everyone seemed to be lost in their own worlds, processing what had just happened. I know I certainly was. My chest felt like it was weighted down by a bowling ball.

Yvonne was sober. Yvonne wanted to be a part of Jupe's life. Everything inside me said *no no no*. Not now. Anything but this. I'd only just gained a small amount of acceptance from the Giovannis—now I had to deal with her, too?

And if I'd felt jealous of Adella and Rose's relationship with Jupe, I felt downright threatened by Yvonne. And it wasn't just because of Jupe. My thoughts were sliding into dark places, wondering if seeing her ignited any feelings in Lon. It was easy enough to hate someone who'd wronged you when they were still doing all the things that made you hate them in the first place. But what if she really *was* making an honest effort to change? Lon didn't want the old Evil Yvonne, but did he want new Humble

Yvonne? They had a shared history. A child together. Could I compete with that?

Logically, I knew I was jumping the gun, but the bowling ball on my chest just got heavier and heavier.

Silence and brooding ruled inside the SUV until the restaurant was a few miles out of sight. Then Jupe broke the ice. "I'm really sorry, you guys. I didn't call her. She called me. And I'm sorry I didn't say anything, but I just wanted Christmas to be normal and good. She said she wanted to visit, but you've got to believe me—I told her not to come. Listen to my feelings, Dad. You know I'm telling the truth!"

"You didn't do anything wrong, baby," Rose said.

Lon stared straight ahead, eyes on the road. "I'm not mad at you."

That seemed to calm Jupe down a little. After awhile he said, "Do you think she's really sober?"

No one answered. Adella was still angry, and like Lon, was keeping herself tightly wound. Mr. and Mrs. Holiday glanced at each other as if they were wondering whether they should jump in. I never knew them to stay quiet about anything, so it was disconcerting that they were holding back.

After a few moments, Rose finally said, "I don't know." She put her arm around Jupe's shoulders and pulled him closer, stroking his arm in one of those grandmotherly ways. I never knew my grandparents, but I always fantasized that they'd be that way, kind and comforting.

It was weird that a few hours ago, I was still angry with this woman. Now I saw her in a different light. God only knew what she'd had to deal with when it came to Yvonne. She could have just let Lon and Jupe slip out of her life. But she stuck around. Jupe thought she was the best thing since sliced bread. So she was a little stubborn. Maybe I'd be stubborn too if I was in her shoes.

"I want to believe her," Jupe admitted after a while. "Does that make me a sucker? Every time I believe her, she lets me down."

"Me too," Rose answered. "Me too."

Lon remained silent for the remainder of the ride. He was dark and stormy and circled by a solid stone wall and a moat filled with snapping crocodiles. Completely unreachable. I hated that Yvonne had that effect on him. I desperately wanted to talk to him in private, but when we got home, Lon asked the Holidays to take Foxglove out back with Jupe. Once he was out of earshot, we stood on the front walkway with the Giovannis.

"How did you do it, Rose?" Lon asked.

"Do what?"

Lon's eyes narrowed. "You know damn well what I mean. Resist her knack. How did you do it?"

Rose pushed her glasses up. If I had to guess, I'd say she was almost embarrassed. "Oh, all right." She sighed theatrically, then reached inside her purse and pulled out an object that fit in her palm. It was metal. It glowed softly with Heka.

"A charm?" I said.

Rose was embarrassed. "Just a little one."

"Mama!" Adella said, peering into her hand. "Why didn't you tell me?"

She shrugged. "I bought it from a magick shop in Portland. The woman who owns it is a witch, and she said she bought it from an estate sale. She wasn't sure if it would work. But I had it on me last time I saw Yvonne and it worked . . . well, like a charm."

"Can I see it?" I asked

She handed it to me. "It" was a silver signet ring, the band almost worn through in the back. The front was a flat hammered circle with a magical sigil engraved in the middle. "This is a variation of Solomon's Seal."

Lon squinted at it as I turned it in my fingers. "I'll be damned. I think you're right."

"And just what does that mean?" Adella asked.

"King Solomon supposedly had a ring that allowed him to control demons and talk to animals. Whoever made this seems to have adapted it for use on Earthbounds."

"That's why I couldn't hear your emotions when Yvonne showed up," Lon said.

"When I saw her walk onto the patio, I grabbed the ring from my purse. It only works if it's touching your skin. That's what the witch told me, anyway."

Lon was astonished. "Damn, Rose. Do you know how many hours I've spent thumbing through old grimoires trying to find something that would do this?"

"Believe me, I wish I'd had it years ago. More

than that, I wish I knew someone who could just get rid of her knack once and for all." She slid a sly glance my way. "Do I know someone who could?"

"Me? Christ, I don't know. I've never seen a spell that could do that. Plus she's got—" I gave Lon a questioning look. He told me that, like the Holidays, they knew about the transmutation spell. Yvonne was fond of showing off, apparently.

"She's got magick in her already," Lon finished for me.

Magick I never wanted to experience. Her regular knack was powerful enough.

"That would have to be reversed first, I think, and . . ." My words trailed off as I thought about it. Could I? If I could slow time, then maybe I could do this, too. But so much could go wrong. It was like performing a surgery you've never done before. Or that's what I imagined, anyway. Besides, there was no way Yvonne would ever agree to such a thing, so what was the point of thinking about it?

"Just a thought," Rose said.

I handed the ring back.

"What I'm dying to know is what *you* heard," Adella said to Lon. "Spill it. Was she lying about any of it?"

Lon glanced around at all of us. My nerves were jumping, buzzing with dread.

"She was sincere."

Godammit. I knew it was selfish, but my heart still dropped.

Lon's fingers grazed the back of my neck. "Being sincere in a moment doesn't mean lasting change."

"He's right about that," Adella murmured.

Rose sighed. "I'm going to the hotel to talk to her."

"Mama—"

"I want to know what her plan is. I'm not going to let her spoil Christmas for Jupe."

"I thought you expected me do that," I joked lamely. A second after it was out of my mouth, I wondered if it was too soon. But she waved her hand dismissively, almost as if she was embarrassed.

Adella hoisted her purse higher up on her shoulder. "Here's the difference. If Yvonne shows up for Christmas, there's a good chance she'll put everyone in a foul mood. And apparently the only way *you* could do that is by not showing up, because all Jupe did today was whine that you weren't with us."

Ah, crap. I was getting *verklempt* again. It was like some sort of sensitive housewife had taken over my body and was sitting around watching Lifetime movies and Hallmark commercials.

"So you're stuck with us now," Rose said. "Which means that Yvonne is your problem as much as she is ours. Be prepared to play defense if she's planning on showing up Christmas Day. Legally, she has the right. But I've got this ring now, which means for once in my life, I've got the upper hand, and I plan on using it. You with us?"

The three of them looked at me expectantly, as

if it was the most serious request in the world. As if they were asking me to get a pitchfork and join them in pursuit of the village monster. And at that point, to be honest, they probably could've asked me to murder Mother Teresa.

I gave Rose a decisive chin nod. "I'm your girl."

I briefly worried that Lon would want to go along to talk with Yvonne, too. But when Adella relented to drive her mother—"I'll wait in the parking lot while you talk to her," Adella told Rose—he didn't even act as if he'd considered it. I asked him if he was okay. He took a moment to answer, but when he said he was, I believed him.

So while Adella drove off with Rose to the Village to talk with Yvonne at her hotel, the Holidays walked back to their cabin. And after I changed into a less salacious outfit, a T-shirt and yoga pants—which had never undergone a single minute of yoga, just for the record—Lon and I made our way across the driveway.

Connected to the main house, Lon's three-car garage would make a perfectly nice studio apartment, with polished floors and central air and a couch salvaged from his parents' place. I'd napped on that couch once, and I have to say it was way more comfortable than Kar Yee's. It was also where we found Jupe, sitting cross-legged as he squinted at a book of Pontiac engine diagrams. An old TV sat upon a workbench to one side, tuned to a channel that was showing *The Nightmare Before Christmas*. This was

Jupe's little home-away-from-home, as he'd claimed the first empty bay as a hangout area, and his rusted-out '67 GTO sat on blocks in the second bay. The bay at the far end housed Lon's silver Audi sports coupe, rarely driven.

"Whatcha doin'?" I asked, plopping down on one side of him.

"I can't figure out what this is." He held up a rusted metal disk to Lon. "I found it under the car, like it had fallen off of something."

Lon inspected it for a few moments. "I think it's part of the A/C. Four hoses fit inside those holes to draw in fresh air."

"Oooh. I'll put it in the pile with the compressor junk."

Lon handed it back and sat down on the opposite side of him.

"You okay?" I asked.

"Depends," he said, turning to Lon. "Am I in trouble for talking to her?"

"I told you no already."

"Just making sure. Where's Gramma and Auntie?"

"They went to talk to her."

"Oh." He stretched out long legs and tossed the manual onto the floor.

"I don't want you to get your hopes up, Jupe."

He shrugged. "I know. But it's not wrong to hope. That's what you've said before—not about her, but it still applies, right?"

Lon made a frustrated noise.

"What do you think, Cady?" Jupe asked, long-lashed eyes looking up to mine.

"God, I don't know." What was I supposed to say here? "I guess I've heard too many stories about her. She makes me feel angry for the two of you, and a little jealous, too."

His nose wrinkled up. "Why would you be jealous?"

God, was I really allowing myself to be dragged into this? "Because she's beautiful and—" And what? What was I going to say? That, hey, your father probably fucked her brains out God knows how many times over the years? He'd been in crazy in love with her, and—unlike Lon and I with our you're-my-favorite-person code—the two of them probably professed their undying supermodel-photographer love, before everything went bad. They'd slept in the same bed, and maybe he even cooked dinner for her, like he did for me.

And, then, the big one: she gave birth to you. Because of that, Lon and Yvonne shared a bond that Lon and I didn't have. How does a person compete with a couple's history that would never be left in the past?

But I didn't say any of that. I just said, "I'm jealous because you both loved her."

"You don't understand," Jupe said. "She's messed up, bad." He tapped his temple. "Wrong in the head."

"I know," I said. "And I'm sorry."

He shook his head and sighed. I looked across his skinny frame and caught Lon staring at me, concern tightening his brow.

I picked up Jupe's hand and slid my palm against

his, spreading out his fingers to line up with mine. "I just want you to be happy. I think your dad does, too. That's all."

"I am. It's just . . . hard to explain," he finally finished.

I nodded.

He threaded slender fingers through mine. "You're staying home tonight, right?"

"Yes." Oh, yes. I was. If I'd had any doubts about that before Yvonne walked in the restaurant, they were long gone. I might never let Lon out of my sight again.

Lon ran his palm over Jupe's forehead, pushing back curls. "What do you say we go watch TV in the living room? That crack in your screen is driving me nuts."

Jupe glanced at the old television set, where Jack the Pumpkin King was announcing his plans to usurp Sandy Claws. "You said that crack added character."

"I lied." Lon slapped his son's leg and stood up. "Come on. If we hurry, we can watch something R-rated before Gramma comes back and stops us."

"What about *Black Christmas*?" Jupe said with a big cheesy smile.

"Only if Cady says yes."

Jupe turned his eager smile on me. Like I was going to say no to anything at this point. "Is this a horror movie?"

"It's made by the same guy who made *A Christmas Story*. It's great!"

Lon crossed his arms over his chest. "And . . ." he prodded.

"And it's a slasher flick from 1974. Sorority house murders." He waggled his brows.

"Go find it and meet us in the living room."

"Woo-hoo!" Jupe sailed off the couch and exited the garage with Foxglove running alongside. For the moment, everything was temporarily patched up in his teenage mind. And I was okay with that. I wished like hell a movie could do the same for me.

"I hate to bring it up, but I still need to call Hajo," I said to Lon as he helped me off the couch.

"Hajo," he repeated, as if it were a dirty word. But I could tell by the look on his face that he was a little relieved to change the subject. Maybe he wasn't in the mood to rehash Yvonne anymore; I damn sure wasn't. "Go on and get it over with," he said. "Maybe the boy can actually help us out."

"He's my age, you know. Not a boy."

"Don't remind me." He slung his arm around my shoulders. "And if he won't talk about it on the phone, try to arrange a meeting with him in the afternoon."

A drug dealer and user, Hajo hated talking about anything remotely illegal on the phone. "Why afternoon?"

"Because Merrimoth's funeral is tomorrow morning, and I should probably go."

A cool, dark anger prickled my thoughts. "Why? Have you been talking to Dare?"

"Nope. Not a word," he said. "I'm only going

because it's the right thing to do. You don't have to come with me."

Maybe not *right*, exactly, but paying respect to someone you knew is normal. But me? Paying respect to someone I had a hand in killing? Not so much. I thought about it as I left a message for Hajo and headed back into the house. Normal or not, I damn sure wasn't going to let Lon go to the funeral alone. Just because I'd quit working for Dare didn't mean I had to avoid every demon in the Hellfire Club. Nearly impossible in La Sirena, anyway. And it was part of Lon's past, whether I liked it or not. Part of mine, too.

And I suppose, after pondering all this, it was only natural that I had nightmares that night.

At first I dreamed I was attending Merrimoth's funeral, a rainy and gray graveside service in a crumbling cemetery. Most of the attendees had blue and green halos that glowed beneath the cover of their umbrellas. But when I looked around at the gravestones, I noticed sinister occult symbols chiseled into the rain-darkened granite instead of names.

I stepped to the front of the crowd and discovered that it wasn't a preacher leading the service, but my father, dressed in black ritual robes.

The grave opened at my feet. They weren't burying a body. They were hoisting up an old casket. And when they pried open the moldering lid, I stared down at my mother's rotting skeleton.

Her arm moved. One bony finger traced an invisible sigil in the air. I shivered, feeling a current of strong, dark magick undulating in the air between us, and watched as her muscles and organs grew between her bones. Veins and arteries appeared, filling with blood. Her heart pumped. Her skin knit itself together, spreading pale and thin over her Phoenix-like body.

Blank eyes filled the dead sockets inside her skull. They stared up at me, looking like wobbly, slick eggs. And when her mouth opened to speak, I screamed and woke up in a cold sweat.

16

Most people would agree that funerals aren't cheery occasions. But when we made it to David Merrimoth's the next morning, it was the polar opposite of my dream: the atmosphere was more like an awards ceremony than a memorial service.

Cars packed the sunny parking lot of the largest church in La Sirena. Every important Earthbound in a hundred-mile vicinity had shown up, dressed to the nines. I smiled at them; they stared at my silver halo. Did any of these people realize I was the last person to see Merrimoth alive?

"You have nothing to feel guilty about, so cut that out," Lon said in a low voice.

"I don't feel guilty."

"Could've fooled me. You didn't kill Merrimoth. He did that himself."

Dammit. Okay, maybe I did feel guilty, but it was so mixed up with a thousand other negative feelings—my creepy-ass dream about my mother, concern for Kar Yee, the stress of getting the bar fixed back up, the disappointment in losing Telly yesterday afternoon . . . the meeting I'd scheduled with Hajo later that night.

And Yvonne.

The Giovannis came back well after midnight from talking with Yvonne, and their pronouncement was that Yvonne was more lucid and humble than she'd been in years.

Good for her. Truly.

But you'll have to excuse me if I wasn't turning cartwheels and breaking out champagne.

Anyway, it just soured my already anxious mood. And how Lon's empathic knack managed to hone in on "guilt over Merrimoth" inside my woebegone stew of emotional negativity was beyond me. I sighed dramatically.

Lon hit the button to set the alarm on the silver Audi. To be honest, I preferred his mud-spattered SUV with Jupe's comics lining the floorboards. Or maybe it's just that I hated the fact that every time I'd been a passenger inside the Audi, we were going to some event connected to the Hellfire Club.

"Chin up," he said. "This won't last long."

One warm, strong hand wrapped around mine as he led me toward La Sirena All Souls, a sprawling Mission style stucco-and-cedar church surrounded by gently curving palm trees stretching above its terra cotta roof. My heels clicked against rough mosaic tiles that circled a star-shaped fountain in front of the entrance.

Lon wore a perfectly tailored black suit that revealed teasing outlines of hard muscle in his arms and thighs as he moved. I stole a glance up at him, all golden and chiseled, green eyes squinting into California sun, glinting honey hair that kissed the tops of his shoulders. He looked radiant and otherworldly, like a painting of some mythical demigod, crowned with his green and gold halo.

God, but he was a beautiful man. And he treated me like I was both a goddess and his equal. Every morning I woke up in his arms, like this morning—hallelujah!—I was grateful, because how lucky was I? He was a freaking *catch*.

And you know what? So was I. According to him, he saw something good in me the first time we'd met, but maybe I was just starting to realize it, too. It wasn't that long ago I wrestled with insecurities about our age difference, but even though we liked to tease each other, our May-December scandal didn't bother me.

Because now, as I glanced at a well-to-do woman in designer pumps and a haircut that probably cost more than my monthly car insurance payment, I thought, you know, why should I be intimidated? I mean, I looked pretty good. Owned a successful business. Had mad magical skills, as Jupe put it. And I was decent person. So why shouldn't I have an awesome boyfriend with an awesome kid, not to mention a few friends who cared about me? And who the hell else did I know who'd been *half* as betrayed as I'd been by my own parents and managed to hold her head up and keep going? No one, that's who.

And, dammit, even if I did bind David Merrimoth when he was jumping from his balcony, he was trying to kill us—*for no good reason*! Sure, I wish things hadn't turned out like they did for him, but I did the best I could at the time.

Lon was right: I wasn't a killer. Merrimoth's death was not my fault. I was not turning into my crazy, bloodthirsty parents. I was just a girl trying to do the right thing in spite of very abnormal circumstances.

The hollows of Lon's cheeks deepened when he smiled down at me. I tightened my hand around his and put all the bad stuff out of my mind.

We slowed our pace in front of the church. People mingled outside heavy wooden double-doors, chatting and smoking valrivia cigarettes. Lon shook a few hands and grunted at several Hellfire Club members, tilting his chin up in answer to people who waved from afar. The few brief conversations we had with other attendees all started out with "Such a shame about David" and "I just can't believe he's gone," but quickly progressed to "Where are they serving lunch after the burial?" And these were Merrimoth's peers.

The inside of the sanctuary was packed. We decided to forgo the pews and stand along the back wall. We weren't the only ones. When a couple squeezed in next to us, Lon shifted me in front of him, pulling my back against his solid chest. I relaxed, grateful for the comfort his warm body provided. He ran his thumb down the side of my arm from my elbow to my wrist and up again, a slow, soothing stroke.

"You look nice," he murmured in my ear, so low and close it tickled. I turned my head sideways, trapping his cheek with mine. He smelled really good, like clean laundry and soap . . . and like Lon—that same identifiable scent I caught yesterday when Telly was tearing the bridge down over us. I breathed him in, a small pleasure, as he whispered, "Wish we were dressed up for a restaurant instead of a funeral."

"Me too," I whispered back.

A few seconds passed, then he said, "Better yet, I wish we were alone."

"Mmm?"

"Completely alone. No Jupe. No Mr. and Mrs. Holiday. No in-laws. What do you think?"

"Right now?" Funerals were turning out to be *way* better than I imagined.

"A vacation."

"Oh?"

Sometimes communicating with Lon was like pulling teeth. But I'd learned if I stayed quiet, he'd eventually spit out what he was trying to say. So I didn't answer. I just waited, watching people file into the crowded sanctuary.

After a long pause, he continued murmuring in my ear. "I got an offer for a photo shoot in the Alps.

Thought maybe you'd like to come along and we could make a vacation out of it."

"As in Europe?"

"I could choose Switzerland or France. I thought maybe you'd like to go to France."

Hmm. My parents' families were both originally from France (my mother grew up in Paris, and my father's parents were from Marseille) and they used to speak French when they were alone. My mother had a heavy French accent up to the last day I'd seen her alive. I'd always been curious about France. I still had family there—distant cousins and whatnot—and I often wondered what they were like. But I'd never been out of the states.

Lon raised a finger and shifted a lock of hair away from my ear, then continued to speak in a low, quiet voice. "A small village in the Alps. Just the two of us. I was thinking we could rent a villa. A nice one. Indoor pool. Big fireplace. Drink wine. Go skiing."

"Skiing?" I said incredulously. I doubted I could roller skate, much less ski.

Then he admitted, "Mostly I was just thinking about getting naked."

My throat made a strangled sound, something between a laugh and a gasp. A little thrill zinged through me. "A sex vacation?" I whispered.

He chuckled. "No Jupe, no Tambuku. Just you and me."

"I've never been on a vacation before."

"Ever?"

"Never." My parents had always left me at home with someone from our esoteric order when they went on vacations, and then, of course, I separated from them when I turned seventeen. Being on the run and living under an alias doesn't exactly lend itself to relaxing vacation time.

"Another first," Lon whispered in a sultry voice. It was one of his favorite pastimes, cataloging any "first" experiences I shared with him. He kept a mental list. I think it was some kind of male pride thing. Kind of endearing.

"France at the end of January," he said. "It's settled."

It was a glorious thought, this little vacation fantasy of his. "Sure," I said. "I'll talk to Kar Yee."

"I already asked her. She said it was fine."

I cocked my head, confused for a moment until I remembered Kar Yee's words last week before the robbery: *I know a secret you don't know.* "Well, damn," I muttered, a nervous happiness spreading through my chest.

"Eight nights, and I only have to work two of those. I've got everything booked already. Just wanted to make sure you'd be okay with it."

My heart squeezed. I turned my face up to his and kissed him on the bottom of his chin, right below one point of his pirate mustache. "Nicest surprise ever."

He hugged me closer as a familiar face bobbed into view. Lon's head snapped back from mine as he looked where I was gazing, toward a smiling man strolling down the side aisle, waving in our direction.

"Father Carrow!"

It took the good Father a few seconds to pick his way over to us, wending his way around the crowd gathering behind the pews. The sight of his silver hair and cornflower-blue halo made me happy. Yes, he was an Earthbound *and* a former priest. The first one I'd ever met, but there were others, like the current priest of this church. Being retired, Father Carrow was dressed in a suit today instead of robes. He waved a fedora he held in hand as he greeted us. "Cady and Lon, two of my favorite people."

I hugged Father Carrow's neck. "It's good to see you," I said, and meant it. He lived a couple blocks from me back in Morella, and we used to talk frequently. But since I'd unofficially moved in with Lon and Jupe, I saw less and less of him.

He gave Lon's hand a hearty shake. "How's life been treating you?"

"Can't complain," Lon answered, running a hand down my back.

"And I can't tell you how happy it makes me to know I've played cupid so successfully." Father Carrow had introduced us several months ago.

One side of Lon's mouth tilted up briefly. "We agree."

Father Carrow grinned in reply.

"Are you, uh, working here today?" I asked.

"They often ask me to lend a hand for big events.

I'm helping out at the gravesite. Did you know Mr. Merrimoth personally?"

"I did," Lon answered.

"I'm so sorry," Father Carrow said, his brow furrowing.

Lon shook his head. "We weren't close. I'd go so far to say that we almost enemies, unfortunately."

Father Carrow leaned in closer. "Then you won't mind me saying that there were some nasty rumors going around about his knack before he died. Folks say he set fire to his own house."

I'm not sure why that surprised me. I wondered if it was Dare who yapped, or one of his henchmen. Word spread fast in a small community like this. I hoped there weren't accompanying rumors about some silver-haloed witch helping him jump to his death.

Lon grunted. "You hear similar rumors about anyone else around town?"

Father Carrow squinted. "Setting fire to things? Or . . ."

"Knacks being stronger than they should," I clarified. "Way stronger." I quickly filled him in about Tambuku being robbed, touching on Noel Saint-Hill's grim death. I didn't think it was a good idea to volunteer the bionic drug information, so I skipped over that detail.

"That's definitely unusual. And to your question, Lon, there is a rumor that comes to mind now. Do you know Peter Little?"

"Former city councilman?"

Father Carrow nodded and explained to me, "He has a luck knack. Folks say that's how he got his position."

"Among other things," Lon agreed. From the dour look on his face, he wasn't a fan.

"But have you heard that his luck has gotten . . . luckier?" Father Carrow asked.

Lon's melon-green eyes narrowed. He waited for more.

"He won the lottery."

Not a surprise for someone with a luck knack, I thought to myself. It wasn't a common ability, but I knew a Tambuku regular who won a lot of bets at the horse track.

"I heard about the lottery win," Lon said. "Three hundred grand, right? Last week."

"Yes, but that's not the only instance. He's won three times this month. First was five thousand on a scratch-off ticket. Second was that three hundred thousand you mentioned. And the third time was two days ago."

"Huh."

"I'm surprised you don't know," Father Carrow said. "It was all over the news. He won the Mega Millions jackpot. Fifty-nine million."

"Holy shit," Lon mumbled, then quickly apologized to Carrow, who made a shooing motion with his hand.

"Seems a bit odd," Father Carrow said. "Even

with a luck knack, how many people win the lottery three times in two weeks?" He glanced at the door. "They're waving for me. Service is about to start. Maybe we'll talk again later?"

Lon nodded.

Father Carrow patted Lon on the shoulder before squeezing my hand. "Come visit me, Cadybell. I miss chatting with you."

I did too. I hugged him, then watched his blue halo trail behind him as he left.

"Peter Little," Lon murmured.

"Is he into drugs?" I asked.

"He's a dirty politician."

"Hellfire?"

"No. He doesn't live far from here, though. We could drop by. Congratulate him. Ask if he's bought any strange red potions lately."

Follow the drug, find Telly.

"Couldn't hurt, I suppose."

Lon pulled me back against his chest and wrapped his arms around my waist as the organist walked across the stage behind the altar at the front of the sanctuary. I let out a long breath, thinking about Peter Little's knack, and about Telly's bottle of bionic juice. Several heads turned when someone walked into the sanctuary. Curious, I glanced to see who was causing all the hubbub and spotted Dare's shiny bald head. My muscles turned to stone.

The Hellfire leader slowed his already casual gait as he glanced in our direction. I flinched but didn't look away. Not even when his black, hate-filled gaze drilled into my skull. It only lasted a moment, that look he gave me, before he turned and continued on to the front of the church without another glance.

I knew right then and there that Ambrose Dare damn well hadn't forgiven me.

17

I half expected someone named Peter Little to reside inside a toadstool in Smurf Village, but after the funeral, Lon drove us to a fancy condo overlooking the La Sirena boardwalk. The building that housed the condo was five stories high and secured by gate. Instead of stopping at the guardhouse, Lon drove the silver Audi to the striped gate arm and typed four numbers into a little metal box.

"How do you have a security password to get inside here?" I asked as the arm began rising.

He gave me a faster-than-light sideways glance. "Used to date someone who lives here."

Ah-*ha*.

"Megan Pierce," he elaborated, surprising me. "She laughed like a hyena at every damn thing I said. Drove me crazy."

"Hate her already. Will rip her eyes out if we see her inside. Just a warning."

"Mmm, catfight."

"Rawrr."

He chuckled. "Have I told you lately that you're my favorite person?"

I smiled as he drove toward the building, swerving through empty parking spaces to avoid speed bumps before pulling into a spot near the entrance. Freshly planted yellow and purple petunias lined the sidewalk. I skirted around a misfiring automatic sprinkler and spotted a white van with a Morella Channel 5 logo driving away from the condos. "Father Carrow wasn't lying," I remarked, pointing it out to Lon.

"Everyone loves a winner." He typed in another code and held the door open for me.

The lobby, if you could call it that, was a single room ringed with four elevators. A lush cluster of palms and tropical plants anchored the middle of the room below a skylight. Opera floated from hidden speakers. We took an elevator up to the top floor, then stepped out into a chandelier-lit corridor with two apartments. Lon strode to a door flanked by an umbrella stand and pressed a gently chiming door-bell.

Bass-heavy music thumped through the walls. Lon cocked a brow. Yeah, it didn't sound good to me, either. This might've been a bad idea. After a few seconds, a voice crackled from a small speaker near the doorframe. "Yes?"

"It's Lon Butler."

There was a short pause, then the sound of a lock turning. The door flew open to reveal a very tan, *very* blond man, maybe a few years older than Lon.

Long navy board shorts hung to his knees. An unbuttoned short sleeve shirt flapped open to a broad chest dusted with graying blond hair. Mr. Little clearly spent a lot of time at the gym doing ab workouts. He was also in the middle of hosting a party, it seemed. A girl in a bathing suit walked past a doorway behind him, and I could hear distant laughter from somewhere deeper inside.

"Butler," he said enthusiastically as some obnoxious Top Forty club music filled the air. "How the hell are you?"

"Not as good as you, apparently."

Mr. Little looked me up and down. A slow, lecherous grin spread across his face. "Please, come on in and join the party." He closed the door behind me and locked it. "I'm Peter, by the way."

"Cady," I replied, looking around. His condo had blinding white-on-white walls, furniture, rugs, floor, occasionally broken up by a startling accent color, a shade of turquoise blue that matched both his halo and his too-blue eyes.

"Don't even think about it or I'll fucking punch your teeth in."

I twisted around to look at Lon. His eyes were narrowed to slits. A proprietary grip on my wrist tugged me closer to his side.

Peter held up his hands. "Whoa, calm down. I wasn't—" He glanced at me, then gave Lon a sheepish smile. "Okay, I was, but . . . Dammit, Butler. I forgot how much I hate your knack."

Feminine voices tinkled from another room.

Peter glanced over his shoulder and shrugged. "I've got my hands full anyway." He shouted over the music at the girl in the bikini. When she came over, he whispered something into her ear. She looked at Lon and smiled, then nodded at Peter and meandered off somewhere. What the hell was that all about? I glanced at Lon for guidance, but he had a funny look on his face. That better not have been that hobag, Megan Pierce.

"You two heading out or coming from somewhere?" Peter asked, gesturing for us to come farther inside. The volume of the thumpy dance music lowered.

"David Merrimoth's funeral," Lon answered as we followed Peter into a sunken living room capped by a wide, white fireplace. Sunlight spilled through long windows. How in the world he lived in a sterile place like this was beyond me. But when I looked closer, I noticed a lot of clothes scattered around. Mostly women's clothes.

"Oh, the funeral. That was today?" Peter said, flopping down on a sofa. His shirt fell open a few more inches. Four empty wine glasses sat on a glass coffee table next to a wine bottle. Where was the party? I briefly saw a figure move through a hallway at the back of the room, and thought I heard talking in what seemed to be the kitchen, but I didn't see anyone.

Peter sniffled and wiped his nose. "I meant to attend, but . . ."

Lon perched on white leather loveseat across from him. "I guess I'd forget too if I'd just won fifty million dollars."

An enormous shit-eating grin lit up Peter's face. "I still can't believe it." He puckered his lips and exhaled a long, slow breath. "They don't give you the money right away, you know. Have to deal with lawyers and accountants. More red tape than I ever saw on city council."

"Rumor has it that this is your third win."

Peter dialed down his smile. "Wishing you could trade knacks with me?"

"No, just wondering why you haven't won the lottery before."

He shrugged. "Never really tried."

"You have a luck knack and never played the lottery before?" I said. "That would probably be the first thing I did." I was sitting on something. Rising up slightly, I pulled out a pair of purple panties from beneath my ass. And immediately chucked them on the floor. God only knows whose crack they'd been up.

Peter didn't seem to notice. "Maybe I played it a few times when I was younger. Won bits here and there, I don't know."

"But suddenly you win three times in a month?" Lon said.

Peter sank back in to the sofa and crossed his ankles. "I'll be fifty this year. Guess I thought why not? You only live once."

"Bullshit."

Tiny lines filled Peter's forehead as he raised his brows. "What are you implying, Lon?"

"I'm not implying anything. I'm telling you, I know something's changed."

"Like what?"

"You tell me. What are you doing to increase your knack?" Lon's tone was unfriendly and accusatory.

I tried to smooth things over. "Because if you've stumbled on something good? Boy, we definitely want in on it," I said, smiling my best flirty smile.

"'We?'" Peter said. "I thought people like *you* used magick to get everything they want."

A quick anger flickered inside my chest. "And just how many magicians do you know?"

He curled his thumb and index finger into an 0. "Unless I count you."

"You don't," Lon said.

"So protective." Peter reached for the wine bottle and tried to pour a drink, but nothing came out. "If you ever get tired of Killjoy over here"—he pointed the bottle at Lon—"give me a call. I could use a little magic in my life."

A long silence fell. I could practically feel Lon's blood pressure rising. Or maybe that was mine.

"Let's cut the shit," I said. "We know you're using a bionic drug. We just want the name of your dealer."

Peter's face twitched in about fifty different places. "I don't know what you're talking about."

A long moment passed. We all stared at each

other. Strange noises floated nearby. Sounded like someone was in pain.

"Bind him."

I looked at Lon. "What?"

"Bind him. He won't talk unless we make him."

Peter straightened in his seat, twitchier and twitchier. "What the hell are you talking about?"

"Daytime, remember?" I whispered hotly to Lon. I wasn't *Sun*child.

"There's more than one way."

Alarm spread over Peter's face like wildfire. He shot up out of his seat and whipped around the sofa to a low credenza behind it. As he was tugging open a drawer, Lon calmly stood, strode three steps, and slammed the drawer closed. Peter barely got his fingers out of the way in time. The blond man retreated a foot or two. "Stay back or—"

"Peter?"

We all looked toward the back of the living room, through an arch that led to the kitchen. A busty girl in a black bikini top held a white towel around her waist. Another girl peered over her shoulder. "The hot tub is done heating," she said dumbly.

Peter said nothing.

"He'll be there in a minute," I told them. The first girl shrugged and they both retreated into the kitchen. As soon as they were out of sight, I said, "Who's your dealer, Peter?"

"I don't have one! I swear to God. I went to a party in Morella a couple weeks back, and everyone was talking about bionic knacks, but nobody knew how it was happening. Some girl invited me into a little side party in a bedroom and they were passing around a drink. She said it would make me luckier, so I took a swig. Everyone did. I didn't feel anything, but I was already pretty drunk. Things got blurry after that. I didn't think much about it until I tried to play the lottery. And, you know . . . it worked, I guess."

"Where was this party at?"

"I don't know. Somewhere in midtown. A really nice place. Some rich guy with connections to Morella politicians. I don't keep track of who's who in city politics anymore, and this was a friend of a friend—they heard about it when we were out at a bar, and someone drove us there. I was really trashed. I wasn't paying attention."

I shared a look with Lon, and he gave me a reluctant nod: Peter was telling the truth. Great.

"No one's offered it to you since?" I asked.

"No."

"And you went to this party two weeks ago?"

"Yeah. A day before the first lottery win."

Which meant the potion lasted a hell of lot longer than I'd hoped. Not exactly what I'd wanted to hear, but it told me Telly was still dangerous.

Lon gave Peter a long stare. "If you hear of anything else—someone selling it—we'd appreciate a name."

Peter glanced at my halo. "Uh, yeah. Sure."

"We'll let you get back to your teenage Dream Team," I said, kicking the purple panties out of my path.

We headed out the way we came in and didn't talk until we were back inside the glass elevator.

"Why are all your friends creeps?" I asked, a little perturbed.

"He's not my friend."

I punched the Lobby button several times, then the CLOSE DOORS button a few more times.

"I have normal friends," he argued in a calm voice, pulling my hand away from the control panel.

"Like?"

"Mick."

"The doctor?" I'd only seen him briefly from a distance in the emergency room when Jupe's tattoo got infected during the chaos around Halloween.

"His wife is real nice. You'd like her. They've got two daughters. One's Jupe's age, the other's a couple years older."

"Hmph."

The elevator began descending. I crossed my arms over my middle and considered what Peter Little had just told us. "He said the party he went to was swank. Someone connected to politics in Morella. So this bionic elixir is being distributed to rich politicians. I don't think they're buying it from homeless gutter punks like Telly."

"They probably bought it from Telly's distributor."

I groaned in frustration. "So much trouble for a stupid punk kid. I just want to get him locked up."

"What if he just tears down the jail cell?"

"It's got to wear off eventually." I hoped.

"But if the elixir stays on the market, there'll just be another Telly. It's not safe, Cady."

Damn him for being right. "Well, I'm meeting Hajo tonight, so we'll soon see if he knows who's distributing it."

Lon scowled. Guess it was his turn to be grumpy now. Because he definitely wasn't the only one with creepy friends.

18

I was supposed to meet Hajo at a pub, but he texted me as I was driving into Morella and asked if I'd come to his place instead. I hesitated, until he told me he was having some people over that lived in his high-rise. That sounded safer than meeting him alone, and to be honest, I was a little curious about his fancy apartment.

Hajo owned a condo on the twenty-second floor of one of the tallest buildings in downtown Morella. He'd first told me about the penthouse pad a month or so ago, at which time I accused him of being a showoff—he lived down the hall from a semi-famous professional football player with a five million dollar contract. Hajo claimed the real reason he bought it was because it was so far above all the dead bodies.

Hajo is a death dowser. That's his Earthbound knack. He can track death trails all over the city and pinpoint where bones are buried. Though he's tall, dark, and handsome, he spends most days being miserable, highly aware of every dead rat in the sewer.

Hajo is also a dick with a capital *D*.

Lon hates his guts, and he has plenty of reasons to resent the guy. Hajo has few scruples. He can't keep a girlfriend because he has a fatalistic notion of fidelity and will fuck anything that doesn't have the backbone to fend off his less-than-romantic come-ons. And yet, he's too depressing and brooding to be a swinging, happy-go-lucky playboy. You almost feel sorry for him. Almost.

Around seven that night, I pulled the Jetta into the high-class parking garage below Hajo's building. I was surprised Hajo was actually allowing me there, as he's fiercely protective of his privacy. Like I've said, he won't discuss anything illegal on the phone and prefers to meet in shady places. Comes with the territory, I suppose; drug dealers have to be on guard. And judging from the fancy digs, he was way better at his job than I'd first imagined.

I tried to text Lon and tell him about the change in the meeting place, but there was no reception in the elevator. He could've come with me, but in the end we decided that it wasn't cool to ask his in-laws to babysit Jupe while we headed off to meet a drug dealer. Better to tell the smaller lie that I had to step out and take care of something related to the bar. He did warn me, as he always did when I met Hajo, that if I wasn't back in two hours, he was coming to get me and possibly calling the police. I'd never tell

Hajo this, of course; he'd probably take it as some testosterone-fueled compliment that Lon saw him, however remotely, as a potential threat.

The penthouse hallway had a modern art deco feel to it, with plush green carpeting and gold chevron uplit sconces on the walls. An even fancier gold elevator sat in the middle of the floor, manned by a building attendant. I found Hajo's condo and swung the gold knocker against the door several times. It opened, and some waif of a girl stood on the other side. She looked up at my halo and said in an unidentifiable European accent, "Oh. He's inside."

Low, atmospheric trance music pulsed as I entered. I expected to see a few people. I didn't expect to see a freaking party. Then again, it was the holidays. Thirty or forty people were buzzing around the large, dark apartment. The only light came from scattered candles, a few low-light lamps, and the entertainment: a video projector shining a Kenneth Anger film ten feet high across one wall. Jupe would shit a brick if he could see this setup. It was like the kid's beloved drive-in, just indoors.

Damn, Hajo. His drug den was ten kinds of awesome: big and showy, with high ceilings and a long balcony stretching over a stunning city view. Way nicer than Peter Little's place, actually. Lots of rich purple and golden green. Low, sleek furniture and pillows scattered everywhere, like some Middle Eastern palace. I wondered how many of the girls walking around with no shoes were part of his harem.

The waif left me on my own. I felt a little nervous around people who were way richer and hipper than me, drinking and smoking God knew what. I smelled valrivia, and weed, but I didn't smell the very distinct burnt-soil scent of sømna, the highly addictive fungi-derived drug that Hajo was addicted to. Possession of any amount of the drug would get you slammed with the harshest drug laws in the state. He told me he never smoked it at home for that reason. He also told me he was in control of his addiction. I had no idea how true that was, but I never saw him out of control or strung out.

I asked someone if they knew where he was and was pointed in the direction of a room next to the balcony. A long column of golden light stretched from a crack between double doors. I figured if he wanted privacy, he'd shut them all the way, so I pushed one of the doors open and stepped inside. It looked like it was supposed to be a library or home office, with built-in bookshelves, crown molding, and a Persian chandelier in the center of the ceiling. Only, the bookshelves were filled with *objets d'art* instead of books, and there was no desk. Just some stuffed chairs and more floor pillows.

Three large paintings of women were propped against the bookshelves at the far end of the room. With his short, dark hair combed back all Rebel Without A Cause, Hajo stood in front of them, his tall, lean frame dwarfing a man at his elbow. The waif who'd answered the door was draped around his shoulders, her small halo looking pale against Hajo's ultra-watt blue one.

"I like them all, but I only have room for one," he was telling the guy, who was either the artist or the art dealer. From the way he was dressed, in expensive slacks and a button-down shirt, I was going to assume the latter.

The paintings were life-sized: a redhead, a blonde, and a dark-haired Asian woman wearing a surgical mask and a nurse's cap. They were painted with angry strokes, and none of them were particularly attractive. In fact, I'd go so far to say that they were dark and depressing.

"I like her the best," I said.

Hajo turned to look at me, dark, heavy brows lifting. He had great bones and miles of sooty lashes that ringed his eyes like kohl. "Hello, Bell. Which one?"

I pointed to the painting of the Asian nurse.

"Interesting. Why her?"

I studied the paintings. "She doesn't seem as lost as the other two."

"Interesting," Hajo said. He kept his dark sideburns styled into diagonal points, which seemed to stretch when his chiseled face drew up into a slow smile. Then he spoke to the buttoned-up man. "Let me look at them tonight and I'll give you a decision tomorrow."

The man scribbled something on a card. Hajo glanced at me while he waited for it. Light from the punched-metal and glass chandelier cast shadows on his elongated face that made his cheekbones seem impossibly sharp. He could trace his paternal ancestry to the missing Roanoke colony, like the majority of Earthbounds in the US, but his mother was Turkish, or so he said. His mismatched heritage combined pretty pleasantly.

He took the man's business card and jerked his head toward the door. "Out."

The guy looked a little put-out, but he made no comment and retreated as Hajo pried the waif's hands from around his shoulders. "Go on," he told her.

"Hajo—"

"Are you deaf? Get the fuck out of here. And close the door behind you."

The girl seemed genuinely offended, and not for the first time, I thought it was kind of a shame that all this tall, brooding handsomeness went to waste on someone so miserable and douche-y.

Hajo's chest and shoulders broadened as he crossed his arms, stretching the dark fabric of his shirt. His jeans were expensive and Euro-trendy, sitting low over his flat, polished loafers. Everything about his look projected the image that he was some sort of continental business mogul who ordered five-hundred-dollar bottles of champagne in the VIP section of a hipster nightclub. It was the first time I'd ever seen him without his black leather racing jacket. Guess this was Hajo in his natural environment. Or maybe the other Hajo was real, and this was show. Hard to tell.

"Why are you having a party if you don't want to socialize?" I asked as the doors clicked shut.

"The football quarterback suggested it," he said dourly. "I'm worried he knows I deal. He asks too many questions. He's got a coke habit and is also looking for a steroid hookup." Hajo gestured to the party outside the door. "I'm trying to placate him. Get him introduced to people who can steer him away from me. I don't need a high-profile client with a big mouth."

"Tough to be you." I glanced around. "Your place is . . . really freakin' nice."

"Don't act so surprised."

"Well, geez. The first time I met you was in that hellhole in Waxtown."

His chin lifted as he made a vague noise of acknowledgment. "Cristina's place. She was a pig."

"I'm sure she wasn't the only one," I muttered.

His lazy gaze rambled over my body. "Oink."

"Don't start."

"You've got a little extra something going on tonight, Bell," he said, waving his hand up and down between us. "Your energy's sharper. What's up with that?"

Hajo once told me that he could sense living energy trails, not just dead ones. Said my energy was different and he could probably track it, which scared the bejesus out of me, truthfully. And now that he'd noticed something different, I thought of my moon magick and my mother. A dull panic surfaced. "What do you mean?"

"It's just busier. More potent. Riper."

"Maybe you're just higher," I said.

"Maybe. Have you gained weight? Your breasts are starting to balance out that big ass of yours."

I think my mouth fell open. Sure, Kar Yee's shirt made a ridiculous show of my boobs, but this was my own T-shirt. Was I really getting fat? And, *oh my God*, why was I even listening? Who says this kind of stuff?

"It was a compliment," he explained. "Your ass is marvelous."

"What's the matter with you? Stop saying shit like that."

"Me? What's eating *you*? You're in a horrible mood."

Pfft. Like I was going to tell him. I grumbled to myself and jerked my head away, but he just stared at me, waiting. "Lon's ex-wife is in town."

He whistled. "The hot supermodel."

"She's way hotter in person."

"Nice. I mean, not for you. That blows. Are they getting back together or something?"

"Over my dead body. Or hers."

"Mmm, smells like jealousy," he said with a smirk.

"Shut the hell up."

He shrugged and looked at the paintings again. "So, what did you want from me?"

"Nothing, now."

"Oh, come on. Tell me what you're here for. Another dowsing job? That last one didn't turn out so well. I'm not all that jazzed about stumbling into magical cockroaches again."

"Me neither." I reached into my jacket and pulled out the red vial. "Do you know what this is?"

His eyes narrowed. "Looks like an elixir. Already gave one of these back to you, though I'm still fuzzy on why, exactly." He shook his head and swallowed, momentarily lost in remembering. He hadn't figured out that Jupe persuaded him with his knack. I'd definitely like to keep it that way.

Music spilled into the room. I looked up and saw someone standing in the doorway, a man about my age with long blond hair pulled back into a tight ponytail. One of the barefooted girls roaming Hajo's place had her hands all over him, trying to get his shirt unbuttoned.

"Do you not understand what a closed door means? Get the hell out of here, Darren," Hajo snapped. "And don't even think about heading to my bedroom. Go bang in your own apartment."

"Sorry," the man mumbled, high as a kite. I held the red vial behind my back until they retreated and closed the doors again.

"Asshole trust funder," Hajo said under his breath.

"Not a friend, I take it?"

"He lives on the floor below. Always begging me for shit. Spoiled asshole. Just like everyone else here. I hate every last person who lives in this damn building." He nodded to the hand behind my back. "Anyway, you were saying?"

"This isn't my brew," I said, showing him the vial again. "You really haven't seen this?"

He held out his hand. "May I?"

My fingers brushed his when I passed it to him. A little burst of static electricity almost made me drop the bottle.

He sucked in a breath. "Oh, Bell. One of these days . . ."

"One of these days you're going to fall for someone who'll want you back. And if you're lucky, they'll be patient enough to stick around while you wean yourself off the sømna."

Dark lashes blinked as he regarded the bottle with curiosity, holding it to the light. "What am I looking at?"

"Bionic juice."

Every muscle tensed. His gaze locked with mine. "You're joking."

"You've heard of it?"

"Three people have asked me for it tonight. Including the quarterback and that dickwad trustfunder," he said, waving toward the door.

"Shit. You think he saw the vial?"

He shook his head dismissively. "He wouldn't know his ass from his elbow, and he's too wasted to care right now." He tilted the vial and studied the liquid inside. "I know people exaggerate—should I assume this doesn't *really* do what people say it does?"

"Magnifies the strength of Earthbound knacks, if that's what you've heard."

He thrust it back into my hand like it was poison. "Are you serious? Get this shit away from me. That's the last think I'd ever want. Something to dull my knack? Sign me up. But I seriously think I'd rather slit my wrists than have it increased."

"I'm not trying to sell it to you, drama queen."

He sniffled and wiped his nose. "Right. Sorry."

"Some punk kid took a dose of this and was able to lift off half a bridge to crash down over my head. A telekinetic homeless kid. And that was after he lifted a car with his mind and killed his friend."

"What the hell?" Hajo mumbled.

I pocketed the red vial and told him about the robberies on Diablo Avenue, Kar Yee's injury, and the other weird crimes on the news, and how they might be because of this elixir. Told him everything I knew about Telly and exactly where we found him.

He listened quietly, arms crossed over his chest, then mumbled "fuck" when I finished.

"So that's why I called," I said. "I thought maybe you could help me. You ever heard of this telekinetic kid, Telly?"

"You think because I'm a dealer, I know every other dealer in the city? Homeless kids selling meth and ten-dollar hand jobs under a bridge?"

"Ten dollars. Is that all?" No wonder Telly was selling the elixir.

"Really, Cady?"

"Look, I don't know the drug dealer chain of command," I complained, feeling a little sheepish. "Anyway, he said this bottle's worth five grand. Guess he was doling out one-drop doses on sugar cubes and selling them for three hundred a pop."

"What is this? The '70s? Why wasn't he using blotter paper?"

"How the hell should I know? I'm just telling you what was in his backpack."

"And I'm taking it that you don't know how to brew this up?"

"No idea. Never seen anything like it." I told him about Peter Little and his not-so-little luck. "So he claims that he only took one dose, yet he won the big lottery two weeks later. God only knows how long the effects last."

"Shit."

"Yeah. Maybe Telly was undercharging. We overheard him saying that there's only two sources for this. We figure it's the maker and the distributor. I was hoping you might be able to ask around and see if you can get us the name of the dealer."

"I see." He crossed his arms over his chest. "If this stuff is that rare, I bet the kid's pretty pissed at you for stealing it from him."

"Well, I'm pretty freaking pissed at him for hurting Kar Yee and stealing from *me*."

"Can't say I blame you. How is she?"

"Kar Yee? Better. Bob's healing her."

A rare open smile revealed a flash of white teeth. "Dr. Robert Hernandez. Who would've thunk it?"

"Leave him alone. You're such an ass."

"Guilty." But not guilty enough to care much, I supposed. Long fingers molded his hair in place as he studied the nurse painting. "I've never met your partner, but I've seen her at your bar. Hot. Maybe you should set us up."

Never in a million years. "You aren't fit to be in the same room as her. Now can we focus on the bionic elixir? I'd like to find Telly's dealer. Or Telly himself. Then I'd like to bind him until his heart explodes."

"I'll bet. Look, I'll put out some feelers. Try to find who's distributing the stuff, and while I'm at it, see if anyone's heard of this Telly kid. If he's doing business with other dealers, they need to know that he's dangerous. Might take me a few days, but I'll call you when I've got a something."

"Thanks, Hajo. I appreciate it."

He stared at me for a long moment, dark, dilated eyes scheming up something behind the miles and miles of black lashes that fanned over his skin. "So, you wanna—"

"No."

"You don't even know what I was going to say."

"Don't need to know."

"How about a threesome. Me, you, and Lon."

I choked.

"Don't say you haven't thought of it."

"No, Hajo. I can truly say that I *have never thought of it*."

He gave me a sexy little smile. "You will now, though."

"In my nightmares."

Ugh. If that thought ever materialized inside my brain while I was having sex with transmutated, thought-reading Lon, I would die. And Lon would probably come over here and strangle Hajo with his bare hands. Which might not be the worst thing in the world, but still. I shuddered and shook the thought away as I walked toward the double doors leading out of the room.

"Set me up with Kar Yee," Hajo called out from behind me.

I gave him a look over my shoulder as the rolling trance music pulsed through the doors. "Buy the nurse painting," I said with a smile. "And call me when you have a name."

I picked my way through the crowded party and gave a little wave to Hajo's waif to let her know that I was finished with him. Once I was out of the condo, I breathed a sigh of relief. Lon wasn't going to be thrilled to know I'd been here, but at least I came out unscathed, and maybe Hajo would find a name that would help us. I buttoned up my coat and caught the elevator to the parking garage just as someone was stepping out. But when I hit the button to take me underground, a hand stopped the doors from closing.

"Hi there. Mind if I ride down with you?"

It was the man with the blond ponytail—the trust funder. Darren, I think Hajo had called him. And the predatory way he was looking at me made all the hairs on my arms stand on end.

19

He pressed the button to close the elevator doors and blocked me from stepping back out. His pupils were tiny black dots in a sea of bright blue. His halo was weak and pale.

"You were selling something to Hajo," he said when the doors closed.

Shit. He'd seen the red vial when he busted in on Hajo and me. He was also several inches over six feet tall, lording over me like someone who was accustomed to taking what he wanted.

The elevator descended. I lunged for a button—any button, any floor. But he shifted in front of the control panel like a moveable brick wall. Ungodly fast for someone who was wasted. Ungodly fast for someone who wasn't. I backed up into the far corner of the elevator. Classical music, calm and innocuous, filled the small space, mocking me with its false assurance that everything was fine.

"I saw the red juice," he insisted, stretching an arm across the elevator doors, like I'd try to pry them open while the car in was in motion. "Should've known Hajo was holding out."

"Look, you're mistaken—" I started, trying to buy some time while we descended. I could pull some current and shock him, but there was a chance I'd blow the elevator's fuse. Did I really want to risk getting trapped inside here with him?

"I know what I saw. And I want it." His arm shot out, lightning fast. His big hand was around my throat before I could blink. "I don't want to hurt you. Let's play nice. Just give me a dose and I'll leave you alone."

He wasn't choking me. Just showing me he could. And when I went for the portable caduceus inside my jacket pocket, he also showed me how fast he really was. His free hand slapped mine away with unexpected force. Pain rocketed up my arm. I yelped.

"Speed," he said with a cocky smile. "A good enough knack. Would be better if you'd give me a dose of what you've got."

"Get your hands off me," I bit out.

"Hand over the juice, and I will."

"All I'm going to give you is a warning. Because if you don't step back—"

"What will you do? Call the cops and tell them that you refused to sell someone drugs?" He laughed. "I'll tell you what, I'll even pay you for the dose. Name your price. This is just a simple transaction. Don't make it into anything more."

I flailed, trying to knee him in the groin, but he blocked all my moves with ease.

Panic morphed into a black, black anger. Within the span of one second, my intentions had already leapt over the possibility of shocking him with Heka and tunneled into something much worse.

I just couldn't help myself.

Darkness fell. Sound turned in on itself. The blue pinpoint jumped into my line of vision.

I felt Darren slipping fingers inside my jacket, going for the red vial. But as his warm hand ghosted over my stomach, something changed. Something was cool against my skin. It started around my neck and washed over my breasts . . . my stomach. Like someone had spilled a cold drink down my shirt. He felt it too. His arm jerked away, as if he'd been burned.

He withdrew. Dropped his hold on me completely and backed up a step. I could see the blue pinpoint of light beyond him, overlapping where his heart beat inside his chest. And I probably should've been worried when the blue changed to bright silver, but I was distracted.

That thing happened again. Just like in Tambuku: something ran down my leg. Something cold and thick and smooth.

The elevator ground to halt, startling me out of my fear. Darren, too. His blue halo swirled as he shook his head like a dog that had just emerged from a rainstorm. He lunged at me again. Both hands were on my throat now. And any fear or doubt I'd been harboring just went up in smoke. I emptied my mind and focused on the now-silver dot. Internally spoke what I wanted, loud and clear.

Get off.

His big body flew backward. Slammed into the elevator doors. A second later, the doors opened. He lost his balance and fell outside, landing on his back. I felt the impact in my soles of my shoes. Felt something else, too—a growing pressure on my leg. Something moved there. My jean leg tightened uncomfortably. It was cutting off the circulation in my thigh. Throbbing. I limped out of the elevator, following Darren's path as he crab-walked backward into the parking garage.

Before I turned to see what was hurting my leg, Darren reached into his pocket and pulled out his keys. He was fumbling with something on the key ring. Pepper spray.

Big trust fund party-boy was going to mace me? Fuck that.

I meant to kick the mace away. That was definitely my intention. But something popped on the back of my leg. The pressure around my thigh released. And then, lightning-quick, instead of my foot, something else smacked the spray canister.

Something that came from behind me.

Something connected to me.

I felt the cool, jagged edges of his keys before they sailed across the garage. Felt them with what? Did my magick solidify and mold itself into some sort of weapon?

Darren shouted—I saw his mouth open and heard the sound in a distant, removed sort of way through the filter of my moon sight. He was on his feet way too fast, towering over me again. He had something else in his hand and was highly pissed off. His arm lifted. Metal glinted between his whitened knuckles. A pocketknife.

The jerk was going to stab me.

Anger and Heka got jumbled up inside me. Seethed. Boiled. Raged. I couldn't even make any rational, focused thoughts. All I could do was let it out before I went crazy with it.

Energy ebbed from me. A gush of Heka. It reached out for something—moon energy, perhaps—and came back like a boomerang, charged and ready. I made no conscious decision about what to do with it. I just unleashed it.

A cloud of silver swirled around me. I pushed it out across Darren, expanding it. There was nothing but the fog. I was creating it, spinning it . . . and it was part of me. He was a bug on my web. I spun the fog around him, encasing him in tight circles of silver smoke.

I felt Darren's heart pounding furiously, and his life draining away. I'm not sure how I felt it, but it was as if I had my hands on him and was measuring his pulse beneath my fingers. I was strangling him with the fog.

I was going to kill him.

The thing was, for a moment, I wasn't even sure

if I cared. God help me, but I think I almost *wanted* to kill him. And then some tiny voice of reason raised its hand inside me and waved—as if to say, *You sure you want to go this far?*

I didn't.

Straining, I tried to let go of the magick. It was so hard. Unnatural, even. But I kept trying, and my grip on Darren slackened. I felt him fall away and drop to the ground. The dark overlay of the moon magick lifted. My normal sight returned. I could hear a car driving on the parking level above us. It was gone. I'd done it. Pushed it away.

Maybe I really could control it.

And I never heard my mother. Not once. No whispering, no visions.

A small, joyous laugh escaped my lips.

My chest heaved with labored breath as I glanced down to check on Darren. His body lay crumpled at my feet, arms askew, mouth open. I couldn't tell if he was alive or dead. But that wasn't the worst of it.

My silver halo was stunningly bright. Bigger. I could tell because it was outlining the sleeves of my jacket with a silver light. It shone like a spotlight behind my head, one that cast a long shadow over Darren's body and the cement below. And I saw myself in that shadow: the curve of my hips, the shapes of my legs and arms, my hair standing around my head like it sometimes does when I'm channeling electricity.

And the long, rope-like shape of a tail.

A goddamn tail!

Like a reptile. Like a dirty rat.

I suddenly knew what had smacked the keys out of Darren's hand. What had wrapped around his body along with my silver fog.

I panicked. Hard. Cried out in shock.

Without thinking, I called up the moon magick again. It came so fast, like snapping my fingers.

I didn't have any idea what I was doing. I just wanted to retreat—that's all. Never in a million years would I have imagined what power a simple thought could wield.

20

The scent of cool, damp earth filled my senses.

A memory floated by: falling down a summertime grassy hill when I was five or six. Skinning my knees. My face pressing against the ground as I wept. And no one coming to my rescue. I remembered crying until I couldn't cry anymore before I'd picked myself up and walked home alone. My mother had taken one look at me and said, *"Oh, le petit cochon!"* And after that, my father built a fence around our yard, and I wasn't allowed to leave.

That's where I thought I was for a moment. Then I smelled other things: intoxicating lavender and pine, pungent coastal sagebrush. The unmistakable, comforting scent of cool ocean air. And then I realized that the person calling my name wasn't saying "Sélène," but "Cady." And there wasn't anger and disgust beneath the voice, merely pained concern.

Strong, warm hands rolled me over onto my

back. An indigo blue sky dotted with hundreds of stars came into view. I knew where I was from that alone. You couldn't see that many stars in the city. The view here was as breathtakingly beautiful at night as it was in the day. And the best part about it was the man's face hovering over mine.

"Cady!"

I was in Lon's backyard—his lush Garden of Eden that looked out over the cliff across the Pacific. Behind me was the welcoming harbor of a redwood deck and his covered patio, where we drank jasmine tea in the afternoon. Where we watched Jupe play fetch with Foxglove. Where we ate dinner on warm nights and talked and laughed and made plans.

I was safe. Home.

I stared up at Lon for an extended moment, lingering over the long hollows of his cheeks and tight furrow bisecting his worried brow. He was shifted. The green and gold of his flaming halo flickered over his ruddy, spiraling horns. Usually when his halo was big and transmuted like this, it cast long shadows over his face. But his features seemed brighter than usual. Ah, my halo was doing that, lighting his face from the front with a silvery glow.

My halo. Too bright. The parking garage. It all snapped back.

Panicking, I reached a searching hand down my backside. No reptilian tail. But I hadn't imagined it: my fingers found a gaping tear in my jeans where it burst through.

"Oh, God, no," I whispered, the words drowned in a fit of uncontrollable sobbing.

Intense green eyes stared down at me, serious and commanding. "Show me," he said in a low voice.

I'd never been so thankful for his ability. It was a relief to just remember everything, instead of trying to explain it. I didn't have the strength to edit details, so I showed him everything—the conversation with Hajo, the man accosting me in the elevator, and the crazy details of what came after, tail and all.

If he was shocked, he didn't show it. And I was thankful for that, too.

I don't know if I killed him, I said internally. *I don't think I did, but I'm not sure. What if I did?*

"Fucker deserved whatever he got."

But—

"Stop worrying and let me handle that. You're not hurt?"

I shook my head, but I wasn't totally sure. I didn't feel like I could move. Like all my energy had been sapped. Lon sat on the grass and pulled me into his lap. He held me close and ran his hands up and down my back as I blubbered and sniffled. And when I was all cried out, I asked, "Is my car here?"

The bass of his voice vibrated through my cheek. "I don't think so."

"Oh, God." What the hell had I done? Slipped through time? Flown here? Beamed myself thirty miles to the coast without the help of the *Starship Enterprise*?

"I was starting to worry," Lon said. "You weren't

answering your phone. I stepped outside to smoke, thinking I'd try to reach you one more time, and saw a flash of light on the lawn. You just . . . appeared."

"How?"

"Dark yard. Flash of light. You were sprawled on the grass," he summarized efficiently. "I couldn't make out that it was you at first, but the house ward hadn't been set off, so I figured it was okay. Then I recognized how you sounded. Inside. Your emotions," he explained awkwardly before clarifying. "I shifted and heard your thoughts. I knew it was you. Your halo—"

"It's so bright."

"It's . . ." He almost said something more, but seemed to change his mind at the last second. "It's bright," he finished simply in agreement.

"I wished myself here," I whispered. "It's not possible. Is it? Lon? How the hell is that possible?"

He smoothed a hand down my hair. "Don't know. But I think you asked your bird-boy guardian the wrong question. If you mother's alive, she's on another plane. But whatever's going on with you is happening here. You should've asked Priya to find out exactly what your parents bred into you during your conception."

A rotting misery nearly pulled me under. He was right, of course. Maybe I could call Priya back, change the plan. But I was tapped out. Was there even a drop of Heka left inside me?

"Summon him later," Lon said, surprising me. He was reading my thoughts.

He started to push himself off the ground, but I squeezed his arm. "I don't want Jupe to see me this way," I pleaded.

"Hush," he said in a kind voice. "They're all out at a movie together. We're alone."

A small relief. My hands were covered in grass stains. Hair was frazzled, like it got when I released Heka without a caduceus. A dull burning smell wafted from my clothes. "I need a shower."

Without another word, he lifted me up with him and carried me across the wet grass and inside the house.

When he finally set me down, it was in the master bathroom inside his room. My legs were floppy, but he held me up, propping me against the vanity as he flicked on the lights. He unbuttoned and removed my coat. A large red spot stained the front; the vial had broken inside my breast pocket. So much for that. Not like I had any use for it, but still.

"Doesn't matter," he murmured, tossing the jacket in the corner on the dark gray slate bathroom tile. Using his forearm to bolster me across my stomach, he crouched long enough to take off my shoes and socks. Cool porcelain touched my back when he pulled my shirt over my head. I watched his long fingers unhook the front closure of my bra. Kar Yee was right: they were awfully nice hands. Good hands. Lean and muscular, like the rest of him. He made a small noise in response to those thoughts and freed my breasts.

My screwy brain thought of Hajo's comments.

Lon grunted. "The next time I see that dowser, I'm going to bloody his nose."

I was pretty sure I'd enjoy seeing that.

My jeans were trashed. I had a million pairs, so it didn't matter. But as he tossed them in the pile with the rest of my clothes, I once again remembered the surreal feeling of the tail—a goddamn tail!—and felt panic rising again.

"Shh," he said, reaching over his shoulder to pull off his T-shirt. Then he picked me up around the waist and walked me four steps to the shower.

Lon's shower. Nothing better. Standing separate from the big tub in the corner, it was a spacious walk-in tiled in unpolished gray and brown stone, open on one end, no door. Hot water sprayed from both sides and above, the pattern and angles changeable into a billion configurations, but Lon kept it on a no-nonsense setting: steady streams from all directions. A low stone bench was built into the far end, and the alcoves above were always stocked with sandalwood soap and expensive shampoo.

If I could declare my undying allegiance to one shower for the rest of my life, it would be this one.

Lon held me under the jets and began bathing me with efficient precision. I melted against one wall, giving him free reign. He shampooed my hair. Soaped me down with those nice, strong hands of his, foregoing the washcloth, on my face and shoulders and arms. The flat of my stomach, the curve of my hips. When his palms cupped my breasts, I whimpered. He wasn't trying to seduce me, but it felt like possession of a sort. I closed my eyes and allowed it.

"Lon," I murmured. "Please. I need you."

His hand slipped between my thighs. "This?"

Yes. Please just . . . ground me, I thought to him as he methodically went back over the trail of soap he'd left, rinsing it all away. *Bring me back to earth.*

The jets squawked off. He lifted me out of the shower and toweled me dry. It was only then that I stood without help. I heard drip-drip-dripping on the slate floor and saw the drops falling off his horns. Heard more dripping and looked down to find that he was still in his jeans, and they were soaked through, sticking to his thighs. Water ran in rivulets down the hard lines of his chest, rippled over the ridges and valleys of his stomach—down that fine line of honey hair that dipped into the waist of his jeans. I tentatively touched the nasty scar over his ribs, the one Yvonne left. It looked angrier somehow, as if now that I'd seen Yvonne's face and talked to her in person, it was so much more real.

Yvonne. My mother. My magick. My body . . . nothing was within my control anymore.

I felt so lost.

Promise me everything will be all right, I thought to him.

"I promise," he murmured, kissing me gently. It was soft and sweet, but I didn't want tenderness.

Tender was weak, and I wanted strength. Wanted a guarantee, not an airy assurance.

I shoved his shoulder, an angry challenge. "Make me believe you. Show me you mean it."

Steely arms pulled me tight against his body. His mouth covered mine, and he kissed me hard. Shockingly hard. I resisted, but he cupped the back of my head with a firm grip and held me in place. He was brutal. Unyielding.

It was the most perfect thing he could've done, and I absolutely, wholly relented. My mouth opened. His tongue slipped inside, and I kissed him back, just as rough. Just as needy. He moaned into me, and I loved it. It made me feel alive.

He hauled me out of the bathroom and to the bed. Flung me down so hard I bounced on the mattress. A terrible thrill went through me as I watched him peel off the shower-soaked jeans. His thick erection proudly jutted out, curving upward from an impossibly dense patch of hair. And the dark way he was looking at me made me lose whatever was left of my magick-fried mind. My legs fell open.

In a flash, he had my hands pinned over my head with one of his. Opened his mouth and bit me firmly on my cheek. I cried out, and he bit me again on my neck. My shoulder. His skin was damp and hot. I shoved my hips against his as he rolled one of my nipples between his thumb and finger, then pinched. I pushed against him again and whimpered. He butted his forehead against mine, horns brushing against my ears, fingers still holding my nipple hostage, and demanded, "Tell me you're mine."

I'm yours, I thought.

"Say it."

"I'm yours. *I'm yours.*"

As he released my nipple, he sank himself into me, and I nearly came. But he wrestled one of my legs up, as high and wide as it could go. The angle threw me off balance, but it gave him better access. He pushed deeper and held himself inside me, unmoving, until my eyes watered. Then he began thrusting in long, excruciatingly slow strokes.

I made terrible noises. Far worse than my usual loud moans and barked commands. I made sounds that had me worried for myself. Like there was something seriously wrong with me. But a few thrusts more, and it didn't matter. His in-laws could walk in on us, and I wouldn't blink an eye. I'd reached that point of madness, the dangerous headspace where nothing else mattered but his breath, hot on my cheek.

God, *God!* I was just too far gone to care about anything else but us. And when my body clenched around him, it was so intense—so much of everything, all at once—that I tried to retreat. My hands struggled against his iron grip. I attempted to buck him off of me, but it only encouraged him to go deeper. I was trapped. Pinned. Impaled.

His.

I came endlessly. I came until I couldn't breathe.

Until I thought I might pass out. Seconds later, he surrendered and bellowed my name, shuddering violently above me. And everything that had been upended that night—all the sanity I thought I'd lost came floating down and clicked back into place.

He released my hands and pulled out of me with a grunt. Tiny shocks of pleasure continued lazily pulsing through me as I dissolved into the mattress. He collapsed on top of me, cheek flattened against my breast, one spiraling horn lightly digging into my clavicle, and his damp, wavy hair spilling everywhere.

I was alive, and I was okay. The world wasn't falling apart.

"Your halo looks normal now," Lon said a few minutes later.

My hand went to my head, as if I could feel it. "Yeah?"

"Mmm-hmm." He ran a hand down my hair and tucked it behind my ear. "Where's your phone?"

"Mmm?"

"Phone."

"In my jeans." The ones with the big rip in the back. Because I had some freaky-ass tail. No big deal. Totally normal.

Lon kissed my forehead and pushed himself off the bed. I watched him appreciatively as he strolled into the bathroom. After some fumbling noises, I heard his deep voice echo around the tiled walls, but I couldn't make out what he was saying. The shower came on briefly. After a minute or two, my cell rang in the bathroom. More talking, but this time it was brief. The bathroom light shut off, and Lon returned.

"I called Hajo," he said, tugging a pair of charcoal lounge pants over his narrow hips. "He checked the parking garage. Your guy was gone. Parking attendants didn't notice anything out of the ordinary, so no ambulance."

"I didn't kill him." Relief washed over me.

"And your car's still there. We'll get it tomorrow."

"Thank you."

He tossed me my favorite robe—a kimono with wide, gaping sleeves and a black-and-white poppy pattern. "Hajo's curious about your abilities now, but you can deal with that."

No one could lie like I could.

21

I got the call from Hajo early on Christmas Eve. When I answered, all he said was, "I found what you were looking for. Meet me at noon at the usual spot."

The "usual spot" was a dirty pub called the Palm and Cypress in a rundown Morella neighborhood. Hajo liked it because the pub was dark and smoky, filled with shadowed booths, and it had a back door for easy escapes. And the small parking lot in back was not only surrounded by a tall brick wall, but also possessed a secondary exit. A drug dealer's wet dream.

Lon and I waited in the SUV in that small parking lot, in the same spot I'd waited for Hajo a couple times before when I'd done some bindings for him. The ones I'd owed him for finding Jesse Bishop's bones in the cannery last October. He was always punctual, which I suppose is a nice quality for a dealer to possess. But it was ten past noon already, and he hadn't shown.

After pulling his dark blue peacoat closed, Lon lit a second valrivia cigarette and cracked his window. A chilly breeze sifted in. It was colder today. A real winter day. That somehow made things slightly more miserable.

A knock on my window scared the bejesus out of me. Hajo's long face peered inside, backlit by his blue halo. I thumbed toward the back and hit the button to unlock the door.

"Sorry I'm late," he said as he compacted his tall frame to duck inside. Plopping down in Jupe's usual spot, he pushed dark hair out of his eyes and shivered as he set a silver motorcycle helmet on the seat next to him. He was wearing his trusty black racing jacket with the mandarin collar zipped to his throat, three gray stripes running down one sleeve. "Cold as shit today. What the hell's up with this weather?"

"It's warmer on the water," Lon said, offering him a cigarette. "La Sirena's always ten degrees better than Morella in the winter."

Hajo took the valrivia and nodded his thanks. "I'd die a slow death out there. Too many hippies in the Village. No money in weed. Though I could probably make a fortune selling coke to all the rich suits." He loosely slapped my shoulder with the backs of his fingers before flicking a lighter in front of the cigarette dangling from his lips. "Wanna go in business together, Bell?" He turned his head to the side and blew out a cone of smoke, a smile playing on his lips. "You can be my enforcer."

"Pass."

"Too bad. That binding shit you do is effective. I can't tell you how much it's boosted my reputation—no one owes me money right now. You still doing side jobs for someone in La Sirena?"

Lon gave me an askance look. Yeah, maybe I shouldn't have told Hajo that, but I hadn't mentioned Dare or the Hellfire Club. It was easy to open up to Hajo. God only knew why. Maybe it was because I thought he was high half the time I saw him and assumed he'd forget. He never did.

"I bet I could pay you better," Hajo said.

"I bet I wouldn't care."

"How—"

"Where are we going?" Lon said irritably.

Hajo leaned back in his seat, half amused at Lon's impatience. "Hold on. I'm watching for someone."

I swiveled my head to study the parking lot. "Who?"

"Someone was following me. That's why I was late." He craned his neck and spoke to Lon. "Can you move up there so we can see Gilman Avenue? Not too far. The brick wall will hide us."

Lon pulled the SUV to the exit and we anxiously surveyed the street that ran behind the pub.

"Who'd be following you, Hajo?" I thought of the dark sedan and my elusive shadowy follower. My pulse sped up.

"Don't know. I noticed a black car when I was coming out of my parking garage. Stayed so far behind, I couldn't identify a make or model, but it tailed my bike when I made some weird turns. I'm overly paranoid, which I'm sure will come as no surprise to you—"

"Doesn't," Lon said, tossing him a bland look in the rearview.

"But it does mean that I'm good at spotting tails and losing them. Pretty sure I shook him a couple of miles back, but it never hurts to be cautious."

"Why would someone be tailing you?" Lon asked.

Hajo shrugged. "Plenty of reasons, but nothing in particular jumps to mind."

Hazy images from my scuffle in Hajo's parking garage elevator filled my head. "What about that guy Darren? Think he could be wanting the bionic elixir?"

"No way he made bail," Hajo said. "Couldn't be him."

"Bail?"

Hajo looked at Lon. "You didn't tell her?"

Lon sighed.

"Tell me what?"

"We took care of that shit," Hajo said proudly. "It was Lon's idea—I just executed it. Happy to do so. I told you, I've hated that trust funder for a long time now."

"What are you talking about?"

Lon flicked his cigarette out the window. "I asked Hajo to frame him. Seemed better than beating him to a pulp and going to jail myself."

"I had a buddy who owed me a favor," Hajo explained. "He sold a little sømna to Darren. Just enough to get him slapped with ten years in prison. Smoked up with him then left and called the cops. It's pretty fucking scary how easy it was."

I stared at Hajo, who was smirking . . . then Lon, who looked either guilty or defiant—it was hard to tell with him. "Were you going to tell me this at some point?" I asked Lon.

"Figured I'd eventually get around to it." The way he looked at me was loaded. As if he was remembering how long it took me to spill the beans about Dare blackmailing me. Or maybe that was just my guilt talking.

"Come on, Bell. You wanted to just let Darren walk free after he manhandled you?" Hajo said, throwing one arm across the back of his seat and crossing one leg loosely over his knee. His leather jacket made a scrunching noise as he lazily slouched. "Fuck that. If he wanted the bionic elixir so badly that he'd attack you, then what would he do to get it from me? I gotta protect my own interests."

"So you did all this for *you*?" I said.

"For me . . . for you." Hajo waved his hand dismissively. "Either way, Lon was a hundred percent right. Darren deserved worse than the spanking you gave him."

Lon gave me a tight smile. "Sometimes you do stupid things for people you care about."

It was a dirty thing to do, framing Darren. But

I wasn't going to lose sleep over it. I leaned over the armrest and pecked Lon's cheek. He cupped my jaw and pulled me back for a firmer kiss on the lips.

"This is arousing," Hajo said behind us. "Don't mind me. I can entertain myself while you two go at it."

"I would punch him, but now I owe him," Lon mumbled against my lips.

"Welcome to my world," I mumbled back as he released me.

"It's the secret to my success," Hajo said with a boastful grin that was far too handsome for his grating personality. "Everyone always owes me."

"Thank you," I told Hajo. "I mean it."

He looked away, as if embarrassed. Not an emotion I was used to seeing on him, but it didn't last long. "So, anyway, this bionic elixir of yours. After I started asking around, I found everyone wanted it, but no one knew who was selling. No word of the Telly kid. But today I had a bunch of people call me at once with a name: Tabor. I talked to him briefly. Claims he's the only one in town holding. He wouldn't go into detail, but I figured we might be able to get more information out of him in person. So I told him I'm bringing in two people who want to buy."

"Us?" I said. "You're brokering a drug deal for us?"

"Don't act so high and mighty. You don't have

to buy it, but you're definitely going to want to shell out some cash if you want him to question him about that telekinetic kid of yours. Money talks."

"I've got fifteen dollars in ones," I said. "How much information will that get me?"

Lon glanced at Hajo in the rearview mirror. "It's fine. I've got cash."

"See, Daddy will pay." Hajo waved toward the street. "Looks like I shook the guy following me, so can we get moving? Because the sooner we go talk to my guy, the sooner you get the information you want. And the sooner I get a date with the delicious Kar Yee Tsang. Don't think I've forgotten."

Like I said, he never forgets.

We drove through the rain, watching to see if anyone tailed us. Not a soul.

Hajo led us to an old highway on the eastern side of Morella. I don't think I'd ever been on it, nor did I ever want to again, considering the dismal scenery that surrounded it. Past the exit ramps, disused strip malls, and unpopular fast food restaurants that dotted the roadside was our apparent destination: the Sleepy Hollow trailer park.

I'd visited a trailer park with Kar Yee once in college. It was dirty and cheap, and filled with college students who wanted the independence of living off campus but didn't have the funds to get an actual apartment. We were there for some party, and I remember walking into a trailer cloaked in smoke with ten guys watching some Italian film that I would've called soft-core porn, but apparently it was art. Either way, Kar Yee and I were the only females and ten pairs of eyes looked at us like we were pizza being delivered. That was the first time she'd used her fear knack in front of me. Once the effect wore off and we were long gone, I was impressed.

We pulled up next to a doublewide and dashed through the rain to the small awning that covered temporary wooden steps. Hajo briefly surveyed the area, eyes narrow and cautious. I wondered how many places like this he visited on a daily basis. Such a stark contrast to his penthouse.

Closed blinds shielded our view through the small boxy window flanking the door, but light shone through the slats; someone was home. But I stopped paying attention to the trailer when Hajo moaned beside me. His eyes were closed. "Shit," he murmured as he swayed on his feet for a moment. "No, no."

I'd seen him look this way before . . . using his death dowsing knack.

A muffled crash sounded from somewhere inside. Another door slammed. I turned to question Hajo and found Lon gone. Dammit. Swiveling, I spotted him racing around the trailer, Lupara in hand.

"For fuck's sake," Hajo muttered, pulling a slim gun out of a holster hidden under his jacket in the small of his back. He darted after Lon.

Now there were two too many guns out. And Hajo had sensed death. A warm panic heated my chest as I jogged after them, my only thought a repeated prayer that Lon remain safe.

As I rounded the side of the trailer, cold rain pelting my face, I nearly slammed into Lon. One shoulder pressed against the corner of the trailer, he was standing with Hajo. They were peering into a field of dry grass that merged with a wooded ravine.

A winding section of the grass was trampled. I thought I heard someone running through the brush in the distance, but rumbling thunder masked the noise.

"Someone ran through there," Lon said in a quiet voice as I caught my breath. "I heard the panic. Panic mixed with elation. Sounded like . . . the person was happy to have gotten away with something."

Hajo peeked around the corner. He made a sour face, as if he smelled something repulsive. "Can you hear any emotions inside the trailer?"

"It's clear."

Hajo's shoulder's slumped. "Well I hate to be the bearer of bad news, but there's a dead body in there."

"What the hell is going on?" I whispered.

"You sure you don't sense any emotions at all around here?" Hajo asked Lon in a low voice. "I don't want to walk into a trap."

Lon glanced at me through hooded eyes. Questioning.

"Go on," I said, checking behind us. "You either trust Hajo or you don't. And apparently we do. One big happy family."

"Trust me for wha—" Hajo said, but his words bottomed out when Lon transmutated in front of him. I was thrilled Hajo was getting to see this. Let him shit his pants a little. It would be good for him to know that Lon was someone he should respect. And from the awestruck arch of his brows, that's exactly what he was thinking as he stared at Lon's fiery halo, defiantly flaming tall around his shoulders, and the curling burnished horns that deflected drops of rain.

I glanced at Hajo and snorted. "Hajo Kemme with nothing to say?"

He opened his mouth, made a long, low sound, then mumbled, "Damn, am I glad we're all friends."

Lon tilted his head toward the trailer. "We're clear. Closest around is two people in the distance—in the next trailer down the road, I think." He slipped the Lupara inside his peacoat. "I can barely hear the person running away—getting too far out of my range."

"Just how far is your range when you're . . . like this?" Hajo quizzed.

"Far enough."

"He can read your thoughts now," I informed Hajo.

"Ah." His shock lasted about five seconds before a slow smile curled the corners of his mouth. "I'm rethinking my business plan. Bell, you're still the enforcer. But this . . ." He spread his hands, gesturing toward Lon as if he were a prize on a game show.

"This is a beautiful thing. Very useful. Why the hell are you a photographer again?"

Lon squinted in amusement at Hajo. "So I don't have to hang around places like this to earn a dollar."

"Point taken. Let's go inside. Might as well see who's dead."

22

We cautiously approached the back steps. The screen door was standing open, flapping against the side of the trailer when the wind blew. Lon dug in his coat pockets and pulled out a pair of leather gloves. After tugging them on, he opened the door and peered inside.

"You can hear if someone's coming, right?" Hajo asked, still scanning the area.

Lon didn't answer. He stepped inside the trailer, long legs disappearing into shadows.

"Is that a yes?" Hajo said to me, bemused.

Oh, good. It was sort of nice to see Hajo flailing, unsure of how to interpret Lon's low-level communication style. I smiled to myself and skirted around him up the steps.

"Yep."

The inside smelled musty, but cleaner than I expected. Dark. Sparsely decorated. The door led into a depressing living room. Two couches had been pushed against the walls and a large, round table that sat in center of the room. Chairs were knocked over. A few bills were scattered on the floor. I leaned down to look at them. Hundreds.

"Christ," Lon said. "Someone got robbed. Explains the emotions I was hearing."

"Not good," Hajo murmured. He pointed to the far end of the room. "Body's in there."

We rounded the breakfast bar counter into kitchen and stepped into what could've been the aftermath of a tornado. Pots and pans were strewn everywhere. Cabinet doors had been ripped off their hinges. The old avocado colored refrigerator had been toppled to the floor. And sprawled beneath it, like the Wicked Witch of the East, was a crushed body.

My heart pounded against my rib cage as I approached. A man's limbs jutted out at awkward angles. Salt-and-pepper hair crowned his head. Blood pooled around his body.

"This your contact?" Lon asked Hajo.

"That would be him." He stooped to look at the man's face. "Poor Tabor. What a way to go. This bionic shit is more holy grail than sømna, and that's saying a lot."

"Telly did this," I said as the shock wore off. "Who else would kill this way? Anyone else who wanted to rob a drug dealer would use a bullet or a knife."

"It's just like the Road Runner and the bridge," Lon agreed. He toed a small gun lying a few feet away from the body. "This was no use against Telly's bionic knack."

Hajo sighed. "Maybe we should look around and see if we can find anything else."

The three of us scoured the trailer. Lon found a stash of amphetamines in the first bedroom. The door was ripped off the second bedroom. Inside, the floor was covered in broken glass. A small desk sat in the center of the room. On it were three glass bottles. Two of them contained clear liquid. The third was red. But next to it sat an open container of food dye.

"Asshole was lying," Hajo said, sniffing one of the bottles. "Tabor wasn't holding—he was going to try to sell us sugar water."

I looked around the room. Red was splattered on the white wall, broken glass beneath it. "Telly must've realized the same thing. Smashed a bottle against the wall."

"Maybe Tabor ran out and couldn't get more," Hajo said. "Thought he could pass this off."

"Too big a coincidence that Telly showed up right before we did," I said. "This isn't Telly's dealer. He acted hesitant when he was talking about him. Said he couldn't go back to him, like he was scared of him. Why would he be scared of a gray-haired man in a trailer with one little gun?"

"You said everyone started giving you Tabor's name all the sudden today," Lon said to Hajo. "Maybe Telly heard the same noise you did. Maybe he came here thinking Tabor was easy pickings."

"No idea," Hajo said. "But frankly, I'm not interested in following this thing any further. Tabor's dead, and I don't want that punk kid dropping something on my head. Not to mention the car that was following me earlier. And even if I wanted to help, this was my only lead. I'll keep my ears open and let you know if I happen to hear anything else. But maybe you need to look outside of Morella if you think this wasn't the dealer."

Outside of Morella. That put us back in La Sirena. And if Mr. Lucky, Peter Little, didn't know who brought the drug to his party two weeks back, then the only other lead connected to the elixir in La Sirena was Merrimoth, and he was dead. That left us with nothing.

"Tomorrow's Christmas," Lon said, reading my thoughts as we went outside while Hajo stepped into the living room to make an anonymous 911 call on the trailer's landline about Tabor's dead body. "If there's one thing I've learned from all the years I spent with Yvonne, people tend to self-medicate during the holidays. I'll make a few phone calls around La Sirena. See if anyone knows any other bionic knack stories."

I gave him a halfhearted smile. "Merry freaking Christmas."

By Christmas morning, I'd managed to block out the image of the drug dealer crushed under the refrigerator and took a break from obsessing over Telly. The Butler household was buzzing and busy. Everyone was in good spirits—even me. Maybe it was because, being the daughter of crazy occultists, I'd never experienced a big Christmas celebration. But Jupe was so damn excited that it was hard not to go with the flow.

Mr. and Mrs. Holiday came over and we did the whole gift exchange thing. I got Jupe a couple of DVDs, graphic novels, and a 1977 Godzilla toy. It was rare and vintage and he totally loved it. I knew he would. He'd tried to buy a similar one last month but lost the bid, so I'd contacted the seller and paid twice as much for him to find another one. Most expensive toy I've ever bought, but it was worth every penny to see his eyes go big when he opened it.

I got Lon a book for his library. *Danger in Our Midst: How to Recognize and Identify Magicians* was a quirky field guide written in 1955 by an Earthbound psychologist. The only copy I'd ever seen was in my occult order's library in Florida, but I found another one online. It had hilarious drawings of 1950s occultists and a plethora of helpful tips for Earthbounds: how to recognize magicians by their clothing, a glossary of occult symbols, a chapter on how to avoid a binding trap and what to do if you found yourself caught in one—"don't panic"—and a list of known occult temples.

"Do you like it?" I asked, curled up on the couch next to him, morning sun spilling across the room from the patio doors. It was a clear day, and the Pacific sparkled jewel-blue in the distance. Near the Christmas tree, Jupe was tearing open another gift from the Holidays, who were in some sort of friendly competition with Rose for the title of Who Can Give Jupe the Most Presents.

Lon carefully turned the pages. "I had no idea this even existed."

"Is that a yes?"

"Love it." He flashed me a lovely smile, then pressed a kiss to my forehead. "Ready for yours?" He handed me two things. The first was a bulging manila envelope filled with travel reservations, luxury chalet brochures, and a guide to the French Alps. It was real: we were actually going to go on a vacation. He corrected me, mouthing "sex vacation" when no one was looking, but I think Rose was too caught up in the gift-giving to have noticed anyway.

"And this," he said, handing me a small, flat box. Inside was a silver bangle bracelet. Two beautifully molded snakes looped around the bangle. Their heads twined at the center over a pair of wings.

"It's a caduceus," I said in surprise. One that was designed to fit a circle instead of the usual straight staff. Around the inside was a Latin phrase: *quod est superius est sicut quod est inferius*. As above, so below.

"It's reputedly from a medieval mage's tomb in Rome," he said as I slipped it on. Good God, this thing was probably worth a small fortune. "It doesn't seem to have any practical uses, but I thought you might like the aesthetics of it."

I threw my arms around his neck. "It's wonderful. I adore it."

"I'm glad," he said, definitely pleased with himself.

"I have something else for you, but I wanted to wait to give it to you . . ." He nodded toward the mayhem in front of the Christmas tree. ". . . when things return to normal around here."

"Might be waiting a long time."

"It'll keep."

Once Jupe noticed we were exchanging gifts, he paused his chaotic present-extravaganza. "Get your laptop, Dad."

Lon reached over me and handed me a computer, while Jupe bookended himself on my opposite side. "What's all this?" I asked.

"Hold on," Jupe said, leaning all over me to type an address into the web browser.

I watched a page pop up on the screen. It was Tambuku's website. But nicer. Way nicer. It wasn't just a static page with our address and a badly lit photo that Kar Yee had taken when we first opened. It had style. Professional photography. A drink menu. And on the page with our hours, it even said that we were temporarily closed for construction and would reopen after the holidays.

"What? How . . . Who did this?"

"I did!" Jupe announced proudly. "I mean, Dad took the photos and helped me with some of the graphics, and he said that I couldn't use Papyrus or Comic Sans for the fonts. And that the background up here couldn't be purple. And that I couldn't post photos of you and Kar Yee because it just encourages weirdos—"

I gave Lon an appreciative look.

"—but I did most of the CSS and I got Kar Yee to send me the drink menu and I got this little map thingy to work and I wrote all the stuff about the bar and it was all my idea," he ended, inhaling a big breath.

I clicked around, going back through all the pages.

"Do you love it?" he asked. Not "like," but "love," as if he meant "isn't it the greatest thing in the world and didn't I do a good job?" It was such a Jupe thing to say, and he was so eager and enthusiastic.

I pressed my forehead against his. "I love it *so* much. It's my favorite gift."

"Really?"

"Really."

"Dad's going to be pissed. His gift cost way more. Like, mine was free, and his—"

"How many times do I have to tell you?" Lon said. "We don't talk about the cost of things."

"Oops." Jupe glanced at the French chalet brochure on the coffee table. "Hey, what's all this?"

"Our vacation stuff," I said. But I wasn't concentrating. I thought I heard a strange noise, but I couldn't figure out where it was coming from. I wanted to shush everyone, but Jupe plowed on.

"We're going to France?

"No, *we're* going to France," Lon said. "As in Cady and me. You're going to stay here with Mr. and Mrs. Holiday."

"Hey, no fair!"

"You let him think he was coming with us?" I said to Lon. Maybe I was just imagining the noise. "That's not nice."

"I—"

"Whoa, whoa, whoa. You never said anything about a vacation," Jupe clarified.

"What do you mean?" I asked, suddenly confused. "Kar Yee said she was keeping a secret for you."

Jupe cringed. "Uh . . . that was nothing. Barely even a secret. Don't ask her about it, though."

While Jupe hedged, the strange noise became clearer. No wonder I couldn't pinpoint the source: it was coming from inside in my head. And when it repeated, louder, I realized what was going on.

May I show myself?

23

"No!" *Hell* no. Not here, in front of everyone. "Hold on!"

Jupe frowned. "What?"

"Not you," I said, handing him the computer as I scrambled off the couch. "Be right back." I jogged to the back of the house, to a place that was the farthest distance from the living room—and, hopefully, far enough away that the clairaudient Earthbound in the house couldn't hear me—and pressed my finger into the security lock on Lon's library door.

"Okay. Now," I commanded, standing in front of the unlit library fireplace, pulse pounding. Polished wood built-in shelves stretched from floor to ceiling, all of them filled with hundreds and hundreds of occult tomes: grimoires and goetic tomes, spellbooks and hand-painted illuminated bibles, all carefully arranged and cataloged according to Lon's exacting standards.

The air shuddered as a black line of light appeared in the middle of my palm. A mass of crackling white light whooshed a few yards in front of me. When it flashed, Priya flew out of it.

Black wings brushed over book spines, knocking several grimoires off the shelves.

He just took up so much space with those wings. It was one thing out on Kar Yee's rooftop, but quite another in this room. Startling, really. He began to fly forward, but his black-haired head clunked against a dangling pendant light. He made a very human face, while gritting a pair of very non-human silver pointy teeth, and said, "Oww."

"Come down and land, for the love of Pete," I said nervously. "Stop flying. Whatever. Just quit wrecking the place. Lon's going to be furious!"

He rubbed a hand over his injured forehead and lowered to the carpet, landing awkwardly as he folded up his wings behind his back. His grimace turned to a smile. "Hello, mistress," he said, bowing his head briefly. The swinging pendant light above cast a moving shadow over his silvery gray chest.

"Thank God," I murmured. "I was worried something had happened to you."

His mouth tilted up. Black hole eyes softened as the corners crinkled. "You were worried about me?"

"Well, yeah. I didn't want you getting killed." I paused. "Again. And you were gone for so long."

"I'm sorry to have disappointed you," he said, hanging his head. "It was a longer journey than I expected, and I can't travel as fast in this body."

"Don't be sorry. I'm just glad you're okay."

He brightened. "As am I. You look lovely," he said, looking at me with unabashed interest.

New Priya was easily distracted. No wonder it took him so long. "Can you tell me what you've learned?"

His shoulders straightened. "Of course. But I fear you will not like what I have to say."

"Oh, God."

"Enola Duval is still alive."

I closed my eyes as a dark disappointment weighed down my bones. I suppose I'd known it all along, since that first vision of her on the beach at Merrimoth's house. I just didn't want to believe it.

"I did not see her personally," he continued. "But I spoke with many who have. I know of her general whereabouts on the demon plane. She has taken control of a citadel in a remote region that is on the brink of war. Rumors are spreading about her. The demons under her snare are threatening another group of demons—a strong legion under the command of a Grand Duke."

My pulse went haywire. Surely there were many, *many* Grand Dukes in the Æthyr. But I had to know. "His name isn't Chora, by chance?"

Priya was surprised. "You know of him?"

"You can't be serious. It's Duke Chora?"

"Yes."

"Sh-h-hit."

"What is wrong, mistress?"

"This Duke almost killed someone I love a couple of months ago."

"Your demon child?"

"What?"

Priya pointed to my palm. "The one bound to you."

"He's not *my* child. I mean, I didn't give birth to him. Anyway, I was talking about someone else."

The door to the library swung open. "She's talking about me." Lon burst inside the room, all fiery halo and spiraling horns, eyes narrowed to slits.

Priya rushed in front of me and snapped his wings open. "Stay back, Kerub."

Lon balked at the reference to his demonic heritage—or perhaps at the fact that Priya was protecting me against him.

"Priya, calm down," I said. "This is Lon. He's, uh . . . well, he's the father of the demon boy under my protection." I couldn't think straight. I was still reeling from Priya's news about my mom. "This is his home."

Priya's wings fluttered and drooped. He stepped aside and lowered his head, black halo trailing. "Forgive me." I couldn't tell if he was hurt or angry, but his mouth was drawn in a tight, straight line, and he was unwilling to take his eyes off Lon.

"It's fine." I put a hand on Priya's arm, which was cooler and smoother than I expected. It was a simple gesture, meant to be casual, but it seemed to surprise both of us, and I quickly moved my hand away. I still couldn't reconcile the familiarity I felt around him with the foreignness of his new body. I did my best to push away my confused feelings and cleared my throat. "Lon, this is Priya. He's one of my oldest friends, so please stop glowering."

Lon glanced at the spilled books on the floor. Yeah. Not happy about that. *An accident,* I said to him in my head.

He made a disgruntled noise then spoke to Priya. "What else have you learned about her mother?" He'd been listening to our conversation, which meant he'd heard me say the L-word. And now he was listening to me obsess over it. Awesome.

Priya glanced at me. "Would you like me to continue to discuss this in front of the Kerub?"

"Yes. Anything you tell me, you can tell Lon. He's empathic, by the way. And he can hear your thoughts." Only fair that he knew.

Priya nodded. Surely he was well acquainted with demonic knacks. Regardless, he wasn't happy. He crossed his arms over his bare chest and turned to me. "As I was saying, rumors are spreading about your mother. Whenever there is a human in the Æthyr, it is momentous. But it has been said that she wields a great power. I am worried that this power is . . ."

"Yes?"

He blinked black, feathery lashes. "I am worried the power she wields is connected to you."

"What power is that, exactly?" My voice came out squeakier than I wanted.

He shook his head. "I do not know. But there is talk that she's given birth to someone who could decimate armies of demons."

Oh, God.

"And since you are her only child . . ." Priya shrugged and narrowed his gaze at me. "You used your Moonchild ability recently."

"What? Yes. A day ago."

He nodded. "I thought I detected your Heka in the Æthyr. Not strong, but if I can sense it, then your mother may likely sense it, as you suspected. And because of this, I would be wary when you are drawing on those powers. Shield yourself. I think you are opening up a channel to the Æthyr when you use moon magick."

I groaned.

"I do not know the repercussions of doing such a thing," he said. "There are magicks that can track energy signatures. Creatures who can follow your Heka and use it to slip between the planes, or to spy on you."

I thought about the spy in the shadows I'd seen at the racetrack after I'd used my moon power. Chills pricked my skin. What if it was something spying on me from the Æthyr? Although that wouldn't explain the mystery sedan I'd seen at Diablo Market, or the one I thought I saw after Telly tore the bridge down. Æthyric creatures don't drive cars.

"Perhaps it is not something to worry about," Priya continued. "But I am concerned it will attract the attention of other beings in the Æthyr who are familiar with the scent of your Heka."

"Like?" Lon prompted.

Priya glanced at him, chin tilted. "Any Æthyric demon she has summoned might remember her scent. I am connected to her. I carry a trace of her Heka in me." He said this as if he were proud of it. Like he was goading Lon. And from the way Lon's jaw tightened, I assumed it worked.

"Priya," I said. "You need to be concerned about your own safety. Do not go near Duke Chora."

"Chora is a respected leader."

"He is also dangerous. Please stay away from him."

"As you wish. I am following another trail that may bring me more information concerning your mother's intentions. Once I know more, I will return to you."

"Okay, but—"

A crackling energy emanated around his halo. He winced. "It is hard for me to remain much longer."

"Crap." I hated this. Now I was going to freak out about his safety, as well as my own. "Look, you've got to be careful. Promise me you will."

A faint smile lifted his mouth. "I promise."

"If you can find out what my mother's intentions are, that would be great. But if you can find out anything about me, that would be better. You don't know, do you? What exactly she bred into me? Whatever *this* is that can 'decimate' armies of demons?"

"No more than you do. But maybe she is sharing

this secret with demons in the Æthyr. I will trace the rumors and see what I can discover."

"Thank you."

"It is my honor to serve you." The air around him crackled again.

"One more thing. What about my father?"

Priya lightly grazed the backs of his fingers over my cheek. "I'm afraid he isn't alive."

I nodded, unsure if this was good or bad, or how I felt about it. "Please be careful."

"You, as well. Guard yourself and call if you need me." In a flash, his entire body just disappeared. Gone. As if he was never there.

I looked up at Lon. He was unhappy. Maybe even a little shocked at seeing Priya's new form—how could he not be? But whatever he was thinking about how my guardian looked, or whatever he'd heard inside his head, he had the good sense to keep it to himself.

"Lon," I said in a voice that sounded smaller than I intended. "I'm scared."

He shifted down, pulled me into his arms, and held me. But he didn't tell me it would be okay this time. He merely said, "I know."

24

After Priya's unwelcome news, Lon and I rejoined the group and carried on like nothing was wrong. At least for awhile. Rose and Lon made a huge Caribbean feast for Christmas dinner: rice and peas, plantains, coconut snapper, curry, and some chicken that was so spicy, I nearly choked—much to everyone's great amusement.

But when we were clearing the table, a knock on the door made my stomach flip. Jupe ran to answer it. A couple of seconds later, Yvonne entered the house: designer clothes, gold-framed sunglasses perched on top of her perfectly coiffed hair, arms filled with presents.

She paused in front of me. We stared each other down for several beats. Then she said, "Merry Christmas, Arcadia."

"You, too," I managed.

I didn't talk to her directly after that, and I stayed my distance when she was showering Jupe with expensive presents, only hearing his excitement as I helped the Holidays wash up dishes in the kitchen. And when I'd towel-dried every single speck of water off the plates and had no more excuses to stay away, I lurked in the dining room and listened to her chattering with Jupe about new stores in La Sirena. About the pool in her tropical Floridian backyard. About her celebrity neighbors and the season tickets she had for the Miami Heat.

And she was apparently modeling for a national jewelry company, doing print and television ads, so I could look forward to seeing her face during commercial breaks of our family TV time. Maybe she'd even haunt me in Tambuku, too, her too-perfect face and body hawking diamond pendants during the bar's weekly viewing of *Paranormal Patrol*. Then all my regulars could say, "Hey, isn't that Lon's ex-wife? Looks like she's making a comeback."

Everyone loves an underdog.

But how could I be anything but encouraging to Jupe? If anyone knew how he felt, being abandoned by her all these years, it was me. I couldn't deny him a chance for a relationship with her. The Giovannis seemed impressed by her new sober life, and Yvonne might actually be stable and trying.

Even so, there was only so much I could take of her Celebrity Rehab success story. So when everyone decided to move the party outside on the deck, I excused myself and left the house for a couple of hours.

Kar Yee was glad to see me. Bob came over and after I gave them the update on my quest to find Telly, we watched *Miracle on 34th Street* on television. Kar Yee was healing up enough to drive. She'd made plans to get out of the city the next day and go upstate to visit an old college friend of ours. I don't think she knew what to do with herself, since Tambuku wasn't open. Bob neither. He told us he'd made a couple of appointments that week to do some minor healing on people in his group. I was glad. Seemed to keep his spirits up.

Life almost seemed calm for a couple of days. No winged Æthyric being popping up with news about my mother, no crimes fueled by bionic knacks. Just . . . normality. But two days after Christmas, some magazine bigwig called Lon up to San Francisco for the afternoon to meet with the president of an advertising firm. It was only a two-hour drive, and he'd be back early evening.

Meanwhile, I stayed in with the Giovannis. Rose was showing me how to make something called "black cake" when Yvonne called, wanting to take Jupe to the movies. Rose said she trusted her to spend a few hours alone with her son and thought maybe it would be good for both of them.

Maybe they were right. If Jupe wanted a relationship with her, I couldn't stop him. I called Lon and told him what was going on. He said it was okay.

So we let him go.

After the movie ended, Yvonne called Rose and said they were stopping by a diner for a bite to eat. So we waited some more. Two hours later, they still hadn't come back. Rose called her. Several times. No answer. I called Jupe. Texted Jupe. No response. That's when I started full-on panicking. He'd never, *never* failed to respond to my texts. Rose couldn't get a decent cell signal in the house, so she stepped out on the back patio and called the diner while Adella paced the living room.

His life wasn't in danger. I knew this because the thread that connected us wasn't visible like it was when he got demon-snatched by Duke Chora on Halloween. I considered sharing this with the Giovannis, but I wasn't sure how they'd react to knowing he'd tattooed my sigil on his hip, and I didn't want to get into the sordid events from Halloween. That would only make them more worried.

"I knew better than to trust her," Adella said, as she paced, volcanic curls jostling beneath the blue-and-white striped scarf she'd tied to keep them off her forehead.

"I'm sure there's a rational explanation," I told her. And if the diner couldn't confirm they were still there, I'd drive out to the Village to find them; I already had my keys in my pocket.

She snorted. "You don't know my sister very well. Expect the worst, and you won't be disappointed."

How the hell I'd put myself in the position to defend Yvonne was beyond me. "You said before that you'd never forgive her. I don't mean to pry, but I've been curious. Was there something she did to you specifically, or . . . ?"

Adella stopped pacing behind the couch. "She slept with my husband fifteen years ago."

I didn't know what to say to that. I hadn't even realized she'd been married. Lon and Jupe never mentioned it.

She gave me a tight smile. "We met in college, Samuel and I. It was love at first sight. We'd been married for a year when she came to stay with us. I think she'd been seeing Lon on and off at the time, but this was before she got pregnant with Jupe." She stopped in front of a black-and-white photo of Jupe, one Lon took when he was a baby. "I, on the other hand, *was* pregnant. Three months. She seduced Samuel with her knack. He said he couldn't stop himself. I believed him—you felt what she can do, right?"

"Yes."

"Now imagine her when she goes all—" She mimicked horns with her fingers. "I confronted her. We fought. It could've been the end of it. Samuel and I would've pieced our life back together. But she was so angry. Petty. She slept with him again. He killed himself later that night. I lost the baby the next day."

"Oh, *God*. Adella, I—"

She shook her head. "Don't feel sorry for me. I survived—I didn't let her pull me under. But maybe you understand a little better now. I know Lon probably keeps most of those old stories under his hat. He's just that way."

"He tells me some things, but it's difficult for him to dredge it all up."

"Oh, I know. I love Lon like a brother, but I think I'd go crazy if I had to live with him, all quiet about everything."

I gave her a gentle smile. "He's getting better."

"You're good for him. Good for Jupe, too. I'm really glad you're in their lives."

"Me too." I wanted to say something more, but a silence hung between us for a moment. It was broken by the sound of the patio door sliding open.

Rose stepped inside the living room. The fringe of white bangs that normally was perfectly styled around her forehead was messily pushed to one side. Her glasses dangled from a slender chain around her neck. Her face was still as a stone. "Owner talked with all the waitresses. No pair with their description came in."

Fuck. What the hell was going on?

"Someone needs to stay here in case they come back," I said heading toward the foyer. "I'll drive down to the Village. There's only one way here, so if Yvonne's on that road, I should see her."

"I'll come with you," Adella said reaching for her purse. "Mama, you stay."

"It's eight," I said, glancing at the clock on the mantle. "Lon should be finished with his business dinner and on his way home soon."

"I'm not calling him," Rose said. "I don't want him worried while he's on the highway. He drives like a bat out of hell when he's upset."

That was true. "He keeps his ringer off most of

the time anyway, so it doesn't matter. I'm sure Jupe is fine," I said, more for me than them. "There's a logical explanation for why he's not answering my texts, and—"

"Car!" Rose shouted out of the blue. "Someone's pulling up the driveway."

I didn't hear it, but I didn't have her knack. We all raced out the front door to find Yvonne helping Jupe out of her car. Relief washed over me. Christ, I'd gotten way too worked up.

"Why haven't you answered your phone?" Rose shouted angrily at Yvonne. "It's been two hours. I know you weren't at the diner, so don't tell me you were."

"I'm sorry," Yvonne said as shut Jupe's door. Why was she holding onto him like that? I couldn't see what was going on. The driveway lights were on, but they weren't bright. Everything was cloaked in shadow. "Time got away from me. I ran into someone Lon and I used to know from the Hellfire Club. We were chatting, and I guess I didn't hear the phone."

She turned around and was mumbling something to Jupe, blocking my view of him.

"What's going on?" I said. This was all wrong. Jupe should be bounding over to see us. Why was he so quiet?

"What the hell?" Rose said. "What did you do, Yvonne? What—"

"There's no need to throw a big hissy fit," Yvonne snapped as she turned around. That's when I saw

Jupe's face for the first time. His head bobbed. He took a step and faltered.

I was already running toward them.

"He had a couple of glasses of wine, that's all."

"What?" I reached out and caught him just as he was stumbling. Couple of glasses of wine? He smelled like he'd been smashing grapes in a vineyard. His body was limp. He fell into my arms like a sack of bricks. I hoisted him as Adella ran up and helped.

"What in the devil are you talking about?" Rose shouted. She didn't believe it. She hadn't caught up—couldn't see him. He was stinking drunk. Moaning and weak. "Where did you go that serves wine? It sure wasn't the diner."

Yvonne was panicked. Her cool, aloof exterior had melted away completely. "We went to a different restaurant. It was Evan's idea, and I hadn't seen him in—"

Rose slapped Yvonne across the face.

And again.

Yvonne slid down the side of the car and crouched into ball, covering her head with her arms as Rose continued to flail at her.

Christ.

"Come on," I said against Jupe's ear, as calm as I could. "Let's get you inside, okay?"

I half carried, half dragged him across the driveway in a daze. He could walk a few steps, then his legs would turn to noodles and give out. He was trying to say something, but his words were slurred. Everything seemed surreal. Like time had slowed. I could hear Rose screaming at Yvonne behind me.

"I've got him," I told Adella firmly. "I do this at the bar all the time. I can handle this. Go stop your mother from hurting her. If she's drunk as well, better call her a cab and get her out of here before Lon gets back, or he'll kill her."

Getting him up the stairs was the hardest part, but I managed. He seemed to sober up a little and started talking in a small, roughened voice. Mostly just little drunken observations that made no sense, like his shoes were too big, and that was the reason he was having trouble walking. And was he at home? Where were we going?

"Here's your room," I said, kicking open his door and dragging him through in the dark. It was cleaner than usual, due to the Giovannis' visit, so I didn't have to wade through piles of clothes and teetering stacks of comics. Right before I made it to his bed, he made a horrible noise, tried to push me back, and vomited all over my arm. Twice. Good *God*, it stunk of wine.

"I'm sorry," he said brokenly. "So sorry."

"Hush. It's not the first time someone's done that," I said. "Bartender, remember? I'm a vomit cleaning expert. Sit down on the bed. Can you do that? Mind the nightstand." I got him down, half sprawled on his pillows. Wrangled his shirt off and used it to mop up vomit around his mouth and off my arm. It took some work to prop him up against the headboard. I turned on the lamp next to his bed. He squeezed his eyes shut and groaned.

"Don't move," I said. "I'm going to get something that will make you feel better."

My medicinals from the bar were locked up in a drawer in Lon's walk-in closet. I didn't want to leave them in Tambuku while it was closed, just in case we got robbed again—whether it be Telly on a revenge mission or some other hopped-up Earthbound deciding we looked weak enough to hit. I quickly changed shirts and washed my arm in the bathroom sink, then rummaged through the vials until I found one that I used to sober up bar patrons.

When I got back to his room, he was staring at the ceiling. I went into his bathroom and filled up two disposable cups with water then set those down on his nightstand. In one, I measured two drops of the medicinal. "Here, drink this. It will make you feel better."

He drank it down, slow at first, then faster. "I'm so thirsty," he said, as if it was a great revelation.

"I know. Here's more water." I gave him the second cup and filled up two more while he drank it, setting them on his nightstand. "You're going to want to sleep now, but when you wake up, drink more water." I tugged off his sneakers and pulled the covers over his legs, then perched next to him on the edge of the bed.

"Are you mad at me?" he asked.

"I'm mad at your mother. What happened? I tried to call you, but you didn't answer."

He sloppily dug his phone out of the pocket of his jeans. The screen lit up. "Oh, no," he moaned. "I had it on silent. I usually feel it."

I took the phone away and placed it on the night-stand. "Why were you drinking? Did you use your knack to make her let you drink?"

"It was that Evan guy. Dad thinks he's an ass-hole, but he was okay at first. He said kids in Europe drink wine at dinner, so I tasted Yvonne's"—he still wouldn't call her "mom," I noticed—"and it was pretty good, so she let me be in charge of refilling the glasses from the bottle, and they kept bringing more bottles, and they were expensive, but Evan said he'd pay for dinner."

"Tasting is one thing, but you can't drink. You're a kid," I said, struggling for the right thing to say. "You're not supposed to drink." Christ, I felt like such a hypocrite. I got people drunk for a living. How was I going to explain the difference?

"They stopped talking to me, Cady," he argued, gesturing loosely. "I mean, she was s'posed to be spending time with *me*, not him. But he was mak-ing her laugh, and she just forgot I was even there. It was like being a kid all over again. Like nothing changed."

"So you had more wine, and she didn't notice?" I

said, combing my fingers through his curls, pushing them away from his face.

"I didn't mean to drink so much, but they told me to stay at the table. And I tried to stop her. That's when I used my knack. But it didn't work, Cady. Just like when I tried to use it on my dad on the boat, remember?"

Could have been because he was too soused to use it, but I didn't say this. "You've only had your knack a couple of months. It'll take time to learn to manage. Don't worry about it. What happened then?"

"When my knack didn't work, I couldn't stop them. They left for a long time. And the waiter brought another bottle of wine. I didn't mean to drink the whole thing, but it went fast." He groaned again and closed his eyes. "It feels good and bad at the same time."

"I know. When you drink too much, that's what happens."

"Dad is going to be Hulk angry."

"Yeah, he is," I agreed.

"I wanted her to be okay."

I thought of my own mother, and how badly I wanted her to be okay, even after I knew she'd killed people. Even after I knew she was irretrievably lost.

"She said she was sober, but that Evan guy was selling her drugs. I saw him. I went to find them, and he was giving her a tiny bottle of something. Like that." He pointed to my medicinal.

I stilled.

"What color was the bottle, Jupe? Do you remember?"

"Red. Like a little bottle of red wine."

Oh my God. Could it be? The bionic elixir? "Did she drink any of it? This is important, Jupe."

"No, I don't think so. We started fighting, and she told him she'd come by his place later after she got me home."

Jesus. My pulse jackhammered against my temples as I tried to sort it all out in my head.

"Dad's going to . . ." He didn't finish.

"I'll deal with your dad. Go on and sleep. You'll feel better when you wake up."

"Okay."

"I'm going to leave the light on, in case you need to go to the bathroom. Don't want you to trip over Mr. Piggy's crate and smush him."

He mumbled something and shut his eyes. After I'd made it halfway to the door, he said, "Cady?"

"Yeah?"

"I'm not giving her any more chances."

I blew out a long breath, not knowing what to say. He probably wouldn't remember it anyway. "Go to sleep. I'll check back in on you later."

When I closed the door behind me, Rose was striding down the hallway. Pissed off as hell, from the looks of it. "He'll be okay," I assured her. "I gave him something that will help him detox. He threw up, so that's good. Got some of it out of his system."

"Did he tell you what happened?"

"A little—"

"Yvonne said they left Jupe at the table while they went to talk to someone else in the restaurant, and that's when he sneaked the wine."

"Look, I'm not saying she's a liar, but Jupe said that Evan guy encouraged Yvonne to let him drink. They left him at the table with the wine bottle, and they were gone long enough for him to empty it. And—" I stopped and decided against telling her about the elixir. It just complicated things, and I needed to see it for my own eyes first. Jupe *was* drunk, after all.

She swore under her breath. Her anger was contagious, because now that I was satisfied Jupe would be okay, I was furious. "I don't know who this Evan guy is, or what they were thinking, but Jupe says Lon hates him. And given the fact that he's Hellfire, and nobody I've met from that bloody club has a decent bone in their body—"

And if he had a whole bottle of elixir on him, did that make him the distributor? Was this the guy Telly originally robbed to get his supply? If he was Hellfire, it would explain how Merrimoth got it, back when this all started. Could also explain its presence at Peter Little's Richie Rich party.

"I *knew* she was lying," Rose said. "She just tried to use her knack on us."

"Out there?"

"Just now. Anytime she does anything wrong,

that's what she falls back on—the knack. Only it didn't work on me because of my charmed ring. When she didn't get what she wanted, she pressed on and shifted herself."

"Transmutated?"

Rose nodded. "Almost too much for the ring to fight. It was tough, but I did."

"Where is she now?"

"Sitting in the backseat of her rental. Adella's got the ring. She's guarding her. I've got her car keys." She opened her palm to show me. We stared at each other for a long moment. Long enough to hear Jupe snoring through the closed door. Rose eventually said, "You remember what we talked about?"

"Excuse me?"

"You said you could strip away that magick from her. So she can't shift like that."

"Whoa," I said, throwing up both hands. "I said I *possibly* could."

"Lon tells me you're special. Different. He says you can do incredible things that other magicians can't even dream about doing."

"But—"

"Do you want me to beg you? Because I will. She could've hurt him," she said, pointing at Jupe's door. "What if he'd ended up in the hospital getting his stomach pumped? What if she got drunk too and crashed her car?"

That thought made me sick.

"She's a danger to everyone around her, and she's

going to end up killing someone or herself before it's all over."

"I don't know," I mumbled, trying to move things around in my head. To make sense of everything. I was overwhelmed. Could I do what she was asking? I knew I couldn't with a traditional spell. It would have to be the Moonchild power. As much as I didn't want to admit it after what happened in Hajo's parking garage, I'd had success using it. In fact, I'd instinctually been able to get the results I'd wanted every time. They weren't always results I knew were possible: freezing time to help Lon, trapping Noel with smoke at the car rally, squeezing the trust funder to the brink of death, teleporting myself home.

But could I use it to poke around the innermost workings of a human being? Could I "will" Yvonne's transmutation spell out of her? Or would I melt a few organs in the process?

Even if I *could*, there was the other sticking point. Priya warned me: I was calling attention to myself in the Æthyr when I used it. Specifically, my mother's attention.

Rose became frantic. "What do you think Lon's going to do when he gets back? Huh? You think he's going to just let her go back to Miami? He's going to end up in jail, that's what's going to happen. You want to lose him to her? Because if she has her way, she'll take him down however she can." She leaned in closer, putting her face right in front of mine, intense green eyes on mine. Swirls of her halo cast a glow on the tip of my nose. "God forbid she catches Lon alone. If he doesn't have something like this ring to protect him, she'll have him on his knees in seconds. And if you want to know how that story ends, you go ask Adella."

I didn't have to. Adella's story was still fresh in my mind. And it wasn't like I hadn't made myself sick worrying about Yvonne's possible control over Lon.

My hands were shaking with anger. I walked around Rose, heading back down the hall. She trailed me downstairs to the living room as I dialed Lon's number. "Pick up, pick up," I muttered. But he didn't. I tried again and hung up when his voicemail came on a second time. Then I stopped in the middle of the living room and stared at Rose for several beats, fingernail clicking on the screen of my phone.

"Her knack by itself, I can handle," Rose said. "Even without this ring. But when she shifts, there's nobody in this world that can stand between her and what she sets her mind to have. And as much as she's done to hurt this family, I still want her to get better. But without getting rid of that magick inside her, it's just not going to happen. God help me, but she's my daughter."

"Rose—"

"If you won't do it for me," she said in a deceptively calm voice, "then do it for Jupiter."

I glanced upstairs like I could see him. My heart constricted painfully.

Then Rose said, "He's counting on you. Lord knows he can't count on her."

And sometimes you do stupid things for people you love.

25

Golden light from the entry faded as my low-top sneakers crunched over white gravel. Adella's poofy curls were silhouetted against the headlights from Yvonne's rental.

"Everything okay?" Rose called out over my shoulder.

Muffled pounding sounded from the backseat of the car. Shouting followed.

"She's angry as a bull," Adella replied.

I could just make out the movement of Yvonne's halo inside the dark car. When I stepped closer, I saw more. She was blindfolded. I glanced at Adella; the scarf around her hair was gone. I remembered how her knack kicked in when I looked up at her at the seafood restaurant that first night.

"She's like Medusa," I said dumbly.

Rose huffed. "Turning people to stone might actually be useful. She's like Medusa's evil twin. It came from my late husband's family tree."

"Avoiding eye contact only delays the inevitable,"

Adella explained. "Unless you've got a solid wall be-tween you, she'll eventually ensnare you. She's gotten me when I've had my back turned. You doing this? Stripping away the transmutation spell?"

"I can't guarantee anything," I warned. "Are we straight on that?"

They both nodded. Rose gave me the rental keys.

"And I'll need the Solomon Seal ring," I said. "Maybe it's best you two head inside the house. Keep trying Lon. Check on Jupe." I thought of the tail and twitched. No jeans to hide it this time; I was wearing mini cargo shorts that barely covered my ass. An ass that was, by the way, currently freezing in the cool night air. "Don't come out until I tell you it's safe."

Adella slipped off the ring and gave a wary look toward the car as she handed it over.

"Go!" I said. "Before she changes your minds."

I slid the ring on my index finger and waited until I heard the front door shut. Then I approached the car and hit the unlock button on the key ring. The car's interior lights came on, illuminating Yvonne. Her sister's blue-and-white striped headscarf had been torn in two. Half of it covered her eyes; the other half bound her wrists together behind her back. It was a shame that the Giovannis felt they had to do this. I almost felt sorry for Yvonne.

Almost.

"Get out," I shouted.

She didn't move for several seconds. I swung the door open and stepped back.

"Where are they?" she asked. The bottom edge of her makeshift blindfold was damp with tears. Mascara seeped beneath it, running down her cheeks.

"Inside. It's just you and me. Please get out. We need to talk."

"Untie me," she bit out between clenched teeth. She was angry now. Her halo was dancing. I watched it carefully, worried that she might transmutate any second.

"You don't need your arms to stand. Out of the car, please."

She struggled to move her legs around, but finally managed a sloppy exit and teetered on high heels against the side of the car. "I don't know what you expect to accomplish by talking to me," she said, chest heaving. "But this is between me and my family."

"Wrong. It's between you and *my* family."

"He'll always be my son."

"But when are you going to start acting like his mother?"

"It was just wine, for the hundredth time!" She slammed her heel against the car frame in aggravation.

"He's falling down drunk!"

"I never said he could have more than a glass."

"You left him alone at the table."

"Just for a minute!"

"Liar. He told me what happened." I stepped closer and stuck my hand in her coat pocket.

"What are you doing?" she said, squirming.

"Where is it? Jupe told me you were buying drugs. Is Evan a dealer?" I tried the other pocket. "He promise you something that would amp up your knack?"

She jerked away from me with a grunt. But I managed to get a hand inside her dress pocket. Bingo. The glass vial, filled with red liquid. Exactly the same as the other bottle of bionic juice.

"I didn't use any!" she protested desperately. "I'm clean, I swear."

I pocketed the vial. "It's not something you should be allowed anywhere near. Your knack is already amped up enough as it is."

"Ethan said it was magic, not a drug. He said I couldn't get addicted to it. I just wouldn't have to worry about showing my horns to use my knack."

I couldn't think of anything more destructive for someone like her. "What's the matter with you, for the love of God? You encouraged Jupe to drink and left him alone so you could cut a drug deal?"

"I don't need to watch Jupe every second. He's a teenager, not a baby."

"And he wanted to spend time with you. How often do you see him, Yvonne? Once a year? You didn't see him last year at all—I know that much. Why? What could be so important to you that you couldn't come visit? He's a fucking joy to be around."

She choked out a laugh. "Don't tell me what he's like. I know. I carried him inside me. I raised him."

"No, Lon raised him."

"I was there whenever I could be—I had a demanding career. And I made a few mistakes. I can't keep paying for them."

"Then stop making them."

"Who the hell are you to be passing judgment on me? How long have you even been in the picture? A few months? You think because you're Lon's newer model, you can just waltz in here and take my place? A twenty-five-year-old bartender? Think again, honey."

Dark anger coursed through me. "You should be grateful for every second you spend with him, because you don't deserve him. And you're breaking his heart."

"Spare me." She wriggled against the bonds on her wrists. "Jupiter's always been emotional and needy. He'll do whatever it takes to get attention. He used to fake tears all the time when he was little."

"He's not little anymore. But you wouldn't know that, because you don't know him."

"I know he's more like me than anyone cares to admit. He'll do whatever it takes to get what he wants. And what are you going to do when he comes into his knack? What if he inherits mine? If the whole family treats him like they've treated me, he'll come running to his mother, because I'm the only one who understands what it's like to wield this kind of power."

Jupe hadn't told her about his knack? I was

stunned. I thought surely that would be the first thing he spilled when they spent time alone. He brags about it whenever he gets the chance. Hell, he'd have it printed on a T-shirt if he could.

Then it struck me: *Jupe doesn't trust her.* Lon has told him time and time again to be careful about revealing it to people who might use it against him. Jesus. For all the dumbass mistakes that kid made, there were just as many times he made smart decisions.

"Maybe you don't fully get what I can do," she said, misinterpreting my silence.

"Believe me. I've heard all about it."

"Seeing is believing."

Her halo flickered. The air shuddered, just like it did when Lon transmutated. It felt like a cavalry of galloping horses—something enormous approaching. I knew it from the first beat, when the gold in her halo began to dominate the green and rose up over her head and shoulders like a gilded campfire.

Her blindfold ripped as milky brown horns sprouted into existence. But where Lon's came in above his temples and looped into burnished spirals, hers were straight and tilted back and up toward the crown of her head, maybe a foot or longer in length.

Impressive. Even more so when her torn blindfold fell to her neck. Her green eyes were now golden. She was stunning. So incredibly beautiful. Dazzling. A rapturous shudder went through me.

And if she hadn't snapped her wrist bonds, I

might've fallen under her sway, despite the ring. But that simple motion caught my gaze, and the second my eyes dropped from hers, I came to my senses.

The Moonchild power roared toward me. I embraced it like a friend, delighting in the darkness that fell. Just as I had in Hajo's elevator, I felt a foreign coolness rippling down my torso, and God help me, I felt the freaking tail sliding out from the hem of my shorts. Now that I knew it was coming, it wasn't so bad . . . weird, but not bad. Weird I could handle, especially if it made me feel this crazily alive and powerful.

Very, *very* powerful.

No blue dot appeared. But within a blink, my vision morphed. It was still dark, but everything solid was swathed in silver, as if someone had dumped a vat of mercury over my surroundings—the cars, the trees, the circle of Lon's driveway and every bump of gravel that paved it.

I didn't create the silver light: I *was* the light. And I cast myself over the landscape, illuminating everything in my path.

Including Yvonne.

Her skin gleamed like Priya's, bathed in an unearthly quicksilver glow. Her horns jutted backward like two slender candlesticks molded from pewter. And when my gaze locked with hers, I watched emotion play over her eyes in quick succession. Certainty slipped into confusion . . . confusion dimmed to fear.

She *should* be afraid. I was dangerous.

"What is this?" I heard her say in a faraway voice. She tried to retreat, but there was nowhere to go. Her back hit the car. I took a step toward her and she bolted.

She darted across the driveway toward the tree line, racing into the shadows. I flew after her like a bullet, with no thought to her long legs outpacing mine. I lunged and snagged her mid-thigh, tackling her to the wet grass. She shouted angrily. Screamed. Twisted in my grip to face me. To fight me. Her arms flailed as I straddled her. She reared back and punched the side of my head. The pain was shocking, but not enough to distract me when she tried it again with her other hand. I blocked her with my arms and quickly pinned both of hers to the ground.

Heka flew out of me and came back fully charged with moon energy. I was vaguely aware that my mother might be listening somewhere in the Æthyr. Best to be quick about this, before I heard her horrible voice in my head.

Or before I fell prey to Yvonne's knack.

Already, the soft perfume of her skin and hair were worming their way inside me like a siren's call, beckoning me to succumb to her. I squeezed my eyes shut and concentrated.

How to remove the transmutation spell? Shit. I didn't know. I pushed kindled Heka through my hands into Yvonne, sending out a magical search party inside her veins, poking around for the transmutation magick.

Something solidified between us. The Heka was creating a bridge. For several moments, I felt intimately bonded to her . . . not in a sexual way, but that was the closest comparison I could fathom. I suddenly knew more about her than I could learn about her from years of conversation. It was overwhelming. I briefly wondered if this is how Lon felt using his knack. Did he see inside people this way?

And if he could see Yvonne like I was seeing her right at that moment, I wondered if he would do what I was going to do, or if he would pull the plug and stop right there.

Because buried within her cells, I saw her demonic soul. And the stitching that secured it to her body was drenched in a deep, impenetrable sadness.

My eyes welled with tears. It was so overwhelming, I almost pulled back.

But, just out of reach, I suddenly felt the buried magick. The transmutation spell. It was a living, breathing thing, attached to her like a parasite. And its function was like a spiritual dam between her soul and body. A switch that opened and closed, letting the demon soul expand at will.

And I could almost taste the magic that gave it life.

I had no time to flounder or doubt myself. I heard things in the distance. Things watching and approaching. Maybe I was paranoid, thinking of what Priya had told me. But I didn't want to find out. I just wanted to get the hell of there.

Using all my willpower, I poured kindled Heka into that magical dam inside Yvonne, and I ripped it out by the roots.

She screamed like I'd struck her.

My eyes snapped open. I snatched my hand up and regarded a soft pink glow grasped within my fingers. My mind homed in on the memories of the pink magick I'd seen months ago, inside the cannery, where giant magical cockroaches spilled out of Jesse Bishop's bones. And then in the putt-putt golf course, where the earthquake spell decimated an impossible stretch of land and nearly pulled me underground.

Æthyric magic is pink. Or, at least the magic used by archdemon Duke Chora.

The transmutation spell wasn't an earthly spell.

Terrified, I flung the pink glow from my hand. It exploded like the head of a dandelion, pink splinters floating away, then disappearing into shadows. And it wasn't the only thing disappearing: Yvonne's horns withdrew into her head as her halo went crazy: green and gold flashed intermittently, like a stoplight on the fritz. She flailed. Kicked. Cussed.

The gold sizzled like a campfire being doused. Nothing remained but a soft, dull green nimbus. I'd done it!

Then her hands flew to my throat, cutting off my oxygen.

Damn! She was stronger than she looked. I gripped her forearms and tried to force her back, but her muscles were stone. Pain ringed my neck. My larynx felt like it was close to exploding. A horrible tingling sensation spread down my arms. She scissored her legs around me and pushed. Before I knew it, I was on my back and she was choking the fucking life out me.

Instead of panicking—and I probably should've been panicking at this point—I became incensed.

It happened instinctually, just like in Hajo's parking garage. My tail lashed out like a whip and wrapped around her chest. I felt the material of her dress beneath it. Felt the bouncy give in her ribs as I constricted around them. I could tell the breaking point was coming soon. But it wasn't enough. I was blind with fury.

I wanted to obliterate her.

My halo expanded and whooshed around her head like clouds covering a mountain peak. Silver fog. I couldn't see her face anymore, but I felt my halo seeping into her mind. It wasn't the slow, exploratory push I'd used when seeking the transmutation spell inside her. It was a brutal invasion.

And I wasn't controlling it.

Screaming her lungs out, she let go of my throat, but I didn't stop. I couldn't. Something else was the puppet master. I felt another presence, foreign and distinct and strong. Panic budded beneath all the rage and I tried to pull back, but I was both weak and out of control at the same time.

Blinding light spilled over her back and beamed through my silver fog. I dimly heard a metallic squeal and felt something coming toward us, but I didn't realize what was happening until an explosion filled my head.

Not an explosion, but a voice. And the voice bellowed, "Cady!"

My Moonchild magick fell away like an avalanche. The silver vision fizzled into shadow and sounds plumped up to normal volumes. Everything became solid and real again. And Yvonne was ripped from me, green halo trailing.

But I barely noticed. I was too busy looking at my skin. Tiny, smooth ridges stretched over my chest, between my breasts. What the hell? This was the coolness that I'd felt in the elevator with the guy from Hajo's place.

As I yanked down my top, trying to get a better look at it, out of the corner of my eye, I caught a movement that distracted me to the point of madness.

My tail retracting.

Ringed in alternating black and white stripes, it was covered in tiny, glossy scales so lustrous, they almost looked wet. I reached out and managed to grab the last few inches of it. The magick was pulling it back inside me, much like Lon's horns withdrawing when he shifted down. But I touched it, just for a moment, as it slid through my fingers. I expected it to feel slimy, but it didn't. It was smooth and silky, and it tapered off into a rounded point. Like a snake.

Just like a snake.

Shouting diverted my attention. "Yvonne!"

Lon's voice.

He was crouched over her body. She was convulsing.

What the hell had I done?

26

Rose rode in the ambulance with Yvonne. Lon and I followed in his SUV with Adella. The Holidays stayed behind with Jupe. The hospital was a ten-minute drive. But even though Lon was driving up the ambulance's ass, it still felt like ten hours. When he asked, I gave him a barebones account of what happened. He made no comment.

"We asked her to do it, Lon," Adella said.

He didn't respond. I wished I knew what he was thinking, but I supposed it had to keep. He wasn't going to say anything in front of Adella, especially if he was pissed. And if he was? I understood, but I wasn't sorry for stripping the transmutation spell. Just sorry that I lost control after it was done. I suppose I'd be a lot sorrier if I'd fucked her up enough to do some permanent damage, but that remained to be seen. I wasn't going to jump the gun and start falling apart just yet.

When we got to the hospital, Lon strode away to find his friend, "Dr. Mick," as Jupe called him. Moments later, I watched Yvonne's body being rushed in, strapped to a gurney with Rose trailing behind the ER team. They wheeled her behind a swinging door, and that was all I knew for the better part of an hour.

Adella and I sat together in a mauve-colored waiting room, smelling that depressing antiseptic hospital scent, staring at the TV like zombies . . . watching other people wait for bad news. I finally couldn't stand the silence anymore, so I returned the Solomon's Seal ring and attempted a conversation.

"Thanks," she said. "I'll give it back to Mama."

I nodded and took a deep breath. "Adella?"

"Yeah?"

"Did you see me out in the yard with Yvonne?"

She gave me a confused look. "After Lon yelled for us to come."

Okay, good. She hadn't seen my reptilian form, or whatever the hell it was.

"Does my halo look funny?"

She glanced up. "It's a little brighter and jumping around the edges."

At least the tail was gone.

"I'm not upset at you," Adella said, eyes weary but kind. "I just want you to know that. Whatever happens with her, it was the right thing to do. You said you'd try, and you did. So thank you."

I started to reply, but that's when Lon finally made his way to the waiting room and gave us the only update we'd had: Yvonne was stable. He promptly left us alone again. I watched him walk away, and sadness crept inside my chest.

I hadn't killed her. But God only knew if I'd turned her into a vegetable. All I could hope for now was that she could be healed. And even if she could, I might've unintentionally made her into a martyr— one who suddenly had everyone's sympathy and attention. Exactly what she wanted. How beautifully ironic.

Adella got up and paced the waiting room while I buried my face in my hands, trying to regroup and focus. To push away all the dissonant thoughts clamoring for attention inside my overtaxed brain. Maybe I could call the Holidays again, check on Jupe. Last I'd heard, he was still asleep. No more vomiting. That was something, I supposed.

"Here."

I flinched and looked up. Lon was sitting next to me, offering a paper cup of hot chocolate. I'm an admitted hot chocolate junkie and will imbibe it in any form. Lon's homemade hot chocolate was probably one of my favorite things in the world. Even the watered-down powdery instant chocolate from the hospital vending machine was a welcome distraction.

And a peace offering.

His fingers brushed mine when he gave me the cup. I was so needy for his attention, the tiniest touch sent a wave of longing crashing through me. His eyes met mine for a moment, anxious and searching. I wanted to be alone with him. To talk about everything that happened and find out what was going on behind his impenetrable poker face. But even that small, arbitrary touch and momentary shared gaze was a kind of sustenance.

It was alarming how much better I felt when he was around. I wasn't used to this level of emotional dependence. So I looked away in embarrassment, unwilling to submit to it for too long. When I glanced back at him moments later, he was focused on drinking his own hot tea out of a matching paper cup, blowing on the surface to cool it.

We said nothing. Several minutes passed. As I was starting to make headway on my drink, a tall doctor with dark reddish-brown hair and a bright blue halo strode toward us.

"She's out of the woods," the doctor announced with a calm smile.

I could practically feel Lon's sigh of relief aligning with mine.

"This is her sister," Lon said to the doctor as she strode back to over to join us. "Adella Giovanni. Mick Bright."

The infamous Dr. Mick. Lon's friend, and one of the best healers in La Sirena.

"I think we've met before," he said, squinting at her.

"We did," Adella confirmed. "You pumped Yvonne's stomach when she overdosed on New Year's Eve about ten years ago. She nearly died."

The doctor scratched his ear and nodded. "Yeah, I actually remember that quite vividly. You'll be happy to know that this is more hopeful news. She had a seizure. Thought maybe it was an aneurism, but I've studied all the scans and they're clear. Looks like she did, however, suffer a concussion. She's also severely dehydrated and has some bruised ribs, but nothing major. We're going to keep her here to watch the concussion."

"Did my mama tell you she can't have any pain medication?"

"Yes, I'm very familiar with her medical history," he said. "She's resting. You can go talk to her if you'd like. Your mother's with her now."

He waved down a nurse to escort her. Adella thanked him and made her way back.

Mick turned to me with an outstretched hand. "You must be Cady." He surprised me with a big, toothy smile and shook my hand with a slightly jarring amount of strength. "Wish we were meeting under better circumstances, but I'll take what I can get. You're even lovelier in person than in the photos I've seen."

I wanted to ask about these mysterious photos, but he just kept talking. And I let him, because he was so blindingly handsome, with ruddy hair tinged with gray near the temples and a perfect square jaw. A little too clean-cut and friendly for my preferences, but on him it was somehow appealing. Maybe it was the white doctor coat.

"I've been telling Lon we should all have dinner but our schedules haven't synched. Maybe we can plan something after the holidays, when things cool down. Before you head out to France."

He knows about France? I felt like I'd entered some weird alternate reality in which Lon had a normal relationship with a close friend he confided in. Sadly, this almost made me jealous, because I selfishly thought *I* was his only confidant. Every time I believed I had Lon all mapped out, along came a new road that led to some strange place I didn't know existed. The secret Oreo stash I'd recently uncovered was one thing, but this? Fairly unnerving.

"Dinner sounds good," I said. "But can we back up a moment? Because I think you should understand that I might've caused Yvonne's concussion. I don't know how much you know about what I am—"

"In regards to the mage thing, or the bartender thing?"

"Uh, the mage thing."

"I know a little," he said with a sly smile. He crossed his arms and nodded toward Lon. "He's extremely protective of you. I suppose that's no surprise."

Lon grunted. I cleared my throat. God, we were so dysfunctional. "Well, anyway. I sort of used magick on her. That's what caused the seizure. And probably the concussion."

"I see. And on the bright side, should I assume that's why her halo's back to normal?"

Was Mick Hellfire? I tried to remember. I didn't think he was, but surely he knew the story behind Lon's dual-colored halo; if so, he also knew about Yvonne's. "Yes," I said simply.

"Don't worry yourself," Mick assured me. "I handled it. She'll be fine. And your secret's safe with me. Impressive, by the way."

I didn't know what to say to that.

He slapped Lon on the shoulder with affection and a startling familiarity. "Go home to Jupe. Nothing you can do here. If Rose and Adella want to spend the night in her room, they're welcome. But I gotta get back now. Duty calls."

"Thanks," Lon said.

"Don't worry. I'm charging you double for making me save her. Joyce would have a cow if she knew Yvonne was anywhere near the hospital. It's a miracle I never got caught in her web. I'd like to maintain my clean record."

He hadn't slept with Yvonne? I liked him more and more.

"If only I'd been so lucky," Lon mumbled. "Go on, then. Heal the dead with your smile, or whatever the hell it is you do around here."

Mick leaned toward me conspiratorially. "I don't know what you see in this guy, but I'm damn grateful. Please don't leave him. I'll pay you."

I laughed anxiously as he gave Lon a thumbs-up and walked away.

"What do you want to do?" I asked Lon.

"Get the hell out of here. I can't handle hospitals. Let me go tell Rose."

Of course he was overwhelmed with everyone's miserable emotions. Why didn't I realize that? I was so stuck in my own worries that I didn't realize what kind of toll a place like this could have on his knack.

He reappeared a few minutes later and rushed me out the door, telling me that the Giovannis were staying with Yvonne tonight. Once we got a few yards away from the building, he visibly relaxed. I stopped him in the shadows between two parked cars. "What did you see earlier? What did I look like?"

His eyes searched mine. "You were . . . your skin was . . ." He paused, clicking his jaw to one side. "Your eyes were silver. Your halo was almost too bright to look at. It hurt my eyes. And I saw the tail."

Ugh.

"I've never seen a tail like that on anything I've ever summoned," I said in a small voice.

He didn't comment. Didn't have to. It was weird, and we both knew it. My mind leapt past the physical issues, to the reason we were here.

"Look, I'd lost control when you drove up and found us," I said. "But I did what I thought was best at the time. Rose was right—you would've ended up in jail if I left it for you to handle. You didn't see him, Lon. He was stumbling drunk, sick as a dog." Angry tears pricked the backs of my eyelids. "She encouraged him to drink. Then she left him in the restaurant alone, when she should've been spending time with him. But the point is . . . the point is—"

He grabbed my face. Gold flecks from his halo glittered above his head. "You think I'm angry that you stepped up to defend Jupe? That you stopped me from hurting her or going to jail trying? Because, that would've been a real option. And sure, I'm upset about the situation. It was a stupid, ballsy thing for you to do."

"I know, but—"

"But, I'm damn glad you did it. And I'm mostly upset because you're going through something big, and I feel powerless to help you. All I can do is sit around in my library, combing through old books looking for a clue to whatever the hell is happening to you, and I'm coming up empty."

"I—"

"And in the middle of all this, you have to deal with my baggage. I'm ashamed of it. And it worries me. Because I know you could be seeing some nice human with no crazy ex-wife, no hyper kid. Someone who won't be a senior citizen when you're still in your prime."

"You know I don't care about that."

Hands tightened around my jaw. His look was so intense it almost frightened me. "Do you understand how lucky I am that you put up with all this bullshit? How fucking grateful I am? How much I love you?"

I stilled. His eyes widened. He hadn't meant to say it. He was as surprised as I was. A low, deep shudder worked its way through my chest. My throat made a small, broken noise when I inhaled. I could barely get words out. "What did you just say?"

His eyes became unfocused. He blinked several times in rapid succession, then exhaled heavily, as if he was giving in, making peace with the idea. His gaze lifted and returned to mine. "I said I love you."

"You do?"

"Yes."

"Are you sure?" I grabbed his hands and pulled them away from my cheeks.

He let out a strained laugh and nodded. "Very sure."

I didn't have to say it back; he knew my feelings better than I did. But to hear it from him? It was like I'd just been given an endless supply of cool water and, until I drank a sip, hadn't realized I'd been wasting away in a desert, dying of thirst.

My head dropped against him, falling into the space in the center of his chest where his breastbone dipped. A space that almost felt like it was made just for me. Where I could feel his heart beating. His arms wound around my back. He pulled me closer and kissed the top of my head. And for a long moment, only the two of us existed, and nothing else mattered.

He loved me. How wonderful was that?

I wanted to stay like that, wrapped in his arms, feeling safe and good. But then I remembered the vial in my pocket.

27

I pulled away to look at Lon. "I need to tell you something important. When Yvonne left Jupe alone in the restaurant, it was because she wanted to be alone with some Hellfire guy named Evan—"

Lon's eyes narrowed to slits. "Evan Johnson?"

"I don't know. Jupe said you hate him."

"Definitely Evan Johnson."

I pulled the red vial out of my pocket. "She was buying this from him."

A rare look of surprise crossed Lon's face. He took it from me and studied it. "Is this . . ."

"Don't know if it's fake or real, but yeah. She admitted that's what she was buying."

"Evan's the dealer?"

"I don't know. Maybe."

"Christ. He's Hellfire. Just a regular club member—not an officer, and not all that active in the club."

"Maybe he's Telly's original source. Do you know where the guy lives?"

"Yes, I know." Lon nodded and pocketed the vial. "Guess you and I will be paying Evan a little visit."

My biggest worry about confronting Evan Johnson was that he'd be wielding some juiced-up knack, but Lon informed me that Evan didn't have one. It was one reason why Lon suspected the guy had never been a regular attendee of the Hellfire Club's monthly Succubi and Drugs parties at the Hellfire caves. "Hellfire members without any special gifts tend to be ignored," Lon explained. "They're outsiders."

Like I needed another reason to hate that stupid club.

Evan's house was a few blocks from the hospital. It was almost midnight, but I reasoned since Jupe had overheard Yvonne telling the guy she'd stop by his place later, he'd still be up.

We rang the doorbell. When the door swung open, we found ourselves staring down the barrel of shotgun.

"Lon Butler?"

The gun lowered to reveal a dark haired, paunchy man who looked to be a little older than Lon. He might've been handsome, but his T-shirt and boxers weren't flattering, and his eyes looked tired and panicked. A wary gaze flicked my way, then over our shoulders. "You alone?"

"Nice to see you, too, Evan," Lon said, then slugged him in the face.

Evan hollered as he staggered backward, dropping the shotgun to block his face.

This was not part of our plan.

"What the hell?" Evan managed to spit out as he stumbled and collided into a wall.

Lon shook out his hand. "That's for getting my kid drunk."

Evan pulled his hand away from his face and stared down at the blood covering his fingers. Lon had got him good, all right. And as he stalked Evan down the hallway, he began transmutating.

"I'm sorry, I'm sorry!" Evan shouted, holding up his hands in surrender. "It was Yvonne who encouraged it, I swear. And I wasn't trying to put the moves on her, or anything." He made a pained noise. "Jesus, Butler—I think you broke my nose. Please stop. I can't . . . just, please."

Lon's horns were out now. I pulled the front door shut so no one would walk in on us.

As I did, Lon cornered Evan against the wall. "I don't really give a shit what Yvonne does, but I could have you arrested. My boy is at home sick. And on top of that, you're selling Yvonne *this*?" He pulled the red vial from his pocket and shoved it in front of Evan's face.

Evan made a sobbing noise. "Get that out of here! I gave it to Yvonne—I don't want any part of it anymore. Please!"

Lon stared at Evan for several moments, reading his thoughts. "What the—" Lon flinched. His head swiveled toward an open arch that led into a living room. "Jesus!"

I peeked around the corner, desperate to see what Lon saw. The living room was torn apart like someone had searched it: drawers pulled out, cushions removed, furniture broken.

And sprawled on the carpet was a teenage boy with a bullet between his eyes.

Telly.

I glanced at Evan. "You killed him?"

"I found him like this," Evan argued. "Lon, you've got to believe me. Isn't that how your knack works? Can't you tell? I wouldn't kill my own stepson."

"Hold on," I said. "Telly's your stepson?"

"His mother and I are separated," Evan mumbled, slumping against the wall as he looked down at the body. "He's been nothing but trouble since the day I met him. But now this . . ."

"He originally stole the bionic elixir from you?" I said, remembering Telly's words from the camp under the bridge.

Evan looked surprised. "You know what it does?"

"Your kid nearly killed us with his knack after using it. He robbed my bar in Morella. He's killed other people."

"Oh, God. That elixir . . . I wish I'd never laid eyes on it."

I glanced at Lon. *Go on,* I encouraged without speaking. *Use your transmutated knack and get him to talk to you. If he resists, I'll bind him.*

Lon clamped a hand around Evan's shoulder, causing the man to jump. "We need to know everything about the elixir, and you want to tell us." He'd tapped down his anger and now sounded patient and coaxing. "Why don't you start from the beginning, yeah?"

Whether or not Evan knew about Lon's latent persuasive abilities, he didn't resist. "It started at Thanksgiving. I'd just signed the separation papers. I hadn't been to a meeting down at the Hellfire caves in months, but I didn't have anything else to do. I somehow ended up in one of the Succubi rooms with David and whatever woman he was attempting to seduce that night."

I stilled. "David Merrimoth?"

"Yeah. He normally wouldn't give me the time of day, but we were all loaded, you know. Anyway, that's where I first heard it mentioned. He was telling us about this rare elixir that amped up your knack. I didn't see any that night. It was just a story, and I probably wouldn't have thought about it again."

"Keep going," Lon encouraged. "When did you hear about it again?"

"Before we left the Succubus cavern, Merrimoth invited us to a party at his house. A private party—we were the only Hellfire members invited." Evan wiped away blood trickling from his nose. "He'd never even spoken to me before that night. I felt like the luckiest guy in the world. But when I showed up for the party, he couldn't remember my name. He thought I was from the catering company. It was humiliating. I was going to leave, but he was showing off, making it snow inside his house. When he wasn't looking, I sneaked upstairs and looked around. Found the elixir stash in his closet. Ten vials. I took five."

"Out of revenge?" I asked.

"Not really. I thought if the elixir could do that for Merrimoth, maybe it could help me. Everyone in my family has knacks—I'm the only one without one. I thought maybe if I took the elixir, it would bring out something in me."

"Did it?" Lon asked.

Evan shook his head. "I took a whole bottle. Nothing happened. My wife came over to get some things from the attic and caught me with it, so I told her what it was. Telly was with her. He must've overheard us arguing, because the following night he broke into my house and stole three bottles. Next thing I know, I'm hearing about all these crazy knacks being used to commit crimes in Morella. I knew it was Telly. He's been in and out of juvie. Runs away from his mom's house for days at a time. Kicked out of school twice." He stared at Telly's body, a look of pity on his face. "Stupid kid. If he would've just minded his own business . . ."

"Wait a minute," I said. "If Telly stole it from you, and we heard him talking about going straight to the source to steal it, he couldn't have been talking about Merrimoth. He's dead."

"No," Evan said softly. "Merrimoth wasn't the source."

Lon groaned. He was seeing the answers inside Evan's head before the man could get them out. And the way Lon looked at me, I knew it wasn't good.

I looked at Evan. "Who's the source?"

The question hung between us for a moment before he answered. "Dare."

28

My world shrank. Hair on my arms stood on end. "Dare? How?"

Evan swallowed. "Merrimoth claimed Dare had some magician cook it up a few years ago. Merrimoth had the idea to stop administering the Transmutation Spell to new initiates of the Body."

The transmutated higher-ups in the Hellfire Club formed the Body. Only thirteen seats, and Lon held one of them. At least he used to. He hadn't been active in the club for years, and hadn't attended a monthly full moon "meeting" since he took me along several months back. I don't think either of us knew where he stood in the club now that I'd told Dare to screw himself.

Evan's thin, rough voice sounded even wearier than he looked. "It was a way to be transmutated in public. No horns, you know." He glanced at Lon's, shrugging. "Merrimoth was complaining that Dare hoarded it, and it wasn't fair, because it was Merrimoth's idea. They've been on the outs since Dare punished him for . . ." Evan's attention turned to me, realization widening his eyes. "You're the girl who broke the summoning circles in the caves. The reason Merrimoth got punished."

And the one who killed Merrimoth when he was jumping off the second-floor balcony of his house into the ocean, but I didn't volunteer this information.

"Don't worry about her," Lon said.

"Sure, sure," Evan mumbled. "Anyway, Merrimoth took it from Dare. He made it sound like Dare was clueless about the theft, but I guess Dare eventually caught on when he heard about stuff on the news with the robberies. When I heard, I knew Telly had been selling it. I tried to get it back, but he ran away again. Told his mother that a black car had been following him."

Black car. Oh . . . fuck. I looked at Lon. *Dare's been trailing me.*

Evan touched his nose and winced. "Once I found out Dare was looking for the elixir, I just wanted to get rid of it. So when I saw Yvonne was in town, I thought, well—she lives in Florida, and she'd take it with her. Get it out of Dare's territory, you know."

"Why didn't you just throw it away?" I said.

Evan scratched his arm, avoiding Lon's gaze.

"Because he wanted to sleep with Yvonne," Lon answered.

"I'm sorry, man. You don't understand what it's

like to be in that club and watch everyone else having fun. Everyone else making friends. Everyone else getting the good jobs. I'm a nobody. Useless. No family. Separated. I'm almost fifty, and all I do is crunch numbers in a cube all day. I just wanted to be part of everything, just once."

We all sat in silence for a long moment.

"If Dare had Telly killed, he'll kill you, too," I said.

"Don't you think I know that? I was packing when you showed up. I thought Dare had sent you here. I need to get out of town. Please, I'm begging— let me get out of here."

"What about Telly's body?" Lon said. "You're just going to leave him?"

"I was going to call my wife after I left."

"You have any more elixir hidden?"

Evan shook his head. "Telly stole the rest. All I had was what I gave Yvonne."

Lon threw Yvonne's vial of elixir on the floor and crushed the glass beneath his foot. Red liquid seeped into the pale carpet. "It's not right to leave the boy like this," he said.

"Police will be able to tell the bullet didn't come from your gun," I added.

"I know, but what am I supposed to do? Tell them Dare's behind it? Who are they going to believe? I have no evidence. I don't stand a chance against him."

Lon's horns spiraled away. His fiery halo receded

to its normal gold and green as he let go of Evan.
"You can run, but if Dare catches up to you, you're on
your own. Don't contact Yvonne again."

"I won't."

Lon tapped my hand and spoke in a low voice.
"Let's go."

"Good luck," I told Evan.

He made a small noise, but didn't look up from
Telly's body.

Outside, Lon rushed me into the SUV before
driving to the end of the block and parking.

"What are you doing?"

"Watching Evan's house. I want to see if anyone's
been trailing us. I didn't hear anything when I was
transmutated, but I just want to be sure."

I peered into shadows down the street, searching
for movement. "He sent us to Merrimoth's to find the
leak."

"What?"

"Dare. He said he wanted us to find out why Merrimoth's knack was amped up, but he already knew
why—had to. Maybe he realized someone had stolen
his elixir when he started hearing rumors about Merrimoth's knack getting wilder. But when he heard
about the crazy crimes in Morella, he knew he had a
bigger problem. That would explain why he was so
angry when we failed to get any information out of
Merrimoth."

"Then he heard your bar had been hit and knew
you'd go after the robbers."

"I first saw the black car outside Diablo Market. And I saw someone at the car rally when I was chasing down Noel in the parking lot."

Lon stared out over the steering wheel. "He was already following Hajo before we went to the trailer park. Probably trailed you to Hajo's apartment."

"We led Dare to Telly." Sure, Telly was an asshole, and I had every reason to hate him, but he was just a kid. A dark, nauseating feeling bubbled up inside me.

"If it wasn't us, it would've been someone else," Lon said. "Dare is petty. He's big on retribution. Killing Telly was sending a message to Evan."

Dare. That arrogant asshole had done nothing but make my life miserable.

He was the one responsible for all this. For Merrimoth. For Tambuku being robbed. For Kar Yee being hurt. For Telly's path of destruction. At that moment, I even blamed him for Jupe getting drunk, and for pushing my hand to do what I did to Yvonne.

"Cady," Lon said.

"Don't defend him," I snapped. "What about us? If he finds out Evan gave a vial to Yvonne, will he send a message to you by putting a bullet in her head?"

"No, he . . . I don't know," he admitted. "Dare isn't the man I used to know. I don't know how far he'd go to protect his secrets, and I don't know how far he'd go to punish people who wronged him."

"He's already got a hate-on for me. Maybe he'll just take me out like Telly."

Lon grabbed my arm. "Like hell. I'll kill him my-self before that happens."

"Not if I get him first."

He might be rich, he might surround himself with bodyguards, but what was all that to someone like me?

"Cady," Lon warned. "I can hear what you're feeling, but you can't act on that."

"Why not? Who else can stop him? The police?"

"We can't just ram down his door and kill him. That makes us no better than he is. And we have other things to think about."

"Like?"

"Like Jupe. Telly was only a couple of years older."

"Dare wouldn't—"

"You want to bet on that? How do we know what he won't do? Even if he won't pull the trigger, what's to stop him from arranging some kind of accident when Jupe's at school? You think a man who doesn't give a shit about killing one teenager is going to hesi-tate to kill another one?"

"But he was your father's best friend. You're fam-ily to him."

"You willing to bet Jupe's life on that? Mr. and Mrs. Holiday? The Giovannis?"

I stared at him across the darkened car for several moments before shaking my head.

"I'm responsible for too many people, Cady, and that includes you. I'm not taking a chance until I've had time to think it all through."

I couldn't argue. He was right. But as we drove home in silence, another part of me wondered if us being cautious just meant Dare had won. Again.

When we got home, I played phone tag with Kar Yee, leaving her a message that I had news about Telly. She left me one in return that she'd stop by Lon's house tomorrow afternoon on her way back from visiting our friend upstate.

We checked in on Jupe—he was snoring off his night with Yvonne—sent the Holidays back to their own house, and crashed. I fell asleep angry, still thinking of Dare, but ended up dreaming about someone worse.

I was lying on my back in a field of cheery wild-flowers, red and yellow and purple. A soft breeze rustled through the green grass and stems swaying around my limbs. Lon's hand clasped mine. He lay at my side, eyes closed, wind fluttering his honey hair.

The bright blue sky began to darken around the edges, cerulean shot through with dreary gray. Something approached—something that I couldn't immediately see, sneaking through the field. Fear blanketed me as I watched tall stalks of grass bending. The flowers around us drooped and withered. The green grass turned to straw.

Something was coming.

I shook Lon, trying to wake him, but he remained asleep.

Two legs appeared in the dead grass. My gaze followed them. My mother's long face peered down at me, a smirk curling her lips.

The sky behind her continued to darken, but it wasn't night. I said, "Why are you here? The moon's not out, and I'm not doing magick. You can't see me."

"The moon is not visible here," she corrected, her white toga shifting in the breeze. "But it's night on your plane."

"But I'm not doing magick."

"This makes no difference to me. Not anymore. As long as the moon is visible, I can track your Heka here."

"Where is this?"

"Between the planes."

"Liar," I said. "This is a dream."

She squinted. "Me, a liar? Look at yourself. You are the one with the tail and the forked tongue like the serpent in the garden. The great deceiver, filled with venom."

Forked tongue. I remembered biting my lip at the racetrack. It still wasn't fully healed.

My tail slithered down the side of my thigh. Black and white stripes rotated as it grew until it was longer than my legs. My mother watched it carefully, taking a step back to stay out of its reach.

"What am I? What did you put inside me?" I whispered.

"Why, Sélène—don't you like your serpentine form? It is the real you, after all. And every night you will shed your human skin and become your true self, my little one."

I shook my head. "I'm not yours."

"You'll always be mine. I called forth beings you can't imagine and trapped their magick to create you inside my womb. I birthed your body."

"A pact with what? What am I? What did you create?"

Instead of answering me directly, she talked around my question. "After all my hard work, how do you repay me? Cause me nothing but misery."

She murmured words that sounded like a spell, crouched at my feet, and cruelly clamped my tail to the ground. Pain spiked through it, all the way into my spine. I tried to move away, but I was paralyzed. She'd done something to me with magick.

Terror overtook me. I strained to look at Lon. He was still sleeping.

My mother growled at my feet, still holding my tail to the ground. "You sold your own parents to a demon," she said, anger darkening her eyes. "Once she took us into the Æthyr, Nivella killed your father. Sliced him into shreds like he was meat." She leaned over me. "Do you not care? The man who raised you is dead."

"No, I don't care," I said coldly. "I'm glad he's dead. I wish you were."

She growled in my face. "It is your fault. Your father's blood is on your hands. And you may not care, but I do. He was my lover. My soul mate. My reason for living."

"Why are you still alive, then?"

"I live for you, now, darling. Only you." She crawled over me and whispered into my ear. "And I want what's mine. I created you, spent the last twenty-five years of my life waiting for you. And you may think you've gotten away, but it's only a matter of time before I will have you under my control again. And to prove it, I will take from you what you took from me. An eye for an eye . . . a heart for a heart."

She pushed off the ground and stood, releasing my tail. I felt something cold in my hand and looked down. I was holding a knife. One that looked remarkably like the ceremonial dagger she'd used when she was slicing my breast, trying to sacrifice me to steal my moon powers.

"Your human form betrayed your father. Betrayed me," she said. "But your true form inside cannot, because it is bound to me by ancient rules. We are connected, you and I. And that connection will only get stronger. It's just a matter of time."

Her eyes closed. She raised her hands to the sky. Foreign Æthyric words tumbled out of her mouth. Another spell.

I scrambled to move away, but it wasn't soon enough. Heka hit me like a punch in the gut. My too-slow limbs felt like they were caught in syrup. Then her spoken chant ended and she spoke to me. "I command you to offer me a sacrifice. In payment for your father's death, you will now kill who *you* love."

I sat up in the dead grass, not by will, but by

force. She was controlling me. I was a puppet, and the strings she pulled made me move toward Lon. I called his name, tried to warn him, but he still didn't wake. Holding the dagger, I raised my arms high and aimed for his chest.

This couldn't be happening. It was just a dream.

Wake up, wake up, wake up! I told myself.

And I did. The field fizzled away. My mother disappeared.

I was in Lon's dark bedroom. Moonlight spilled across the sheets, illuminating the kitchen knife I held in my hands as I straddled Lon's sleeping form.

29

Shock and horror held me frozen for several moments. This wasn't a dream.

This was real.

Lon grunted when I jumped off him. Then he rolled to his side and fell back into sleep, utterly unaware of what I was doing.

I was in full Moonchild mode. Everything had a silvery tinge. I started to sever the connection, push it away, when I caught a glimpse of myself in the long dressing mirror standing next to the bed.

I gasped. Took a shaky step forward to get a better look.

It was me, naked. Me, but not me. My skin was covered in tiny, iridescent reptilian scales. Mostly black, I thought—it was hard to tell with the silver vision. A reticulated pattern began around my face, neck, and shoulders, where the black was interspersed with white and gray, and—I turned to peer over my shoulder—this eventually became black and white stripes on my back . . . and tail.

The tail seamlessly jutted out from my lower back and was a couple of inches in diameter. Black and white rings, all the way to the tip. It was now wrapped around my ankle, clinging to my leg, making me look like a dog with its tail tucked.

But that wasn't the startling part. Nor was the silver eyes or the massive dancing silver halo. None of that shocked me. Lon had told me about those things.

He didn't tell me about the horns.

Not spiraling. Not even two. A series of ridges began on my forehead, just above my eyes. They made a wide V shape there, increasing in size and length until they became black spines. A few inches above my hairline, the spines changed to black horns, gently curving backward like crests on a dragon. Three black, glossy horns flaring in neat little rows on each side of my head. The ones at the crown of my head were the longest—maybe two feet tall.

My hair stood out from my head, licking around the horns as my halo whorled like an angry storm cloud.

Terrified of my own reflection, I pushed the moon power away as fast as I could. The weight changed on my head as the horns retracted. Scales disappeared, as well as the tail.

Fuck, fuck, fuck.

I stood by the bed, a slow tremor wracking my body as I looked down at Lon. I could've killed him. Stabbed him while he slept. My fingers uncurled around the handle of the blade I'd forgotten I'd been holding. Not my mother's ceremonial dagger, but a knife from Lon's kitchen—one of his fancy, expensive knives. How the hell . . . had I sleepwalked? Did my mother orchestrate all this?

Her voice rang in my head, clear and strong, as if we'd actually spoken. And maybe we had. She said it was a place between the planes. I stared at the knife. My hand was shaking so badly, I nearly dropped it.

This was so bad. I'd never felt so out of control.

Chest heaving, pulse jittery, I backed away from the bed and headed to the bedroom door. I felt like an intruder in my own home. Lon's home. Jupe's home. Dear God, he was sleeping two doors away. What if he'd seen me . . . looking like *that*?

Worse: what if he wasn't safe either?

Stifling a sob, I grabbed my robe off the back of the door and covered myself, quietly fleeing downstairs in the darkness. I headed straight for the kitchen, where Lon kept a small light over the sink constantly switched on like a nightlight. The magnetic strip that held his knives was attached to the wall nearby. Sure enough, a narrow space on the strip was blank, exactly the space where this one belonged. He kept them arranged in a specific order, which is why he'd known I'd taken the paring knife that night I called up Priya on Kar Yee's roof.

I pressed the blade to the strip until it clicked. Nausea gripped my stomach. I barely had time to hunch over the sink before the vomiting began—once, twice. A third time. Weak and sick, I washed it down the drain and thrust my head under the tap to drink straight from the faucet. Rinsed my mouth out. Drank more. I didn't understand why'd I'd be experiencing post-magick nausea. I hadn't done any magick. Besides, the moon power didn't make me sick like Heka-fueled magick did. Maybe it was my mother's magick.

I waited until the nausea subsided, thinking of my reflection in the mirror.

My true serpentine form. That's what my mother called it.

I ran through a shortlist of deities or mythological beings associated with snakes, but none of them were directly associated with magick. And whatever I had pinging around under my skin was definitely a magick-wielder.

A reptilian, serpent magick-wielder.

Padding to the bottom of the stairs, I paused, listening. No movement upstairs. Lon's jacket hung on a peg in the foyer. I put it on and quietly slipped out the sliding glass doors to the back patio.

The dark Pacific crashed against rocks in the distance. The tree line blocked the moon. I was glad for that, all things considered. Damp grass sent cold shivers up my legs as I wiped saliva over my guardian's sigil. "Priya. Come."

His black line appeared in the middle of my palm as he swooped down from a crack in the sky. "Mistress," he said, folding up his wings behind his back as he landed in the grass a few feet away. He stalked forward and stopped in front of me, black halo swirling above his crazy shocked hair. "What is wrong?"

"My mother visited me in a dream tonight. She's got some sort of control over me in the Æthyr. She's trying to make me do bad things. I'm scared, Priya. Have you found out anything more?"

"Where is your lover? The Kerub."

"Lon is inside," I said nodding toward the house as I crossed my arms over my chest to fend off the biting wind blowing off the ocean.

"He does not like me."

"That's not true," I said. "He's just protective of me, that's all. He doesn't hate you. He's thankful you're helping me in the Æthyr."

"He is right to feel protective, for you are in danger."

"Tell me."

"This is what I know. Your mother is claiming that she has dominion over you through an unbreakable bond. The magick that she used to conceive you is very old. It is similar to the spell used to draw demons into human bodies."

"To create Earthbounds?"

He nodded. "She is bragging that she still has control over you. She has claimed that her control is strengthening."

"It definitely is."

"I think I know why. The spell she used to conceive you is degenerative. Your human body weakens as it ages while the other part of you strengthens. The stronger it becomes, the more control she has over you, because the bond between you will solidify. Your willpower will crumble."

"She can control me in my sleep."

"Because you are unaware and weak. The Moonchild part of you uses lunar power to open up a connection between the planes. You can call up the power when you are awake. But she can use a spell to open that same connection when you are weak."

"When I am asleep."

"Asleep, weary. Inebriated. Impassioned. Any time you are not in full control of your own willpower." He held out his palm, showing me the black thread that connected us. "Her connection to you is like ours, but only temporary. The more you grow into the Moonchild, the stronger the bond becomes. And more permanent."

I curled my hands inside the too long sleeves of Lon's coat and paced. "But only when it's night, right?"

"That would be logical since it is a lunar power, and, as you told me, it does not work in the day."

My throat was dry. "Okay, so I just sleep in the day, when she can't hack into me. I stay vigilant at night. Don't use the moon power at all."

"Even if you do not sleep at night, you will still need to worry." Priya stepped in front of me and leveled his gaze with mine. "Your loved ones and friends are not safe. She can see into your thoughts and feelings when she is connected to you."

I blinked at him. He was talking from experience, wasn't he? He could see into my thoughts and feelings now?

His voice softened. "She can feel who you care about, especially if thoughts of them are fresh in your mind. She will search for your weaknesses, and she will have you destroy them."

"I can't run again," I said miserably. "I can't do that. I have a family now. I need them. They need me."

"You should not risk their lives for a moment of comfort. You must erase them from your mind. Get as far away from them as you can."

"And do what? Wait until this thing inside me is completely under her command?" I was shouting at him. It wasn't his fault. "What am I?"

"They call you Mother of Ahriman."

"Mother of demons," I said. "Is that what I am? A demon? I saw myself, Priya. I was covered in scales. I have a serpent's tail, and horns. What am I?"

"I do not know. 'Mother of Ahriman' is only a story in the Æthyr. A legend. A woman that commands fear and respect. But I do not know exactly who she is, or what manner of being."

"A goddess? Do I have a god inside me? Is there such a thing in the Æthyr?"

"Not in the Æthyr, but maybe on anther plane."

My occult order believed in a multitude of planes, many without names. The Æthyr was merely the nearest one to ours, metaphysically speaking.

Priya exhaled loudly through his nose. "But from the way your mother speaks, I believe that you are something altogether new. She has not invoked the spirit of an old god inside you. She has worked like a surgeon to piece together magicks and create a new being."

It took several moments to sink in. "So I don't have another being inside me?"

"You are something new that has never been seen."

I squeezed my eyes shut in despair.

"My concern is for your immediate safety," Priya said. "If the Moonchild part of you is strengthening, and your mother's control over you with it, then you need to find a way to stop it from developing. Or a way to unmake it."

I thought of what I saw when I was poking around inside Yvonne. "If the spell she used to create me is like the spell to create Earthbounds, it is impossible. Demon souls are fused inside human bodies. I can't get rid of the Moonchild part of me unless I kill myself."

He grasped my shoulders firmly. "You are not like the Kerubs. You are something very different. All magick can be unmade, or at least lessened. Start with the ritual your parents used to conceive you and work backwards."

"I don't know the spell! No one in my order knows it. They kept it secret. The only person who knew about it is dead. It's lost—gone."

"They did not invent the ritual," Priya said softly. "They found it somewhere. Go to your order. Trace their path. Find the ritual. Once you have it, I am certain that we can uncover a way to undo what has been done or, at the very least, cut her bond to you."

A growing hopelessness weighed me down. I wanted it all to go away. I wanted the small life I'd built. I wanted to be me.

I just didn't know who that was anymore.

"This is impossible," I whispered.

"Nothing is impossible, especially for you. You will find a way. And I will help you. I will be your scout, and I will help to protect those you love. The demon boy that is bound to you, I can feel his bond. I can appear to him as I appear to you. If he is in danger, I will cross the veil to protect him. Show him my sigil. He can call me."

"Oh, God."

"But you must act quickly. She has bragged that her connection to you may be strong enough in a matter of days or weeks."

"Strong enough for what?"

Priya's bare torso crackled.

"No, no, no!" I cried. "Don't leave me. I need you."

"I cannot stay."

"What if she finds you? She'll hurt you, too."

"I am careful. At the moment she does not know I am alive or that we have bonded again. I have a new body. It is serving me well. But it does not serve me here, and I must leave." His wings snapped open, blocking out the filtered moonlight. All I could see were two glossy eyes and the silver glint of his teeth. "Sleep in the daytime only. Do not relax your guard at night. Steel your emotions. Learn to hide your thoughts and create lies in your head—if she manages to connect with you again, you will need that skill before you find the Moonchild ritual."

"Priya!"

"You need magical protection from her," he insisted. "Go to your order. If they cannot help you solve the problem, their magicians can shield you until we can find a solution. I will return." Without another word, he snapped away, disappearing in front of my face. Leaving me alone.

Alone and faced with the abysmal thought of going into hiding again.

I was a fool to think I could ever stop running.

I could never have a normal life. Everything I had was lost before I ever found it.

30

I didn't go back to sleep that night. Instead, I walked the meandering road down Lon's cliff, past Mr. and Mrs. Holiday's cabin, to the beach. Foxglove kindly escorted me. I watched her sleek Labrador body exploring the driftwood-strewn sand as I sat on some big rocks where Lon and Jupe and I had once built a small bonfire. And I thought.

And thought.

I remembered my parents talking about some old grimoires they'd found in France that contained the ritual they used to conceive me. God only knew where those books were now. Destroyed, maybe. Brought over to the states? My occult order had taken over my parents' house in Florida after I'd let Nivella take them to the Æthyr. Maybe the Caliph had found something in the house that could be helpful.

It was all such a fucking long shot.

But what else could I do? Sit around until I eventually hurt someone I cared about?

Then I thought of Dare. I couldn't just run off to Florida and leave Lon and Jupe unprotected when that man was going around killing people who've looked at him crooked.

Couldn't stay. Couldn't leave. I didn't know what I was going to do.

I sat thinking for hours. At some point before dawn, Foxglove ran back up the beach path toward the house and returned a couple of minutes later with Lon. I watched his fiery halo flickering across the dark beach as he approached. When he caught up to me, he sat down on the rock next to me. He didn't ask me why I was out there. He merely pulled me into his arms and said, "Show me what's wrong and we will fix it."

Daylight crept over the beach. Feeling fairly confident I was out of my mom's foul reach, Lon and I made the trek back up to the house. We hadn't solved my problem, but at least Lon knew everything. And at that point I was exhausted and spent, and knew I needed to force myself to get rest sometime that day if I was going to stay up all night. I'd watched enough Freddy Krueger movies with Jupe to know that sleep depravation always came back to bite you on the ass.

"Get in bed and sleep," Lon said. "Rose and Adella will be back from the hospital in a few hours. I need to get some work done, but I'll come upstairs and wake you when they come."

I rummaged in my pocket and handed him the medicinal I'd given Jupe. "If he's got a hangover, give him another drop of this in some water. Or crushed ice, if he's throwing up."

He kissed my forehead. "I'll handle him. Go to sleep."

Amazingly enough, I eventually did.

I woke on my own around three. Rose and Adella showed up as I was getting out of the shower. Mr. and Mrs. Holiday were buzzing around the house as well—I could hear Mr. Holiday teasing Jupe in the living room about making him some disgusting hair of the dog drink with raw eggs.

Normalcy had never sounded so good.

Once I rejoined the group, I found out Yvonne would be released from the hospital that afternoon. Her concussion was okay. No permanent damage. A small relief to the lingering guilt I harbored. Rose and Adella were flying Yvonne back home with them to Portland. She was going to stay with her mother for a few weeks. As long as Rose had the Solomon ring, I supposed she was safe from Yvonne's knack, or what remained of it. I spoke to her alone while Lon was helping Adella pack.

"You good?" I asked her. "Need any help?"

Rose pushed her glasses higher on her nose. The Solomon ring was loose around her index finger. "We're going to retrieve Yvonne's clothes from the hotel, then pick her up from the hospital on the way to the Morella airport."

"Doctor says it's okay for her to fly after the concussion?"

"Mick did some healing on her this morning.

Scans look fine, so he said it's okay. Will you be riding out to the city with us?"

Yvonne was the last person I wanted to see right now. "Probably not. My business partner's coming over, and I've got some things to take care of."

She nodded. "I wanted to thank you for what you did. Lon told me that you put yourself in danger by doing that to Yvonne. I didn't know. I wouldn't have asked you if I knew."

After the dream talk with my mother, I now wondered if she was tapped into me during my metaphysical surgery on Yvonne, but what was done, was done. "I just hope you don't regret asking."

"Not one bit." She grasped my hands. Her fingers were firm around mine. "I still don't know if Yvonne can be saved, but you improved her chances, and I'll always be grateful for that, no matter what happens. And if there's ever anything I can do to repay you, please tell me. Because if you're Lon's family, you're my family."

If I hadn't spent half the night emptying myself of tears, I would've cried. But as it was, all I could manage was a "thank you." My early impressions of her had completely faded. I saw her as Lon did now, I supposed: strong, stubborn, beautiful, and utterly dedicated to her family. She was a good mom. I'd trade her for mine in a heartbeat.

Jupe appeared on the back patio and came inside through sliding glass doors.

"How you feeling?" I asked.

"Stupid."

I smiled at him.

"When are we leaving for the airport, Gramma?"

"Soon. Need to be there in a couple of hours."

Which didn't give me much time—a little over an hour before the sun would set, and I had things to do. I stopped Jupe on his way upstairs. "Can I talk to you? In private."

Rose held up her hands. "Don't let me stop you."

I mumbled my thanks and led Jupe to the front door. "Here," I said, snagging his army green field coat off a hook on the way out. "It's cold."

He slipped it on as we marched down the driveway under a dreary afternoon sky. I counted our steps as we went. "You're already way out of her range, if that's what you're worried about," Jupe said.

"Just making sure."

"Is this about last night?" Jupe said in a low voice.

I shook my head as the sound of a car drew our attention to the side gate. "Crap. Kar Yee."

"Kar Yee?" he said, but his excitement soon sputtered. "Does she know about last night? You didn't tell her, did you?"

"I didn't tell her, don't worry."

She sped down the side road and pulled into the circular driveway behind the Giovanni's rental car. When she spotted us, she waved a hand and headed our way. "Nice digs, future boyfriend. I almost got lost on the mountain trying to find your secret back road."

He grinned goofily. "I'm glad you're all healed up now."

"Me too. Good as gold," she said, pinging her collarbone with her fingers. She reached into her jacket and pulled out a red envelope. "This is for you," she said, handing it to Jupe.

"Me?"

"It's movie passes," she said before he even had a chance to open it. "No big deal." She was mildly embarrassed. "You did that stuff for the Tambuku website, and I really liked that opera figure. It was sweet. You're a good kid."

Jupe's breath came a little faster through his open mouth. "Oh, man. That's cool. Thanks."

"No big deal," she insisted again. "What's up with you, by the way? Your halo looks sick."

Jupe's mouth twisted. "Uh . . ."

"Probably just a getting a cold or something," I offered.

"Yeah," he said, sneaking me a grateful look. "Probably just that."

She nodded and tilted her chin my way. "You've got news about that Telly kid?"

I waffled.

"You want me to leave?" Jupe asked me. "I will if you want, but whatever it is, I won't freak out. Dad said you guys had a terrible night."

"We did. But actually, I want to tell you both something that's more important than that, and now's as good a time as any." The tears I didn't think I had anymore were already brimming.

"What's wrong?" Kar Yee asked.

"I need to confess something important."

Jupe looked at Kar Yee, confused. She shrugged her shoulders in answer.

Here goes nothing, I thought. "It's a secret I've been keeping." I looked at Jupe. "Only your dad knows, and a couple of other people."

"As many secrets as you've got, this should be good," Kar Yee said. "I'm all ears."

Jupe pushed curls away from his face, an awkward movement. I was making him nervous. Hell, I was making myself nervous. This was so much easier when I'd first told Lon. Then again, he'd drugged me into spilling the beans. I wished I could drug myself now.

"You know how I've told you that my parents were bad people?" I said to Jupe.

He nodded.

"They were way worse than your mom could ever dream of being. And I need to tell you both who they really were."

"Okay." He was definitely nervous now. Kar Yee, too.

"Are you familiar with the Black Lodge Slayings?"

Jupe's face twisted. "Uh . . . what? Oh!" Something clicked in his head. "The serial killers. The satanic murders of those occultists, or whatever. The Duvets or something."

"Duval. Enola and Alexander Duval."

"Yeah," Jupe said, brightening. "They were on the news a few months ago. They're supposed to be dead, but they were on that parking garage footage."

"Oh, that's right," Kar Yee said. "I know who you're talking about. The murders were all over talk shows back when we were in college."

I waited for them to start piecing things together.

"No," Kar Yee said, her jaw dropping in shock.

Jupe shifted uncomfortably. His mouth tightened to a thin line. Breath quickened through his nostrils. "Your parents . . ."

"Were killers. I didn't know at the time. I thought they were innocent. We all faked our deaths and separated. I've been living on my own since I was seventeen under this name." I looked at Kar Yee. "I met you about a year after it happened."

She said nothing. Just stared at me, frozen.

"I only saw them a few times all those years. And I believed they'd been framed. But then they got spotted on that parking tape and made the news." I nodded toward Jupe. "That's when I met your dad."

"That's why he was helping you?" His voice wavered.

Even then, at that moment, I wanted to lie to him. Tell him I was kidding. Tell him everything was fine and that there was no cause for alarm. But I pushed past it and said, "Yeah. I thought he was going to help me prove their innocence, but we ended up finding out they were guilty."

Kar Yee still said nothing. Jupe shoved his hands into the pockets of his jeans. "Arcadia Bell is a fake name?"

"An alias. I've been using it since I was a teenager."

"What's your real name?"

"It's Cady," I insisted as a hot tear fell down my cheek. "I don't want you to ever think of me as anyone but Cady. No one calls me by my old name. I hate it. I wish I could erase everything from my old life."

A slow breeze fluttered his curls. "How long has my dad known?"

"Since before I came over that first night and met you."

"He knew, and he still let you come over here?"

I nodded.

"If he trusted you and he barely even knew you," Jupe reasoned, "then he could tell you were okay."

"I suppose."

"You told me your parents were dead in college," Kar Yee said. "Then you told me a few months ago that they'd died when you went to San Diego. Now you're telling me that they faked their deaths?"

"I really did think they were dead a few months ago," I argued. "A powerful Æthyric demon took them into the Æthyr. I thought it was safe to assume she'd kill both of them. She killed my dad, but my mom is still alive. Alive there."

"Alive on the demon plane?" Jupe said.

"Yes. And there's more, unfortunately."

I told them everything about the Moonchild powers. The things I could do. About the tail. Jupe listened earnestly, elbows pressed tight against his ribs, every muscle in his jaw flexing. Kar Yee was silent and unreadable at first, but became increasingly distressed. I didn't stop talking until I'd spilled everything. And then I waited for their reaction.

No one said anything for a long moment.

Kar Yee stared at the ground, unable to meet my gaze. "You lied to me all these years. I gave you a million chances to tell me the truth, but you jump into bed with some guy and tell him?"

"Lon's not 'some guy,' and—"

"I don't want to hear it," she shouted, finally looking me in the eye. "I don't need your excuses."

My chest tightened. "I know."

"You could've trusted me. Why didn't you trust me?"

"I'm sorry. It was hard for me to trust anyone. I thought I was protecting them. Me. I thought I was doing the right thing."

She threw up her hands and paced in a circle. "You are living with an illegal name? We share a business! If you get in trouble with the law—"

"I've been careful."

"I don't care." Tears brimmed. Hers hands were fists. "Partners don't lie to each other. If you can't trust me enough to confide in me, then you shouldn't be running a business with me."

"Kar Yee—"

"I don't want to talk about it right now." She spun around and marched back toward her car.

"Please stay," I called after her. "I need to talk to you about it."

"And I need to go to Tambuku, because one of us has to get it running again."

"I'll come with you."

"Don't bother." She got in her car and slammed the door.

That didn't go well. Not that I thought it would, but it still stung. And it wasn't over. Jupe stood silent, staring at the dust Kar Yee's wheels kicked up as she sped away. When he turned to look at me, he wore a pained expression. He almost looked like he was about to cry.

"Please don't be scared of me," I said. "I'm still me. I still care about you as much as I did yesterday."

"I'm not scared," he said.

I nodded, hoping that was true.

"I'm not," he insisted. "I guess I feel like Kar Yee. I just wish you would've told me sooner. It sort of hurts my feelings that you didn't. I mean, you could've trusted me."

"It's not that. I was afraid and . . . I was ashamed of it."

"You were?" He considered this for several moments. "I guess I understand. That's why I never talked about my mom much before, well"—he waved a hand—"all of this happened over Christmas. Sometimes I wish I could erase that part of my life, too."

"At least your mom is trying. She's a very sad person, and she's selfish. I don't know if she'll ever be okay or stop making stupid mistakes. And I don't know if you should give her any more chances—"

"I'm not," he said firmly.

I nodded. "That's up to you. But I guess what I'm trying to say is that it's a whole different thing with my mom. My mom is just evil. And really, really dangerous. She is beyond redemption."

"Wow." He turned away from the wind and kicked at a knotted cypress tree's roots that bulged above the dirt. "This is the biggest secret anyone's ever told me," he said thoughtfully.

"I trust you."

He gave me a funny smile, tight, but honest—as if he was surprised I would trust him, pleased I did, but still in shock about the whole thing.

I exhaled a long breath and glanced back at the house. "I need to tell you about something else. Remember when I once told you about my guardian, Priya?"

He nodded. "One of the sigils on your arm."

I pulled a piece of paper from my pocket. "This sigil. It's his name. And because you're connected to me through our bond"—I nodded to his hip, where my own sigil was tattooed—"Priya is your guardian as much as mine. He can only stay on earth for a few minutes at a time, but if you are in trouble, you can call him. You'll need Heka, and you probably don't have much. You can try to spit on the sigil—"

He made a face.

"Oh, please," I said, straining to eject a single laugh. "You know you love gross stuff. If the spit doesn't work, you'll have to cut yourself and spill a few drops of blood on it. But make a copy of it first so you don't lose the image. Take a photo with your phone or something."

"I just do that and your guardian will cross over to our world?"

"You just say, 'Priya, come,' and he will show up. Don't be frightened of him. He looks like a boy, but he's got wings."

"Oh, shit! No way."

"And he talks a little funny, but you'll do fine. Don't call him more than once every couple of days. He can't stay long—only a couple of minutes, so you'll need to talk fast. But you can tell him anything. You can even ask him to send me a message."

"Why would I need to do that?"

I closed my eyes briefly. "Because I might have to leave."

"What do you mean?"

"My mom can control me. It's getting worse. I'm afraid she's going to make me do something against my will." I attempted to swallow the lump in my throat.

"But—"

"If I stay, it might put people in danger. I'm her puppet. When I tap into moon magick, she can control me."

"So don't. Dad says just because I have a knack doesn't mean I have to use it. Isn't this the same thing?"

"Even if I don't use it, she can get me when I'm

sleeping. She's dangerous, Jupe. You are in danger by being around me. She's crazy and she wants revenge against me. She will try to hurt you."

Jupe was fighting back tears. "You can't leave. Where will you go?"

"To my order in Florida. My godfather might be able to help track down the ritual my parents used to make me this way. Maybe I can use it to fix myself. I don't know."

"Just fight her," he said. "You're strong. You can fight her."

"I don't know if I can, Jupe. And I won't risk putting you and your dad in danger."

"Please don't leave me," he begged in a rough voice. "Please. Don't leave me like she did."

My heart broke into a thousand pieces. "It's not because I don't care. I'm leaving to protect you." I wanted to assure him I'd be coming back—that I could pop down to Florida for a week, pop back up, problem fixed. But I couldn't lie to him. Not after I'd just broken down and told him the truth about my parents.

He stared at me for a moment, eyes glossy and pained. Then he blurted, "He bought you an engagement ring."

My body stilled. "What?" I whispered.

"That was the secret I told Kar Yee. That's the reason Gramma accepted you. Because Dad's going to marry you and we're going to be a family and you can't leave. You can't leave *us*."

Tears spilled down my cheeks. "Jupe."

"You're still going to leave, knowing that? How could you?"

"I—"

"I won't let you!" He gritted his teeth. His pupils flicked back and forth like a pendulum.

He was using his persuasion knack.

"You won't leave us. You'll stay here. You won't leave!"

I turned my head away, an instinctual reaction, as if that could deflect his knack. He'd never used it on me. I wasn't sure how it would feel. But I knew it had to feel like something more than this . . . this nothingness. I looked up at him. It didn't work. I could see it on his face, the way it fell.

And then it hit me. He'd tried to use it on Lon. On Yvonne. On me.

Dr. Spendlove, Jupe's Earthbound psychiatrist, had told Lon that most knacks like Jupe's have a restriction, he just wasn't sure yet what it was.

I was pretty sure we'd just uncovered it.

"Oh, Jupe," I said. "Your knack doesn't work on people you care about."

He made an anguished noise in the back of his throat.

"I'm so sorry." I reached out to touch him.

His face twisted as he bellowed a loud, incoherent growl. He was confused and frustrated and hurt. So was I. And I didn't know how to make it any better for either one of us.

He lunged and shoved me, hard. Shock ripped through me as I stumbled backward. Before I could recover, he was racing across the driveway.

"Jupe!" I called out.

But he didn't listen. He just ran as fast as he could toward the house. The slamming front door sounded like a small explosion.

I fell apart, crouching at the base of the cypress tree. I didn't think I could hurt any more than I did at that moment

31

Jupe needed some time to cool down. And he and Lon had to escort the Giovannis to the airport. When they were done, Lon and I had agreed to sit down and sort out a plan for Dare . . . a plan for Florida. And though I was too shocked to process it, I'd eventually have to tell him I knew about the engagement ring.

Right now, I was concerned about Kar Yee. I needed to make her understand, to tell her how sorry I was. So I headed to Tambuku.

On the drive into Morella, I kept an eye out for Dare's black cars while my brain juggled its crowded contents, struggling to prioritize all my worries. Telly's body. Dare. My mother. My serpentine form. Priya's warnings.

Jupe. Lon.

An engagement ring.

I banged my fists on the steering wheel, screaming at nobody, nearly running off the road. I sobbed. Screamed some more. By some miracle

I reined myself in enough to avoid dying in a fiery wreck.

Half an hour later, I skidded into a parking space in front of Tambuku. Our block was mostly quiet. Other businesses were open, but it was a quarter past four: not primetime for the restaurants and bars that outnumbered the other storefronts on this street. I didn't see Kar Yee's car, but she probably parked in the garage.

As the last trails of sunlight stretched over the sidewalk, I headed down Tambuku's front steps. The door was locked. No surprise. We usually locked it when we weren't open, even if someone was inside working.

"Kar Yee?" I called out. No lights. I flipped on the fishing float pendants over the bar and surveyed the room. The barstools, high-top tables, and chairs had been stacked against the wall in preparation for the paint covered binding triangles to be redone. I called out her name again. No answer. I started to head back to the office; halfway there, I swung around to retrace my steps and lock the front door.

Someone was already opening it.

Shiny bald head. Glasses. Green halo. Expensive suit. Minion at his side.

Dare.

"Miss Bell," he said. "So good to see you again."

It took me several moments to find my voice. "I doubt that."

"I was in the neighborhood."

"Bet you were. You've been following me a lot, lately. I'm flattered you find my comings and goings so damn fascinating."

"You're always fascinating, my dear. Just concerned over your safety."

"If you're concerned as you were about Evan's kid, Telly, then please don't bother."

"Ah, well. That was unfortunate." He slipped his hands inside his pants pockets. "Frankly, I'm surprised you aren't thanking me. He did rob this bar, did he not?"

"I try to avoid killing kids over theft. I thought you felt the same. You had me save several Hellfire kids from being sacrificed in that ritual on Halloween. Telly not worth saving, too?"

"Actually, no. Telly was a dangerous little piece of garbage who sold something that wasn't his to half the Earthbounds in Morella."

"You didn't know it was him. That's why you sent us over to Merrimoth's that night."

"If Merrimoth was my only Judas, I could punish him. The elixir's effects aren't permanent, you see. They wear off after a week or so. But when bizarre crimes started making the news here, I knew I had a bigger problem on my hands. Which is why I sent you out to Merrimoth's that night—so you could bind him while Lon dug around in his head. If you'd just done what I'd asked, we might've narrowed down the problem to Evan Johnson a lot sooner."

"But you would've still killed his kid."

"Oh, I had Evan killed, too. This morning, near Los Angeles."

Jesus!

Dare smiled. "If you run, I always find you. Remember that, Miss Bell."

"Is that why you're here? So you and your thug can teach me a lesson with a bullet?"

"No bullets. I'd merely like to make a deal with you." Dare nodded toward his minion, a middle-aged man with graying hair and the towering, boxy frame of a bodyguard. "Beryl here is an Earthbound, as you can see. But he has some minor magical talent, much like Lon. He'll be the one sealing the deal. I'd like a magical oath from you, once we've agreed upon terms."

I really didn't like the sound of this. I needed to arm myself, and fast. If I could make it behind the bar, I could grab my caduceus staff. Maybe if I could lure them into one of the binding triangles that hadn't been covered in red paint, I could trap them. Fat chance he would be stupid enough to just meander into a trap, but I had to think of something.

"What kind of deal?" I said, backing up a couple of steps.

Dare mumbled something to Beryl. I didn't like them conspiring together.

"I have some information you're going to want to see. In turn, I'd like you to pledge your allegiance to me. I'd like to . . ." He considered his words, then said, "Well, I'd like to adopt you, in a way. Be your symbolic father."

I laughed. "Father? Why in God's name would I want that?"

"Let's be honest—you won't. But you'll be willing to make a compromise to get your hands on what I've got."

"I doubt that. Go on, though. Show me."

Dare pointed at a briefcase Beryl held. "It's a very important piece of documentation. Can Beryl walk it over to you? He's unarmed. To prove we're on the level, he'll even walk into one of your remaining binding triangles. Feel free to bind him at any time."

I hesitated. It felt like *I* was the one walking into a trap—not this Beryl guy.

Dare sighed dramatically. "If I wanted you dead, I could've shot you when I walked in the door."

Beryl walked farther into the bar, holding up one hand in surrender.

It might shock the hell out of me, but I *could* bind him without the caduceus. And seeing how my life might be in danger, I had no qualms about electrocution.

"Say what you're going to say."

"No need to be snippy, Miss Bell," Dare said, then sighed his fake sigh. "So, where to begin? Shall I start with the first time your parents tried to conduct a conception ritual and how miserably that failed? Or are you already familiar with the story of your brother?"

My heart stopped.

"Ah, not aware of Victor Duval?" Beryl came closer, stepping into the second binding triangle before me, as Dare continued to talk. "Victor was damaged goods, apparently. A little screwy in the head. Liked to dissect the neighbors' cats."

I flinched. This couldn't be true. This was bullshit. I would've heard whisperings about this when I was still living with my parents. All the talk shows and exposés and books written about them— someone would've uncovered it . . . right?

"Rather handsome boy," Dare called from the door. "Dark-headed, like you. No silver halo, though. Not at all magically gifted, which meant he was of no use to your parents."

My gaze flicked to Beryl, who was stepping closer to the triangle right in front of me.

"Victor was eight when your folks finally gave up their dreams and drowned the poor child. I do believe that was the first time they killed."

Shock rooted me to the floor.

"Members of their order thought it was an accident. Your mother made an impassioned speech in front of the congregation, asking them to never speak his name again, as it only caused her grief. Quite theatrical. They never claimed the body when local authorities found it. She even destroyed the paper trail proving he ever existed—birth certificate and all. The media would've pounced on that juicy tidbit, don't you think?"

It couldn't be true. Could it? Why was he telling me this?

"But your mother missed a couple of details.

Would you like to see a photo of your brother when he was a boy?" Dare asked.

My stomach tightened.

Beryl stepped into the binding triangle. "That's far enough," I said. He halted and held his briefcase flat on one palm, clicking open the locks.

"Beryl," Dare said, "can you please give Miss Bell what we discussed?"

That was a funny way to put it.

The briefcase popped open.

I tapped into the electrical current as Beryl reached into the briefcase. Electricity raced into me, then slowed. I tugged harder, suddenly panicked that my abilities had changed. That maybe while my Moonchild-self was strengthening, and my natural magical talents were weakening. It definitely shouldn't be so hard to pull current.

Beryl's eyes met mine.

Oh.

It's hard to pull current when someone else is tugging on it.

The briefcase dropped to the floor.

Empty.

Beryl held a reedy wooden stick in his hand. He snapped his wrist and it extended like a metal pointer, several feet long. Now it was a slender cane—some sort of weird magical staff.

I yanked on the current. Hard.

Too late.

He grunted as electricity crackled through the

cane and shot out the end. But it wasn't pointed at me. Why?

My chest restricted. My muscles seized. Pain shot through me. I clutched the flesh over my heart and glanced at the floor.

I was standing in a binding triangle that was now lit up with white Heka. I stepped to the edge. The moment my toe touched the painted boundary, the air crackled. An invisible force shoved me backward. I stumbled to the opposite side of the triangle and pushed with my hands. Heka fortified with electric current zapped me.

Bound!

I was bound I was bound I was bound!

I glanced up at Beryl. He smiled. "Gotcha."

Dare laughed. "Oh, my. If you could see the look on your face right now. You really have no idea what you are. It's delightful. Has no one ever tried to bind you? I'm so glad to be your first. Ironic, since you were the first to bind me in this very bar. Doesn't feel so good, does it? Being trapped like a rat. Terrible on your heart. But you're young—you'll survive. And I've got worse things planned for you. *Much* worse."

He turned around and opened the front door. Three beefy Earthbounds in suits shuffled into the bar. He said to them, "Beryl will mark you."

The binding triangle was big enough to enclose a table—maybe five feet at the base, and another five to the tip of the vertex. I retreated, moving as far away from Dare and his men as I could go. Got zapped again. Yelped in pain.

"Oh, Miss Bell. The mighty Moonchild may possess every knack that ever existed—"

What?

"—but all the Æthyric myths agree that she has two weaknesses. First, her powers aren't as strong during the day. And second, she is susceptible as any common demon to a standard binding."

A whimper got caught in my throat. This couldn't be happening. He was lying again. I blindly reached out and touched the boundary, crying out in pain when I felt the binding react. "I'm not a demon!"

"But you're not human, either, are you?"

When I was able to crack my eyes open, I saw Dare's henchmen gathered around Beryl, who was removing a flat metal tin from his suit pocket. He screwed the top off. Something dark sat inside. Dark red. He pushed his thumb into it, like he was readying himself to offer fingerprints, and then swiped the substance across each of the men's foreheads.

I'd seen this once before, in the Hellfire caves. When Merrimoth threw Lon into the fighting ring with a summoned Æthyric demon. His forehead had been marked.

A mark that allowed the wearer to step inside a binding without breaking it.

The three big men looked up at me with menace behind their eyes.

Shit.

Dare's voice floated behind them. "Word is spreading. You are the most coveted creature between the two planes. Your mother may be making claims about you. But she isn't here. I am. And last I checked, you were my employee. My property. Mine to command, whether you like to think so, or not. Nobody quits until I say they do."

He stepped to the side and leaned against the bar, stuffing his hands in his suit pockets. "I've got a wonderfully inventive portable demon cage in a van out back. You'll be coming home with me tonight."

"Fuck you."

"However, I want you to know that I'm a man of my word," he said, rubbing his hand over his head. "I won't welch on our bargain—I'll tell you what I know about your dead brother. But first, let me show you what happens to people who defy me."

The three marked men approached the binding.

My hackles rose. Brain went blank. Panic sifted through my limbs, turning them to jelly.

Had to use the moon power. No choice. But when I tried to reach for it, the binding reflected it. Pain shot through my chest. I howled.

Trapped.

Bound.

Not a damn thing I could do.

The first man tested his foot against the binding. He smiled and stepped into the triangle with me. As he did, I tried again for the moon power, hoping the binding was weakened enough for me to snag it. No such luck.

His fist felt like iron against my cheek. The pain was sharp and excruciating.

They were on me so fast. Three giant men in such a small space. I tried to defend myself for half a second, but it was no use. One grabbed my hair, then violently wrenched my arms behind my back. The last one punched me in the face. The pain was unreal. Bones cracked. Blood flowed. They were going to bash my face in—maybe they already had. My shoulder popped, and my arm went numb.

Someone jabbed me in the stomach. All the air left my lungs. Blood choked the back of my throat. My arms were released, and the pain in my shoulder rocketed through me. My knees buckled, and I dropped to the floor.

But they didn't stop.

They kicked me in my chest. Ribs cracked.

They kicked me in my back until pain radiated up and down my spine.

Someone stomped on my foot. My ankle cracked and broke. I barely felt it. I couldn't feel anything anymore.

I wasn't afraid to die. I was almost glad it was coming. This would all be over. I would start again, somewhere else. Another plane. Somewhere my mother couldn't touch me. Somewhere Dare couldn't touch me.

My cheek lay against Tambuku's wooden floor. I was curled on my side. I could still see out of one eye. I stared into the spotlight until I imagined it was a tunnel of white, ready to suck me in and whisk me away.

Dare's voice broke through my reverie. "Enough. You're going to kill her."

Please, just do it. I wanted to say it out loud, but one side of my jaw was definitely broken.

I looked up at Dare with my one good eye. He was smiling down at me. Beryl stood by his side. The men who'd beat me were breathing heavy. One shook out his fingers. His knuckles were bloody.

"Go drive the van around and bring the cage inside," Dare said absently.

The air shuddered. A dark shape wavered behind his head. Beryl's hair fluttered. Enormous black wings sounded like a flag snapping in the wind.

They all spun around and looked up at Priya. His face was hardened, jaw tense. He swung his arm around and backhanded Dare across the cheek. The elderly Hellfire leader's face flew sideways. Priya's silvery body darted forward. Beryl and the henchmen cried out and stumbled as he landed.

Two quick strides and his bare foot stamped on the edge of my binding. Heka fizzled and popped. The terrible pressure dropped away.

Free.

Free, but so broken, I couldn't move.

I guess I didn't need to.

The moon power came to me in a rush, coating the room in a blanket of silver light.

All knacks. That's what Dare said. It made sense now. I didn't need a spell. Whatever I could imagine, I could do.

Not demon, but not human, either. Something in-between.

I wanted to tell Priya to get behind me, but I couldn't speak. I didn't need to, though, did I? I screamed at him in my head to move back. His wings extended and flapped, then flew out of sight. My hair blew forward as he landed behind me.

No good would come of letting Dare walk out of here alive. If I lived, he'd keep me chained like a dog and use me to do God only knew what. But if I died, Lon and Jupe would be sitting ducks. Either Lon would kill Dare and end up in jail, or Dare would make their lives miserable—whatever lives he allowed them to have. He was a horrible person, a sadistic asshole with too much power. And he was a killer.

A killer who was pulling a gun out of his suit jacket, looking at me with murder in his eyes.

Eat or be eaten. No choice now.

I mentally marked them all: Dare, Beryl, the three men. And as Dare hesitated, pointing the gun first at me, then behind me at Priya, I thought of Merrimoth that night on the beach, hurling fire at me and Lon. That's what I wanted.

Dare's rage-filled gaze connected with mine. The panic I'd felt before his men destroyed my body was now reflected in his eyes. And with the moon power fueling my Heka, I directed all of my willpower into one single word:

Burn.

Orange and yellow flames lit up the room. Swirled around the five men. Screams of anguish pierced my ears. The heat felt like a blast from an unholy oven. It might burn me up, too.

Someone tried to run—Beryl, I thought—but stumbled after one step.

Burning flesh filled my nostrils as skin melted off their faces. The screaming stopped. They all fell to the ground, one after the other, shaking the floor like sacks of wet cement dropping as fire ripped through them.

Dare was the last to fall. His body dropped in front of mine. I watched him die, infernal flames licking across his body. Watched his eyes dissolve in their sockets. Watched his bones turn black.

Gotcha.

Before I could take more than a handful of strained, pain-filled breaths, the flames were flickering out over five piles of black ash. Smoke curled in the air above them.

I'd killed them all in a matter of seconds.

My hair rustled. I flicked my one good eye upward, away from the ash and smoke. Priya crouched in front of me.

I could tell by the horror-struck look on his face that my body was a mess, but I didn't feel pain anymore. Didn't feel anything. His sinewy silver hand reached out to me, stuttered, and halted.

He simply said, "I will get help."

32

Tall grass tickled my cheek. I opened my eyes to wildflowers swaying in a soft breeze. I tried to lift my head, but I couldn't move. Couldn't move anything: fingers, arms, legs. . . . All I could do was look.

I strained my eyes sideways. Grass. Lon wasn't sleeping next to me this time. I looked up and saw a path of blackened grass and a white dress blowing in the breeze.

My mother stood at my feet.

"*Cassé. Ruiné.*" She sighed and shook her head. "You managed to get yourself mangled, didn't you? How am I supposed to use a broken body?"

I tried to respond, but nothing came out of my mouth.

"You'd better find a healer soon, or I will be very unhappy with you, Sélène Aysul Duval. And while you do that, I will seek a better way to connect with you. This is the back door, so to speak, but I think I know someone who can help me find the front. I will return when you are of some use to me."

She turned and walked away, strolling through the blackened grass until she was out of sight. I lay on the ground, looking at the sky. I thought I heard birds in the distance. But as the sound got louder, I realized it was beeping.

The sound of a machine.

The sound of my pulse being measured.

The grass faded away. The blue sky turned white. I could see out of one eye. Just a slit. It was so difficult to keep it open. I smelled antiseptic and plastic. Saw bodies moving around. They looked busy. Quick, sharp movements. One of them was talking to someone.

"—broken hip, ribs, arms, leg, jaw, fingers. Internal bleeding. Concussion. She's lucky to be alive. I'd like to try to keep her that way. You're going to have to get out of here and let me work. People can't walk in and see you like that."

Like what? I moved my gaze around the room. Dr. Mick. He was staring at a computer screen. Another doctor was hooking me up to another machine. I looked to the side.

"I'm here. You're alive." Lon bent over me, horns spiraling around his ears. "It's okay. Mick will fix you."

My brain was sluggish. *Kar Yee . . . she wasn't at the bar.*

"She's fine." His voice was low and rumbly.

Jupe? The Giovannis?

"Giovannis are on their way back to Portland. Jupe's outside in the waiting room with Kar Yee and the Holidays. I didn't want him to see you."

I glanced down at myself. All I could see was blood soaking through the blue paper wrap they'd used to cover me up. I looked back up at Lon and remembered what happened in Tambuku, my mind flipping through the events in rapid succession.

I killed Dare. Killed all of them.

Lon nodded. "Priya came to Jupe. He told us."

I'm not sorry.

"Me neither."

Dare's gone. Merrimoth's gone. No more Hellfire Club, I suppose. Either that, or you're in charge of it. I laughed silently, feeling mildly delirious. *That's something, huh? You're the head honcho now. Everyone else is dead.*

"It's the least of my worries." He lifted his hand as if he was going to touch my face and halted, fingers hovering above my cheek.

My mom will be coming back. If they fix me, tell them to strap me down. Put anti-magick sigils up around the room. Because I'll be dangerous if she's controlling me.

His voice cracked. "Oh, Cady."

"You need to go, Lon." That was Mick talking. I recognized his voice now.

Lon leaned closer. "I'll find a way to stop your mother. I don't know how, but I will."

I don't know if she can be stopped.

"If there's a way—"

"Lon," Mick said firmly. "Come on, buddy."

I didn't want him to go. *I love you. You know that, right?*

He murmured something anguished I couldn't understand, laboring for breath, as if he'd been running. Mick pulled him away. His horns retracted as they forced him out the door. Two nurses took his place. Mick gave them directions, then stood over me, running a hand through his short hair, which looked more red than brown under the surgery lights. "I know you can't talk, but I think you can hear me. I'm about to put you under."

I blinked. That was the best I could do to answer.

Mick's halo swirled, big and blue. "I also wanted to tell you this before we started. I didn't know if Lon knew, which is why I made him leave."

Knew what?

Mick lowered his voice. "The baby survived. I'm not sure how—you're badly bruised and your hip is broken. But it showed up in the blood work, and I can detect the heartbeat with my knack."

What was he talking about? I stared up at him, unable to ask.

"You're about seven weeks along, I'd guess. Maybe eight."

Impossible—he was crazy. I couldn't be. I was on the Pill! I had a repeating alarm on my phone to remind me. There's the week you don't take it, and the pack gives you sugar pills so you don't get out of the habit, but sometimes I skipped those. Which is fine, as I long as I remembered to take the real pills a week later. And I always did. Well, except that one week after Halloween when my phone alarm went buggy. I missed a few days then, but I doubled up on pills when I finally remembered. Okay, maybe I missed more than a couple of days, but Kar Yee said she forgot and doubled up all the time, and it wasn't a big deal. Besides, I'd been taking it regularly ever since, so I couldn't be pregnant.

I mean, I remembered my last period. It was . . . when was it?

Oh, God.

It was before Halloween.

I looked up at Mick.

"Did you know?" he said. "I thought you did, but now I'm having doubts. I wish I could tell. We'll get a telepath in here later, someone who can read and send, unlike Lon."

Oh, Christ! This couldn't be right. Wouldn't I know if I was pregnant? I thought of Jill, one of the Tambuku waitresses. She'd had a baby earlier in the year. I tried to remember back to when she was pregnant. She was tired all the time. Nauseous. Vomiting. I'd vomited, but not in the mornings—just after magick, which was normal. After my mom visited me in the dream that first night. But that could've been related to whatever magick she'd done to me.

I'd been crying. A lot. Jill cried a lot when she was pregnant.

I remembered Hajo's gross comments about me gaining weight. My breasts were uncomfortable. Maybe even tender. Was that a symptom? I didn't know!

How did I not know?

Beep-beep, beep-beep.

The machine was going crazy.

"Whoa, your pulse is too high. You need to calm down. Your body is . . . I've got a lot of work to do. I'm bringing in a second healer who works here. We'll do what we can, but I can't fix everything at once. Might have to keep you sedated for a few days while we do additional work. I'll do everything I can to save the baby. I just wanted you to know."

Beep-beep, beep-beep.

No, no, no! This couldn't be happening. I couldn't be pregnant. I thought of what Dare's men had done to me. Kicked me in the stomach. In the back. Broke my bones. Oh, God. Tears obscured my vision.

Oh, Christ—did my mother know about this? She hadn't said anything. Maybe she didn't know. Oh, please let her not know. Lon didn't know.

"She's hemorrhaging. We can't wait any longer. "

Wait—hemorrhaging where? What was going on? Was I losing the baby?

"I'm putting her under."

Maybe it was better if I lost it. I was a monster. Lon was a demon. What the hell would we create together? Something unnatural and wrong?

Or something beautiful?

I'd only known about it for a minute. Now it suddenly seemed like the most important thing in the world. More important than killing Dare. More important than my mother's diabolical plans. More important than running off to Florida.

Whatever it was, Lon and I created it. And I wanted it.

I had to tell Mick somehow. He had to save it.

"She's almost under," he said as my eyes closed. "Let's get started."

ACKNOWLEDGMENTS

Without my hard-working agent, Laura Bradford, Arcadia wouldn't exist. I'm eternally grateful for her steadfastness, golden advice, and generous heart.

My new editor at Pocket, Adam Wilson, has faced down wild dogs in the back alleys of Thailand: how badass is that? His keen observations made both this and "Leashing the Tempest" far stronger. Julia Fincher also did some heavy lifting; her edits were sharp, thoughtful, and tough: exactly what was needed. (I secretly call her Julia Awesome.) Big thanks to folks on Team Pocket: Sarah Wright, Mandy Keifetz, Anne Cherry, and everyone else behind the scenes. Kudos to Tony Mauro for the best Arcadia cover yet.

My husband is a genius. He is also patience personified. Not only does he tolerate my insular moods, he also calmly brainstorms me out of plot holes and listens to all my Crazy Writer paranoid ramblings.

The online book community has been terribly generous to me—bloggers, reviewers, readers, and authors. Without their support and word-of-mouth enthusiasm, I'd be nothing. And lastly, thank you to everyone who's taken the time to write love letters to Cady, Lon, and Jupe: long live the Bride of Frankenstein, pirate mustaches, and geeky teenage boys!

More bestselling
URBAN FANTASY
from Pocket Books!

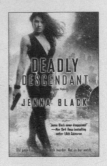

More Bestselling Urban Fantasy from Pocket Books!